FOUR ON THE FLOOR

FOUR
ON THE
FLOOR

Deborah Morgan

WHEELER
CHIVERS

This Large Print edition is published by Wheeler Publishing, Waterville, Maine USA and by BBC Audiobooks Ltd, Bath, England.

Published in 2006 in the U.S. by arrangement with The Berkley Publishing Group, a division of Penguin Group (USA) Inc.

Published in 2006 in the U.K. by arrangement with the author.

U.S. Softcover	1-59722-254-2	(Softcover)
U.K. Hardcover 10:	1 4056 3824 9	(Chivers Large Print)
U.K. Hardcover 13:	978 1 405 63824 1	
U.K. Softcover 10:	1 4056 3825 7	(Camden Large Print)
U.K. Softcover 13:	978 1 405 63825 8	

An Antique Lover's Mystery

The text of this Large Print edition is unabridged.
Other aspects of the book may vary from the original edition.

Set in 16 pt. Plantin by Ramona Watson.

Printed in the United States on permanent paper.

British Library Cataloguing-in-Publication Data available

Library of Congress Cataloging-in-Publication Data

Morgan, Deborah (Deborah A.)
    Four on the floor / by Deborah Morgan.
        p. cm. — (An antique lover's mystery)
      ISBN 1-59722-254-2 (lg. print : sc : alk. paper)
      1. Antique dealers — Fiction.   2. Large type books.
  I. Title.
PS3613.O744F68 2006
   813'.6—dc22   2006008171

Dedication

This one's for my car guys:

Grandson Dylan Ray Brown (my auto museum sidekick), who at three years old could identify any make of pickup on the road, and park his own little two-passenger Jeep on a dime. While in reverse.

Son Kevin Williams, who knows his way around any fender, and willingly shares his knowledge. Thank God we all survived his teenage years behind the wheel.

Brother-in-law Charles "Corky" Estleman, who put me in the 1937 Cadillac that you'll meet in this story.

Husband Loren D. Estleman, who helps keep me in reliable wheels, and understands my frequent need to hit the open road.

Stepfather Dean Morgan, who's always there to help. Always.

And, in memory of my father, G. C. "Bud" Green (1930–2003), who helped me wheel and deal for my first car, and didn't kill me when I wrecked it on my Sweet Sixteenth.

Acknowledgments

Sincere thanks to the following people for contributing their expertise and support to the writing of this book:

Debbie Cauffiel, for the California conversation;

Barbara Conroy, for graciously sharing her knowledge of restaurant china;

Gail Henry, once again, for tracking down research books;

John Lee, editor of *The Woodie Times*, for continued support, and for the great work you do for the National Woodie Club;

J. Michael Moore, dentist and writer, a true ink brother who went above and beyond in order to find information needed for the murder aspect;

and Kym Williams and Loren Estleman, for everything.

One

BETTER TRY
LESS SPEED PER MILE
THAT CAR
MAY HAVE TO
LAST A WHILE

— Burma-Shave

Louie Stella's voice chugged like a Model T Ford. As it choked and sputtered, its owner going on about the virtues of the old classics over the newfangled, high-technology, electronic look-alikes, Jeff Talbot parked the phone between ear and shoulder and allowed his mind to wander.

He'd had his '48 Chevy Fleetmaster, with its splintered wood, caved-in fenders, and buckled chrome bumpers, towed to Louie's Retro Resto and Chop Shop several months earlier after a killer had run him off the road one dark and stormy winter night. Since then, Jeff had survived another Pacific Northwest plaid flannel season, laughed as the rest of the country put so much store in a groundhog, and seen the schools release masses of students from their chalky walls for another summer.

It was high time he got his car back. "So," Jeff prompted Louie, when the grease monkey's motor ran out of gas, "any chance I can pick up the woodie before football season starts?"

"You can pick her up now, if you've got the money to bail her out." Louie chuckled, then the half-lurching noise in his throat sputtered to a stop.

"Now?" Why hadn't Louie said so when he'd called and woke everyone up fifteen minutes earlier?

Jeff should've remembered what conversations with Louie were like. He blamed his lapse in memory on the fact that it was morning, early morning, and he'd just gotten started on the pot of coffee that Greer brought in with the cordless phone and the *Post-Intelligencer*.

He wouldn't give Louie any grief over the wasted time. Jeff was an antiques picker now, but back when he was with the Bureau, Louie was one of his best informants. If Jeff needed a lead on a classic car that had been stolen, Louie was his first contact. If an antique Duesenberg had been lifted from an auto museum as easily as a thumbprint from glass, Louie was as likely as anyone to have gotten wind of the transaction. Jeff's own vintage car was a bonus, kept his visits to Louie's from drawing attention. The primo woodie got the curious stares, not the G-man.

The auto shop had always been a gathering place for all sorts of people from all walks of life, and Louie had created an atmosphere where car people relaxed. If Louie hadn't heard scraps of info about the cars that had disappeared, he knew enough about the whole classic auto world to point Jeff in the general direction. It just took him longer than most to spit it out.

"Sure," Louie now said. "She's all dolled up and ready to go. Better than new, in fact. And the place is like a morgue today, so you won't have to wait. We've been working our butts off to get all the jobs done so's people can squeeze every minute out of showing off their babies — summer cruise nights and car shows are hotter than ever, you know."

Jeff didn't know, but he could trust Louie to. It was no secret that Louie, his two sons (who worked with him), and the other two men he employed were not only passionate about their work, but about old cars, period. Any number of the crew — if not all of them — participated in every auto show and cruise night that came down the pike.

Cars got into people's blood, Jeff knew, much like being a cop did. Having been with the FBI for several years before throwing it all over for the antiques world had taught him that. He didn't miss those days, necessarily, but he recognized the obsessions. To Louie, he said, "What's the damage?"

When Louie rattled off the long string of numbers, Jeff was grateful that he was sitting down. He had insurance — paid more than most because he used his classic car on a daily basis — but this blow would likely raise his premium. "I'll bring a check with me. Should be there in —" Jeff glanced at his watch — "about forty-five minutes."

"Sounds good."

As Jeff started to hang up the phone, he heard Louie's voice calling his name.

"Yeah?" Jeff parked the phone back in the crook of his shoulder.

"I damn near forgot. Tony said tell you he's got a surprise for you when you get here — found a piece of nostalgia while he was working on the left rear door panel."

Tony was the oldest of Louie's two sons (the other boy, Michael, worked in the shop, too, doing grunt work while he learned the finer points of restoration) and had overtaken his old man in skill as far as restoring vehicles was concerned, especially woodies. Tony could turn timber into art on wheels. "Nostalgia? What is it?"

"Damned if I know. He said tell you he put it in the — hang on."

In the what? Jeff waited, heard voices on Louie's end of the line, but he couldn't make out what they were saying.

Finally, Louie's voice was in Jeff's ear again. "Gotta go, Talbot. Kid dropped a transmission." He hung up, leaving Jeff to learn later about what Tony had found.

Jeff showered, shaved, and dressed in record time, then grabbed the tray and telephone that his butler had brought up and headed down the service stairs that led to the kitchen.

"Breakfast will be ready in two minutes," Sheila announced as she removed a pan from the oven.

"Sorry, hon," Jeff said, kissing the nape of her neck below the blonde ponytail, "but I don't have time. The woodie's ready, and I told Louie that I'd head on down."

13

"Ten more minutes won't make that big a difference."

Jeff's jaw tightened. He'd waited *months* for this day, and on top of that, had agreed to pay extra so he wouldn't have to wait even longer. Now, the thought of tacking on ten minutes seemed too much to ask. He was debating how to explain this to his wife when his stomach growled. He dropped the issue.

"What's in the pan?"

"Dutch Babies," she said, looking at him as if his sanity were questionable. "I've only made them for you every Friday morning since the moment I moved in here. Well, except for last winter. Still, it looks like you'd remember."

"Chalk my failings as a husband up to distraction. I hadn't realized how much I missed that car till I heard it's ready to go."

"Come on, then. The quicker we start, the quicker you can leave."

They sat in the breakfast nook slathering the cakes with butter before pouring hot syrup on them (and balancing the indulgence with turkey bacon and fresh cantaloupe), and Jeff tore into his food as if he were bound for the wilderness. "Where's Greer?" he asked around a chunk of melon.

"Washing the car."

"What?" His shoulders dropped, causing the butts of his knife and fork to strike the table. "We don't have time for that."

"He said it wasn't acceptable to drive a dirty vehicle to a restoration shop." Sheila eyed her husband. "He'll be finished before you are — if you eat like a normal person, instead of inhaling everything."

"Sorry." He took a deep breath. Sheila was a chef, and Jeff knew the importance of appreciating the creative efforts she put into everything she prepared. He brought the next forkful toward his mouth more slowly, then paused midair. "I should've checked with you first. Will you be okay while Greer drives me down to Louie's shop?"

"Would you stop asking me that every time you set foot out the door? I'm fine. Anyway, I've got a busy day planned, and it'll help to have the place to myself for awhile. After I list another two dozen items on eBay, I'm packaging the week's sales. After that, I'm providing a Labor Day menu and recipes in a chat room for my agoraphobic chefs' group."

Jeff shook his head. "Always surprises me there's more than one of you."

"Obviously, you mean agoraphobes who are chefs, but I don't know why. We have

15

to eat. And, besides, I spent a lot more time in the kitchen before I started our on-line auction business. Some agoraphobics are into the food and nothing else, which is understandable if you're not into arts or crafts. At least I paint some — or, I did before eBay. Besides, I get some good recipes in our recipe exchange."

Well, Jeff thought, *at least she's back into her old routine.* He listened as she talked animatedly about her plans, thankful that she'd overcome recent traumas, then advanced even further to overcome their physical effects. While holed up in their bedroom for over a month just prior to the previous Christmas, she'd gained fifteen pounds and lost all semblance of normalcy. Now, seven months later, the extra weight was gone (he didn't care about it, except that it had depressed her), and her muscle tone was better than ever. She was all but obsessed with working out. He joined her in the basement's workout room a couple of times a week, and it helped marginally to keep him from gaining weight. Additionally, he'd noticed that a typical flight of stairs no longer left him winded — all a plus, since his "thirty-nine and holding" birthday was only a few months away. He admitted to himself that he'd missed the workouts, which had been a regular habit when he was an agent, but he didn't let on to his wife. Although the euphoria of exercise was addictive, he wasn't about to match her schedule. Besides, he had a decade on her.

Sheila reached over and tugged a lock of his hair. "Weren't you going in for a haircut this morning? You've been putting it off all week."

He waved her off. "I'll have it done on my way back from Louie's."

The back door opened and closed, followed momentarily by Greer approaching the breakfast nook with the coffeepot.

"Greer, can you spare the time to run down to Louie's with me?"

"I'm looking forward to it, sir." Greer poured warm-ups in the cups. "The men over at Woody's Car Wash were asking when you'd be back with the forty-eight. They've missed seeing her."

"That's good of them to say, especially since they don't make any money off the deal." It was company policy that bona fide wooden-bodied cars went through for free.

Jeff swigged coffee, said, "Well, that's one more reason to go get the car," then kissed his wife before hurrying out the back door.

17

Two

LAWYERS, DOCTORS
SHEIKS AND BAKERS
MOUNTAINEERS AND
UNDERTAKERS
MAKE THEIR BRISTLY BEARDS
BEHAVE
BY USING BRUSHLESS

— Burma-Shave

Louie's Garage sat just off an isolated
stretch of road southeast of Renton between communities dotted with strip malls,
Laundromats, and tire stores. The exterior
of the large building from which emerged
gleaming works of pricey auto body art
looked as if it hadn't been painted in thirty
years. The once-white structure was grungy,
and nearly half its milky coat was worn
away, revealing weathered gray boards. Beyond the building was the graveyard: acres
and acres of salvage vehicles — everything
from rusted-out shells gutted for parts to

panel wagons whose sides bore the faded names of businesses that had also faded from the landscape, to pickup skeletons that had given up either their cabs or beds or both.

As Jeff pulled the PT Cruiser off the state road and down the slight incline toward the parking area, Greer said, "Sir, the place looks abandoned."

"Yeah. Louie told me they were pretty much caught up on their work, and most of the cars were picked up last night. Maybe the guys pulled their own vehicles inside to tinker on them."

"True, but why would they have all the doors closed?"

The closed doors — three oversized panels designed to slide to the side, thus allowing room for pulling vehicles in and out — did make the place look abandoned. Beyond them, near the end of the long building, was an entry door with a small window near the top. This door led to a reception area that fronted Louie's office. It was also closed.

Jeff pulled to a stop. "They've probably got the back doors open, so they can keep these closed. You know, make it look like they're not open for business so they can take a breather. Louie sounded beat. He said they'd been working around the clock."

"Yes, sir. Should we park around back, then, in order to keep the ruse going?"

Jeff considered the question. "Nah," he said. "If Louie wanted me to do that, he'd have said so." Jeff parked the Cruiser near the entry door.

"May I join you, sir? I'd like to see what else they're working on."

"Sure." Jeff hid his surprise. Although Greer had shown great skill in maintaining the woodie — keeping it waxed, changing the oil, replacing the plugs and, well, whatever it was he did toward the car's upkeep — Jeff thought he was more likely to show interest in HGTV than in STP.

Greer opened the door for his employer. Chemical fumes hit both of them in the face.

Jeff coughed. "I'll never get used to the smell. How on earth do they work in this and keep from passing out?"

Greer fanned the air. "It's typically not this strong, sir."

Jeff studied his butler as they stepped inside and thought, *How would you know from smells in a garage?* He had to agree, though. "Usually Louie's coffee is worse than the paint fumes and Bondo."

Jeff squinted as his eyes adjusted to the

dim garage. The place was gray, for the most part, with glowing dots here and there where trouble lights hanging on latches of open hoods illuminated the guts of vehicles, and naked bulbs shed weak light on worktables crammed with wrenches, distributor caps, tailpipes, ratchets, oil cans, and a hundred nondescript items, most of which were coated with a mucky layer of grime.

To the far left was a large, partitioned segment that Jeff knew as the dust-free paint room.

"Louie?" Jeff called out, his voice echoing in the cavernous building. It had been laid out with enough right angles so that those working in the smaller rooms weren't visually distracted by those in the main room.

"Perhaps they're taking a coffee break." Greer pointed toward a cubicle in the corner opposite them. He pulled a white handkerchief from his hip pocket and covered his mouth and nose.

Jeff nodded, and the two men walked that direction, the echo of their footsteps bouncing off the rafters. A bright light caught Jeff's attention.

He stopped short. There, in an area spotlighted like a showroom floor, was his car.

This setup was new. Jeff walked toward the showcased vehicle. The varnished ash and mahogany glowed warm and golden next to the Lake Como Blue body. Jeff had instructed Tony to paint the car its original factory color rather than the black that his grandfather, Mercer Talbot, had switched to years before. The chrome replating was the best he'd ever seen, the windows shone like a bartender's polished glass, and new whitewalls all around completed the picture. Jeff was sure she was better than when she'd rolled out of Detroit under Truman.

"Look at her, Greer," he said, only vaguely aware that his throat was getting scratchy. "You can't tell she's ever been wrecked." He coughed, called out Louie's name again as he examined the left front fender, which had taken the brunt of the accident. He rarely referred to the woodie as gender-specific. That jargon was for the obsessed, the possessed, the men — and women (more and more females were getting into the old-car hobby) — who spent every free moment dressing up their toys and entering them in classic auto shows, parading them down the boulevards on cruise nights, vying for trophies and prizes, joining clubs.

But the sight of his '48 Chevy back in working order had its effect. He jingled the extra set of keys in his jeans pocket, anxious to get behind the wheel.

"Yes, sir," Greer said, "but have you noticed that the back doors are closed as well? The fumes are too strong in here."

Jeff buried his nose in the crook of his elbow as he looked around. His eyes stung. He inhaled, coughed, then shouted again: "Louie?"

No response.

"Over there." Greer pointed toward the end of the building farthest from the office. "Hear that hissing? Someone's using a paint sprayer on one of those forty-nines, either the Chevy pickup or that Merc." Greer started toward it, looked up. "That exhaust fan should be on."

Merc? Jeff wondered if Greer, too, had been caught up in the world of classics. The young butler rarely used slang.

Greer walked toward some tanks hooked up to hoses near a paint station. "Hello?" he called.

No response. To Jeff, he said, "The person using it must be wearing earplugs." Greer paused at the tanks, studied the gauges, then flipped a wall switch. The exhaust fan motor started up, its tone raising an octave as it gained rpms and overrode the sound of the Mercury's engine. Greer moved gingerly toward the far side of the car.

Jeff followed, watching as Greer glanced between the two vehicles before moving on toward the far side of the truck.

"Here he is, sir, on a creeper under the pickup."

"Give him a kick, let him know we're here."

Jeff caught up, saw two denim-covered legs and two scuffed brogan work boots extending beyond the wooden platform of the wheeled creeper. Greer gave the sole of one boot a slight kick, got no response.

Jeff stepped forward, nudged the booted foot nearest him that stuck out from under the running board.

The leg fell like dead weight to the concrete floor. Jeff dropped, grabbed the ankles, and pulled. The creeper rolled forward, carrying its cargo out from under the vehicle.

The lifeless load was Michael Stella, Louie's youngest son.

Three

ON CURVES AHEAD
REMEMBER, SONNY
THAT RABBIT'S FOOT
DIDN'T SAVE
THE BUNNY

— Burma-Shave

Jeff checked the Stella boy for a pulse. There was none.

Carbon monoxide and paint fumes. That would do it, all right.

Greer punched 911 on his cell phone, handed it to Jeff, then ran to the back of the building and started opening the large garage doors.

"Nine-one-one. What's your emergency?" The voice was female.

As Jeff jogged toward the partitioned paint room, he told the dispatcher that a body had been found at Louie's garage.

He held on the line, listened as the dispatcher gave the address to a paramedic.

25

Finding no one in the separate room, he rushed to the break room.

The dispatcher turned her attention back to him. "Has something happened to Louie?"

Small community, Jeff reminded himself. "You know Louie?"

"Sure. Everybody knows Louie. I'm not related to anyone down there, if that's what you're hesitant about, so give me what you've got, and do it fast."

"His youngest son is the one we found under the vehicle. I'm checking the rest of the building now." Jeff gave her a play-by-play as he began his search. "Okay, I'm in the break room." He circled the large, round table. "Got another one on the floor, Stan Baker." The man's grease-stained fingers were still curved through the handle of his coffee mug. Jeff squatted. "Checking for a pulse . . ." He sighed. "You better send two ambulances." He stood, then added, "At least."

"What do you mean, 'at least'? You got a third one in there with Stan?"

"No, but I'm almost to the supply room in back. I'll be surprised if I don't find more. Hang on." He stepped around the partially open door and scanned the room.

A young man was seated on the floor at

the far end, leaning against metal shelves that held corrugated boxes with smudged labels showing illustrations of fan belts, hoses, radiator caps, and dozens of other vehicle parts. The man had one ankle crossed over the other, and his chin was resting against his chest as if he were sneaking a catnap.

"Tony?" Jeff called. "Tony, is that you?"

No response.

"It's not Tony." Jeff knelt beside him, and placed two fingers on his neck. "It's that kid Louie hired fresh out of vo-tech last year."

"Oh, yeah, the VanDyke kid," the dispatcher said. "Does he have a pulse?"

"No. That's three, and I haven't gone to Louie's office yet."

"I'll radio for another ambulance."

He was vaguely aware of the dispatcher's voice in the background as he made his way to Louie's office. He dreaded going in there, knew what he was going to find. He was grateful that the third man he'd found who had succumbed to the fumes had *not* been Tony, but sorry that there had been a third victim of this freak accident. And he knew in his gut that there was a fourth.

He stepped inside, scanned the room. First glance turned up no one.

Louie's desk, the size and color of an army Jeep, held a jumble of folders, receipt books, order slips, stained coffee cups, and cardboard take-out containers.

"Well?" the dispatcher prompted as Jeff circled the desk.

There, lumped in a heap on the floor, was Louie Stella.

"Yeah, he's here." Jeff folded the phone, thus ending the conversation. His jaw clenched as he felt the man's neck for a pulse. Nothing. "Damn it, Louie, we were talking to each other an hour ago. How'd you guys let this happen?"

Jeff rubbed his stinging eyes as he stood and went to the window. He pulled the cord on the blinds, worked the latch on the small, dirty pane of glass, and left prints in the grime that coated the aluminum frame as he worked it open. There was no screen, so he stuck his head through the opening and sucked in air. He heard the sirens, checked his watch. He and Greer had been on the premises less than four minutes.

He went back to the main area of the garage, where Greer had now opened the bay doors on the front of the building. Both men stood back as an ambulance rolled into the garage and pulled to a stop.

One paramedic grabbed a large metal case and rushed toward Jeff and Greer, while the second medic went to the back of the panel wagon. That one retrieved a gurney and was wheeling it at the heels of his partner before they reached the location of the first body.

Meanwhile, a sheriff's unit barreled onto the scene, and two uniforms poured out. One loped toward the parking lot entrance, clearly to keep out curious bystanders, as the other, keg-chested and white-haired, lumbered into the building. He worked the leather thong from the trigger of his sidearm as he moved.

"There are three more in back," Jeff told the medics. "No pulses, though."

The first paramedic plugged a stethoscope into his ears, leaned over Michael Stella's body, and worked intently at finding a pulse. He shook his head slightly, then stood. "Show me where the others are."

Jeff started toward the smaller rooms in back.

The sheriff's deputy — H. Cookson, Jeff concluded upon checking the patches and brass on his shirt — surveyed the scene, told Greer to come along, then used a shoulder-mounted radio and made a general announcement for everyone to "get a move on." Finally, he told dispatch to get a detective from headquarters.

Cookson carried on a brief conversation with Louie, much along the lines of what Jeff had said a minute earlier, before escorting Jeff and Greer back to the main room.

Once there, he questioned the two, briskly taking notes as two more ambulances, a coroner's wagon, five cop units, and, obviously, everyone remotely connected to law enforcement and/or rescue in the small community showed up on the scene and burst from their respective vehicles. Add to that reporters from four newspapers and three television stations, and, inside of five minutes, the place buzzed like a luncheon meeting of the local Kiwanis Club.

Despite the sheer number of personnel, whose uniforms represented several different branches and departments, rank and file were quickly sorted out, and people got to the business of giving orders, taking orders, taking statements, giving hell, and, generally, working the process of due process.

Amid all that, a very tall, very slender man who appeared to be the youngest of the whole brigade approached the deputy.

Handing him a business card, he introduced himself as Detective Chris Fleming.

Cookson then introduced the young detective to Jeff and Greer, relayed their statements, and wrapped up with, "No mystery here, really. They all dropped where they stood. They've been working day and night, probably got careless about ventilation. I've been pulling double shifts myself, so my lieutenant could take his family to Disneyland. Summer vacations kill our schedules.

"Anyway," he continued, "there've been so many cars in and out of this joint that if I didn't know better, I'd say it was a front for something."

The detective stared at Cookson an extra second before turning to Jeff. "Were the doors closed on the other three areas?"

Jeff mentally replayed his earlier movements through the building. "No."

"Were the fumes as strong in the smaller rooms?"

"Hard to say. They were strong enough out here to permeate my clothes, probably my skin and hair, too. There's no way of knowing whether they were throughout the building, or whether I was smelling what had already attached itself to me."

Cookson broke in. "Like I said, Detective. Nothing more than a bizarre accident, by the looks of things."

"If that's how it looks to you, why'd you send for me?"

"Because things aren't always as they look." He fished a toothpick from his shirt pocket and poked it between his lips. "Besides, if I've learned anything in this business, it's to cover my butt."

"Any employees not accounted for?"

"Now that you mention it," Cookson said, "Tony's not here. Last name, Stella, oldest son of Louie Stella, the owner."

"And Louie Stella?"

Cookson sighed. "Dead. You'll find him in the office. His wife, Marie, keeps the books, but she's done that from the house for about three years now."

The detective turned his attention to Jeff and Greer. "Driver's licenses, please."

After the two had relinquished their IDs, Fleming said, "Wait here." He pulled a cell phone from his inside breast pocket as he walked to a vacated area of the garage. Jeff watched the man talk, listen, wait, look back at them a few times, and return.

The detective studied Jeff. "So, you're the former agent who bailed."

Jeff raised a brow, wondered how *that* information had been obtained so quickly.

"Bailed. Is that *your* take on it, or is that the word they used in my file?"

"I don't hold it against you, Mr. Talbot. It's not the life for everybody."

Jeff waited him out.

Fleming looked over his notes. "Nearing thirty-nine, threw over the life six years ago for the calm world of antiques."

Jeff couldn't draw a bead on this guy's approach. Was the detective trying to stir him up? "I saw a lot less crime when I was with the Bureau."

"Right." Fleming's tone didn't betray whether he doubted Jeff, or whether he knew all about Jeff's recent knack for uncovering murder evidence while searching for antiques.

"Fleming." Cookson pulled the toothpick from his mouth, went to toss it, then obviously thought better of it, and pocketed the thing instead. "Word's out that you're looking into federal service."

Fleming looked at the deputy but didn't respond. He turned his attention back to Jeff. "Spotless record, too. Same for your butler."

Cookson eyed Greer. "No kidding, you're a butler?"

"Cookson." Fleming's voice carried the full weight of the unspoken warning.

The deputy's irritation was obvious, but he kept quiet.

"Everything checks out in relation to your business here. Give me a few minutes, and we'll get you and your cars out of the mix."

"I'm surprised," Jeff said.

"That I'd give you that car?" Fleming nodded toward the woodie. "I have no reason to doubt the info given me by my sources. If they missed something, however, I'll know where to find you." His gaze went from Jeff to Greer. "One of you, anyway. You're not likely to leave an agoraphobic woman on her own for very long, especially after her kidnapping last fall."

Jeff's jaw locked. What at first felt like identity theft had escalated to voyeurism. He glanced at Greer. The butler, who rarely showed emotion, looked like a thermometer about to pop.

A surprised expression crossed the detective's face. "No offense intended, gentlemen. My mother is agoraphobic."

Four

DON'T LOSE
YOUR HEAD
TO GAIN A MINUTE
YOU NEED YOUR HEAD
YOUR BRAINS ARE IN IT

— Burma-Shave

Fleming left Jeff and Greer to play Rorschach with grease stains on the concrete floor under the watch of a pimple-faced sergeant who'd approached to tell Cookson he was needed outside.

When both Cookson and Fleming returned, the sergeant was dismissed, then Fleming said, "You're right, Cookson. On the surface, this appears to be nothing more than a senseless mistake."

He started walking, summoned them to follow him.

Cookson picked up the thread after they were on the move. "On the surface. Meaning you suspect that something

35

below the surface will tell you it wasn't a mistake?"

"Suspect, no. Expect, yes. Better to anticipate the worst than get careless and corrupt a potential crime scene."

They stepped inside Louie's office, and Fleming said, "It won't bother you to be in here, will it?"

Jeff read Greer's expression, then said to Fleming, "We're fine."

"Good. Don't touch anything. It should only take a minute to square away your business."

The detective leaned over the desk and studied names on the jumble of folders, while Jeff tried to remember whether he'd touched anything other than Louie and the window when he'd been in here earlier.

Something flashed.

Jeff blinked, turned toward a motorized whir. Behind him, a large woman grabbed the square picture that her Polaroid spat out. A second camera was tethered around her neck, and she lifted this one to her face.

Without looking up, Fleming said, "It's about time, Hughes. We need to get done and out so I can turn it over to forensics."

"Four bodies, detective. I saved the best for last."

"Quick shots, please. And watch the wisecracks; there are civilians present."

She turned and mumbled, "Sorry," in the general direction of Jeff and Greer, then set about photographing Louie, the open window, the desk phone, and everything else in the room except the four men standing.

She handed a couple of Polaroids to Fleming — he pocketed them without looking — and left while calling over her shoulder, "Have 'em for you in an hour."

Next came a woman wearing a white lab coat over a brown pantsuit. Kellogg, according to the name embroidered on the coat, made quick work of examining the body. "No blood, no struggle."

"Times four."

"Times four." She stood beside Fleming. "Looks like my son's desk; at least *his* door has a sign that reads Beware of Avalanche."

"There's a certain order here, Kellogg. Each folder matches a car, according to this master sheet, and most of these —" he indicated the mountain of folders filling a quarter of the desktop — "belong to vehicles picked up yesterday."

"Is your son still into cartoons?" Fleming tapped a check that was paper-clipped to a red folder. Jeff recognized the Looney Tunes logo.

"I wish. Some of the bands he listens to look like they've been made up for a horror flick."

Fleming used something that resembled an ice pick to flip open the red folder, then hurried from the room.

Kellogg glanced at the photo taped inside the folder. "Red fifty-five Nomad. It's not out there."

"You sure?" Cookson stepped up, looked at the photo. Jeff and Greer followed suit.

"Believe me," Kellogg said, "if *that* were out there, I'd have noticed it."

Greer said, "She's right, sir. It's not out there."

"Maybe Fleming's trying to read too much into all this," said Cookson. "Obviously, they were all tired. The owner of this one — Donna Tiajuana, it says, as if *that* isn't an alias — could've picked up her car last night, like everybody else, and Louie simply forgot to stamp the order sheet."

Fleming returned, and the group stepped back. He jotted information from the check onto his pad. "It's dated today."

Cookson peered at it again. "She wouldn't be the first to postdate a check."

"Which is against the law."

The cop grunted. "Yeah, well, if every-body obeyed the law, we'd be out of jobs."

"Point taken. Either way, though, I'll need to track her down, find out what gives. I wonder where the rest of the checks are?"

"Oh, damn. It's Friday, isn't it?" Cookson said. "*That's* where Tony is."

The detective raised a brow.

"The bank. He leaves here at ten till nine every Friday to take the deposit in for the old man. He's always the first one in line."

"Which bank?"

Cookson grunted. "The only one in town that hasn't been con-gobble-rated. First State."

"Call them, find out if he showed."

Cookson pushed his radio button. "Barb?"

"Sir?"

"Call First State Bank, see if Tony showed this morning."

"Ten-four."

In less than a minute, Barb's voice again. "That's affirmative."

Cookson hit the button, indicating re-ceipt.

Jeff retrieved a check from his shirt pocket. "Here's payment for mine. Okay with you if we clear out?"

Fleming verified the amount against the

invoice, scribbled info from the check onto his notepad, then put both in the breast pocket of his suit coat. "How'd you find out your car was ready?"

"Louie called this morning around seven forty-five, eight o'clock."

"After reportedly working most of the night? Did he sound tired?"

"Louie always sounded tired."

"He's right, Detective," Cookson said. "Louie sounded like a . . ."

"Like an old junker on a cold morning," Jeff finished. "He admitted he was beat, but that's never stopped him from showing up to work before. This place was what made him breathe."

Fleming said, "Not today, it didn't."

A respectful silence followed, which Cookson broke. "Yeah, it's got today's date on it, all right. Maybe this —" he read the check — "this Donna Tiajuana came in after Tony left."

Fleming leaned against the desk, crossed his arms. "Think about this: The car is gone, the deposit is gone, but the check is still here. If Tony Stella left for the bank at ten till nine, like he always does, then this woman must've come in after that."

"Adds up," said Kellogg. "You think she knows something?"

Cookson said, "Or saw something?"

"Or did something." Fleming fished the woodie's keys from the compartment that corresponded to the folder number. Jeff recalled finding the large, old Spanish oak key box in a hotel that was being salvaged out before a visit from the wrecking ball, and giving Louie the idea of using it for vehicle keys.

Instead of handing them to Jeff, though, Fleming pulled a large manila envelope from the navy and wood-grain folder. Printed across the front in large block letters was JEFF TALBOT. He rattled it. "Know what's in here?"

Jeff took the envelope, rubbed his thumbs over the metal grommets that held two cardboard wheels in place. He didn't know what was inside, and he didn't want anyone else to know — or, at least, to learn at the same time he did. "Knowing Tony, it's full of spare parts."

Cookson all but jabbed Jeff's ribs with an elbow. "That boy's the prankster, all right. You remember that Halloween about a dozen years ago when he and some friends took one of those Seattle pigs off the street and stood it on top of a police unit?"

Kellogg said, "Was there a cop in it at the time?"

"If there were, do you think Tony'd be a free man today?"

"Kellogg." Fleming tossed her the keys. "You might want to check out Talbot's car before he removes it from the scene."

Jeff exhaled, relieved that the attention had been turned away from the envelope. "Well, if you're through with my butler and me, Detective, we'll walk out with her."

Fleming didn't give up that easily. He indicated the envelope. "Let's have a look."

It bothered Jeff that even he didn't have a clue what was inside the envelope. Yet, he knew that if he didn't let the detective see what was inside, he stood a chance of losing possession — not only of it, but of his car, as well. Somewhere in the recesses of his mind he heard the Wicked Witch snap: "And your little dog, too!"

He handed over the envelope.

The detective unwound the thin, waxed cord that held the flap shut, and looked inside. "Nothing but some old photographs and postcards. Probably left in the glove compartment, and someone put them in here for safekeeping."

Greer cleared his throat. "Much like what the dry cleaner does with things left in pockets."

Jeff had mentioned the envelope to

Greer on the drive down, and now appreciated the butler's remark that cemented the safekeeping logic.

"Right." The detective handed the envelope back to Jeff.

Kellogg returned. "Nothing out of the ordinary, sir," she said as she handed the keys to Jeff.

"Don't go too far in that thing, Mr. Talbot," said the detective. "I expect we'll be talking again soon."

Jeff nodded once, then he and Greer left the office.

"Are you holding up okay?" Jeff asked as he unlocked the woodie's door.

"Yes, sir. Granted, it's been quite an experience, but the situation is under control."

"Seems to be, anyway. You can go back to the house. I'll be along a little later. Oh, and don't mention all this to Sheila. I'll tell her this afternoon."

"Yes, sir." Greer bowed slightly, then took his leave.

Jeff climbed behind the wheel, spent a moment refamiliarizing himself with the buttons and knobs, reprogramming himself to take it easy in the big old car. The Cruiser had spoiled him a little with its convenience, its compactness. He took a deep breath, and pulled the woodie through the only garage door still open. Outside, he paused and glanced in his rearview mirror. An officer slid the garage door shut, then strung yellow tape across it.

Cookson approached the woodie, and Jeff rolled down his window. "I like to give the young ones a hard time, but the truth is, I hear good things about that new detective. If there's foul play, he'll track it down."

"That's good to know," Jeff said.

"This is gonna kill Marie. Tony, too. Lose two family members at once."

"No doubt. They've always been a close-knit family."

"Yeah."

After an appropriate moment of silence, Jeff said, "If you don't need anything else, I'll get out of your way."

Cookson stepped back, effectively releasing him. "Too bad you didn't get here sooner, Talbot; might've made a difference."

Cookson walked to his squad car, climbed in, and pulled onto the highway.

Jeff sat motionless, wishing that he'd skipped breakfast after all.

Five

PRICES RISING
O'ER THE NATION
HERE IS ONE
THAT MISSED
INFLATION

— Burma-Shave

There's an area somewhere between electrified and cynical wherein lies most of humanity. It's beyond cautious, but still this side of complacent. It might best be called acceptance, and it's crowded with those who accept the world as a place full of sad occurrences that cannot be explained away by grouping them into an active bed of sinister deeds or lumping them into the latent mire of misanthropic waste. It's an area inhabited by those who trudge along, accepting what fate has to offer, neither digging their teeth into it like an unrelenting dog, nor kicking it into the mounting pile of bones labeled cold cases.

45

Cookson, Jeff decided, was a member of the community of acceptance. Likely, it was how he'd survived almost thirty years with the department without being killed in the line of duty, or stricken down by a stress-induced heart attack. He'd been a small-town cop who likely hadn't seen much more than the occasional drunken brawl or pot party.

Jeff had never belonged to that community. He'd always needed answers, even before he'd been trained to follow leads. If something seemed suspect, he worried at it till it unknotted. He wasn't one to borrow trouble; bad enough that it hounded him like a junkyard dog. Paranoia wasn't part of the equation. But because calamity was always at his heels, he'd come to expect a healthy share of it. He concluded that either way — his expectations, or Cookson's acceptance — beat the added angst that came from constantly expecting the worst, suspecting everything.

Fleming, Jeff concluded, had the right idea: expect it, prepare for it. And no matter which scenario proved out, whether Cookson's acceptance that it was a terrible accident or Fleming's gut instinct to follow the foul play possibilities, the fact didn't change that someone Jeff had known for a long time, someone who'd given him co-vert assistance on many cases, was dead. It was hard to take, harder still to accept the fact that it was an accident that might easily have been avoided.

He welcomed the distraction of the mystery envelope.

He needed coffee, and a place to depressurize, so he pulled into a large diner that resembled an Airstream trailer, then grabbed the envelope and went inside.

The mix in decor was a throwback both to pre-Depression roadside, and sock-hop chic. Black and white tile floors, red Naugahyde booths with individual juke-boxes, gleaming stainless steel and tile, and neon. Everywhere, neon. It seemed appropriate, since he'd just gotten his retro vehicle back — even if the Chevy didn't have a vintage surfboard strapped to its top.

The place smelled of onions, chili, grease, corned beef, fruit salad, apple pie, and Lysol. After the morning's events, Jeff didn't think he'd want to eat for the rest of the day. His senses changed that, though, despite the odd combination they'd been hit with.

A couple of guys in work clothes and hardhats crowded around him and seated themselves on barstools at the counter.

"You guys about missed your break

today." This from a waitress at the end of the counter who looked to be in her late teens.

"Yeah. Something's goin' on down at Louie's, lot of traffic back and forth."

"That's what I heard."

Another waitress came from the back while Jeff took a booth by the front window. The first waitress started toward him as she said to the new one on the scene: "Dottie Jean, you wanna get them a pair of drawers with life preservers while I pick up the booth?"

Jeff swallowed. He *thought* she was using diner slang, and he hoped he wouldn't have to resort to it to place *his* order. He watched as the one called Dottie Jean, who was wearing a dress straight out of TV's *Mel's Diner*, poured two mugs of black coffee, then removed a couple of dough-nuts from a covered cake stand on the countertop.

The first waitress — poodle-skirted and bobby-socked, with the tails of her tight white shirt knotted just above her waist — placed a napkin and silverware on the table in front of Jeff, then retrieved an order pad and pen from the pocket of a little apron. Meg was embroidered in red on the shirt pocket. Apparently, the place was shooting for a wide customer demographic.

"What do I have to say to get a cup of coffee?"

"I'd like a cup of coffee, please."

"Okay, I'd like a cup of coffee, please." He grabbed a laminated menu from the chrome holder on the table's edge against the wall, and told her he'd need a minute.

"Take your time." She started back to the counter. "Dottie Jean, draw one in the dark for the gent with the cool car."

The guys at the counter twisted in tandem, glanced at Jeff, then the woodie outside the window beyond him, before returning to their own business.

The way his waitress trotted out the name "Dottie Jean," Jeff wondered whether it, too, was part of the slang used to anchor the place in the past. He continued the trip down memory lane as he read "The Marilyn Monroe" (chicken croquettes with a stuffed tomato salad on the side), "The Beach Boys" (a double cheeseburger with onion rings and a large malted), and "The James Dean" (a two-way platter, with a steakburger and a foot-long Coney).

Meg returned with the coffee.

"I'll take a cheeseburger deluxe, medium-well, side of fries, a side of this hash you recommend, and a chocolate malt."

49

"Onions on the burger?"

"Sure."

"Mustard, ketchup, mayo?"

"Mustard."

"Coming right up." Meg headed toward the pass-through that opened up on a kitchen. "Kent, burn one, wax it, walk it through the garden, pin a rose on it, and paint it yellow. Put frog sticks in one alley, and a mystery in the other."

Jeff spent several seconds solving that puzzle, decided he'd withhold judgment of the mystery hash till he tasted it, and turned his attention to the manila envelope.

He opened the flap and peered inside.

On first glance, all he could see were the old photos that Detective Fleming had mentioned. They had curled from age into a cylindrical shape. He tilted the envelope and dumped the contents onto the table. An index card landed on top. It had a piece of tape at the top that wrapped around to the back, like it had first been taped to something else. Printed in block letters on the card was:

FOUND IN TALBOT WOODIE
BACK LEFT DOOR PANEL
— TONY

From what Fleming had said, Jeff expected more. All in all, there were two photos, one old postcard, Tony's note, and a miniature version of the manila envelope.

He picked up the photos. The first one was of a man and a woman standing between the headlights of an old car with their arms around each other. They wore swimsuits, dark tans, darker glasses, and huge smiles. Flanking them were two surfboards that stuck up out of the sand like boulders at Stonehenge.

The second photo was more of the same: A group of people, many with surfboards, almost filled the area in front of the driver's side of the car. Behind them was water. Lots of water. The group looked . . . wild, carefree. Hippies, maybe?

Front and center was the man from the first photo, with the woman on one side and a second woman on the other side, their arms looped together. Jeff shook his head and thought, *Why on earth were these in my car?*

A *clang* reverberated off the table. He jerked.

"Sorry. Didn't mean to startle you." The waitress placed a stainless steel container next to the heavy fountain glass. There was enough chocolate malt to fill three con-

51

temporary-sized drink containers at a discount drive-through.

She leaned over and peeked at the photos. "Now, there's a *real* blast from the past!" As she studied the photos, she pulled a paper-wrapped straw from her apron and placed it on the table. "Hey, is that — ?" She paused, looked beyond Jeff and out the plate-glass window, then again at the photos. "It is! It's the same car!"

"I don't think so." Despite his skepticism, Jeff took a closer look. There wasn't much of the car showing in the shots, and he focused on details: the shape of the headlights, the small segments of grille, the spotlight. He said, more to himself than to the young woman standing beside him, "This can't —"

"Sure it is," she said, and looked out the window again. "How fun!" Walking away, she called over her shoulder, "Your lunch'll be up soon."

Who cares? he thought. He'd lost his appetite.

Six

RIOT AT
DRUG STORE
CALLING ALL CARS
100 CUSTOMERS
99 JARS

— Burma-Shave

Mercer Talbot the Second — or Mercy, as Auntie Pim had referred to her brother on the rare occasions when she spoke to Jeff of his father — and his wife, Ellen, had been killed in a boating accident off the Juan de Fucas when Jeff was eight years old. His father was in line to take over the Talbot business, since he was the only male child of the senior Talbot. The patriarch had succeeded in building a thriving lumber trade and had excelled by being a cunning businessman.

After the accident, Jeff was raised by his Grandfather Talbot and his Aunt Primrose — his father's sister, even though she'd been nearly old enough to be Mercy's mother.

Jeff stared at the snapshot that he now held. It seemed his waitress was right. It was the same car. He studied the couple in the photos, tried to determine whether they were his mother and father, tried to remember the two strangers who stared back. There were bits and pieces in his mind, snatches of memories, fragments, held together mostly by the rare stories shared with him by his Auntie Pim when he asked questions in the years following their deaths. As he grew up, the types of questions changed, and there were periods when he didn't ask questions at all. At times, when he was younger, he felt guilty for causing Auntie Pim to cry, even though he was a child whose young mind couldn't wrap itself around the concept of never again seeing his mother and father. Other times, he'd flinch at his grandfather's brusqueness when asked about the couple, sorry that he'd pained the old man, brought back the memories that his only son was dead.

Nowadays, the schools, the courts, the families, would see to it that the suffering child had at his disposal a battalion of counselors and psychologists — whether or not the child had a need for it — but not back then, not thirty years ago.

Jeff had gotten past the emotions that had marched by single file — confusion, anger, sadness, loss, regret, resignation — until, for the most part, his parents were more one-dimensional than three. He wondered at times whether he'd remember them at all if there hadn't been an occasional peek at a picture of them.

He tried to determine at what point he'd lost memory of the sound of his mother's voice. It had rung true throughout his childhood — at least, he thought so — but, as the years passed, it became more of an echo instead of a tone, a warp in an ocean breeze instead of a modulation of her voice.

Scant little was ever revealed to him. His aunt occasionally speculated, usually after Jeff had brought home good marks from school, or done well in a baseball game: "Your father would've appreciated your talent," or "Your mother would've been so proud." These tapered from occasional to rare to nonexistent as he grew older, and by the time he'd entered high school, all expectations were delivered, and comments made upon performance, by the senior Mercer Talbot.

Today, those old-fashioned expectations laid out by the Talbot family patriarch would not only be relaxed but laughed at by many guardians. It wouldn't hurt if some of those were now being enforced, Jeff believed: "Represent the family well," Mercer Talbot cautioned the boy. "Respect your elders, carry on the family name (that one wasn't going to happen), don't disgrace the Talbot name, marry well, take a wife who will respect the family name as much as any woman from the outside might be expected to; determine whether she's capable of raising a child that will adhere to the same principles expected of you." Mercer Talbot Senior had expected a lot, Jeff now realized.

In light of all that, Jeff wondered, *how in the world did my parents get away with* this? He emphasized the last word by thumping the photos with a knuckle. There had to be another explanation.

Jeff studied the shot of the couple. Maybe these two hippies in the photo weren't Mercer and Ellen Talbot. Maybe one of them took the shot. It was possible that these people were friends of Jeff's parents. But, if that were true, then why were they, particularly his father — the child upon which Mercer Senior had pinned all hopes — hanging out with these . . . bohemians? These beach bums?

What if his parents had parked the woodie on the beach and had gone for a walk? That was it! His shoulders relaxed as he realized that anyone could've stood in front of the car, and gotten a friend to take the picture, then showed it around later, jokingly. "Look at my wheels, man!" they'd say to their friends. Yeah, that was it. It made sense, right?

Wait. If that had been the case, then why were the items stowed away in the door panel, and how did they get there? The shoulder muscles knotted again. Absently, he unwrapped the straw, and sucked thick chocolate from the fountain glass.

Maybe Tony Stella was playing a little joke on him after all. Yeah, that was it. Tony the prankster was being true to character. Jeff tried to make that notion stick. Just as quickly, though, he remembered the other items.

The waitress's exclamation that it was the same car had knocked the postcard right out of his thoughts. Now he picked it up.

The stamp had been canceled on the twenty-eighth of either March or May — he couldn't be sure, since the ink hadn't made a full impression — in 1963, in Bakersfield, California. The card was addressed in block letters to M.T., General Delivery, Seattle. There was no salutation, no signature. The message, also printed, was brief:

The treasure is in the vault. Next step: the caper. Meet me at my home in the desert. Will let you know when.

Jeff's hands dropped deadweight to the tabletop. He'd spent all that time focusing on the photos, when the postcard all but said that his parents had been involved in some sort of *robbery?* If the card had been postmarked Seattle, he might've thought that the vault meant the Wells Fargo safe in his own basement. But *Bakersfield?*

M.T. had to be Mercer Talbot. Who'd written the message, though? Who was this guy that his father had obviously been in cahoots with? And what about his home in the desert? Was it someplace they'd met before?

The clue didn't narrow it down much. How big was the desert area of California? Was it desert like Scottsdale, Arizona, or bona fide desert? Sheila's sister, Karen, had wintered down there, doing freelance photography, and had reported that Scottsdale proper wasn't *really* desert any-

more. The climate had been altered in recent years by people who planted greenery,
then watered the hell out of it to get it to
grow. That had created a humidity that
didn't exist forty years ago. Jeff didn't
know but what the same thing had been
done to the desertlike regions of California. Not that it mattered. Unless he
learned something more, he was looking
for a dime on a highway.

He turned the card over. It showed a map
of the western two-thirds of the United
States, with the states shaded one of four
pastel shades so as to discern borders: green,
pink, yellow, and orange. From Chicago to
San Francisco was the Santa Fe Railway
route, with offshoots to Los Angeles, and
through Texas to the Gulf. A boxed message
told him that the red circles — now faded to
coral — all along the route indicated Santa
Fe hotels and/or dining and lunchrooms
under management of Fred Harvey.

Jeff knew very little about Harvey,
mostly that his waitresses were called
Harvey Girls, and that he provided some
of the best food in the country back when
train travel was the thing. You'd be hard-
pressed to get much reality from the movie
of the same name starring Judy Garland;
he knew that much. And that Fred Harvey

collectibles — china, postcards, turquoise jewelry crafted by Indians for the gift shops — were relatively common.

Likely, Jeff deduced, the person who had sent the postcard he now held had been traveling by rail and could've picked it up at any Fred Harvey establishment between Chicago and San Francisco. He turned the card back over to check for a description, but the only thing printed there, other than an elaborately scripted "Post Card" to the left of the two-cent postage stamp, was a stylized circle formed out of the letters in Fred Harvey's name. Smart marketing move; the cards could be sold anywhere along the route.

He read the message again, turning the phrases this way and that, trying to determine whether they could mean something else, *anything* else. No way around it: the message laid out plans for some sort of robbery — a job, a hit, a heist. Jeff was left with one gnawing question: Had his parents actually been involved in something *illegal?*

He picked up the last item, the tiny envelope, and unwound the cord from its figure eight around two discs. He squeezed the sides together and upended it. Out fell a key.

It was a small, silver key. He studied it, turned it over, turned it back again. Nothing indicated what it might open. Was it to a strongbox somewhere? Or an old deposit box at a bank? It seemed too large for a deposit box, but he couldn't be sure. The wards were like new, meaning that whatever the key fit into should open easily. He looked inside the small envelope for a slip of paper with a combination, or an address, or the name of a terminal — *something*.

Nothing.

Okay, *think*.

He'd start with Tony when he went to the Stella home to pay his respects, ask him about his discovery of the items. As they visited, reminisced about Louie and Michael, Jeff was confident that Tony would bring up the subject of the car, ask what Jeff thought about the work, the new color. That's when Jeff could mention the items from the door panel, and, possibly, learn more about them. He'd feel better, anyway, after he talked to the person who'd actually found the stuff.

"You haven't even touched your lunch."

Jeff jumped. He wasn't even aware that the waitress had set a plate in front of him. He looked around. The place was packed, buzzing with noise from chatty diners, two more servers who had joined the ranks, and a litter of half-grown kids pushing noses against the glass-front ice cream counter.

"Sorry, miss."

"That's okay. I can wrap it to go, if you want."

While he was considering this option, the bell attached to the door chimed, and the waitress glanced in its direction. "Lots of people don't like to eat alone," she said. "Would it bother you if I seated another single here?"

Would it? He'd never been asked that before. "I suppose not." Maybe some polite conversation with a stranger would get his mind off the time capsule.

Jeff finished stowing the items in the manila envelope as the newcomer squeezed into the booth opposite him. It was a tight fit. Forty-five seconds into the situation, and he knew he'd made a mistake. The guy talked on and on, moving from one subject to another with no visible indication that he was breathing. It was like being on the phone with Louie Stella.

Thinking about Louie made Jeff think about the four men who'd lost their lives that morning, and all because someone had gotten sloppy about taking precautions.

Jeff interrupted the nonstop flow. "I just remembered that I have to be somewhere." Lame, he knew, but what choice did he have?

"What? Oh. But you haven't even touched your lunch. Meg will sack it up for you, if —"

"Nah, thanks." Jeff grabbed the manila envelope and slid out of the booth.

After he'd stopped at the register to pay his check and leave a tip, he looked back. His booth partner grabbed a French fry from Jeff's abandoned basket, then followed up by sliding the whole thing to his own side of the table.

Outside, Jeff took a deep breath. What had started as a good day, with nothing more on his plate than running a few errands and scoping out some estate sale addresses for the following morning, had turned into the deaths of an old acquaintance, his son, and two others, and a mystery found inside a door panel of the car he'd driven for almost fifteen years.

Jeff's grandfather had purchased the car new, Jeff knew that much, and, until today, it had never crossed his mind that anyone but his grandfather had driven it. At some point, though, it appeared that Jeff's parents had had access to it — and for enough time to have dismantled the rear door panel and stashed the puzzling time capsule. Mercer Senior worshiped the car, wouldn't even let Jeff drive it. It was only after Jeff, being sole heir, inherited everything, that he'd climbed behind the wheel.

That was in 1988. He was with the Bureau, working a case that involved the museum theft of several Indian artifacts: blankets and rugs woven by the Navaho, deerskin dresses and shirts beaded by the Sioux, and several pieces of Zuni turquoise and silver jewelry with its finely cut and inlaid stones.

He received word that the old man had died, and he'd caught the next flight out of Albuquerque. The news hadn't come as a surprise. The Talbot family patriarch, born on the cusp of the twentieth century, had suffered failing health steadily after his daughter, Primrose, succumbed to arthritis the year before. So, at twenty-five, Jeff was the last surviving Talbot.

Memories of his parents were one-dimensional: their wedding portrait, which he recalled hanging on the dining room wall until their deaths, when it had been stored away. He'd found it in the basement, along with every other thing pertaining to the couple, after his grand-father's death, and assumed then that the visible memories of the pair had been too much for the family to bear. Or that his grandfather and aunt had been afraid that the constant reminders might scar him, since he was so young, and they knew that some semblance of a normal upbringing had to be continued.

He sometimes wondered what it'd be like to have a normal family: grandparents still living, who looked forward to the children and grandchildren coming home for the holidays, parents who invited grown children along on vacation. He hadn't given it much thought before, but there had been a lot of death in his family, a *lot* of death. In Sheila's family, too.

Practically from the moment Jeff returned to school after his parents' funeral, he was in a different century. He was an outsider after that. Most of his classmates didn't know what to think about the new restraints put on him, the archaic way in which he was raised, in how he was dressed. The senior Mercer was seventy-one then, and, although he was still ruling his lumber empire with an iron fist, it was a fist splotched with age and showing the first signs of tremor. The female influence in Jeff's life from that pivotal moment was his father's spinster sister.

It bothered Jeff that he couldn't remember more about his parents. *Don't let it,* he counseled himself. *It's been over thirty years.*

As he drove up the main drag of Queen Anne Avenue, he caught his reflection in the plate-glass windows of the shops. It amazed him for an instant, seeing himself in the woodie.

He pulled into his driveway and toward the carriage house in back. Greer walked out as Jeff brought the car to a stop.

The butler approached, examined the left front fender just above the wheel well. "As you said at the shop, sir, the body work on her is flawless. I dare say the joinery of the wood is better than when she was new. How did she handle on the drive home?"

"Good and sound. Nothing more than the usual creaks of an old wooden-bodied car."

"That's the real test. A car can look good, but it's of no use if it doesn't run well and handle properly."

"I never realized that you knew so much about cars."

"Yes, sir."

Jeff considered asking the butler to elaborate, but decided not to take the time just yet. "Are you okay, Greer? I mean, after what happened this morning?" Jeff wasn't sure whether the young man had ever seen a dead body before, but he knew it could be traumatic, even if the cause of death was natural. Finding four bodies boggled the mind.

"Yes, sir. Bear in mind, I've been trained to attend any situation."

"I forget that. I'm grateful for it, though."

"If you'll excuse me, sir, I promised the missus that I'd haul some packages downstairs. UPS will be here soon to pick them up."

"Tell her I'll be up in a few minutes."

"Yes, sir."

Jeff walked around the car, checking the work from every angle, opening and closing the doors, the back hatch, the hood. When he opened the left rear door, his thoughts returned to the things found in the panel, things stored there back when it was Mercer Talbot's car, when no one else was allowed behind the wheel. His parents' access to the woodie wouldn't have been a problem, however. It wouldn't have taken that long, he didn't think, to stash something inside a door panel. The question was, Why? And why the woodie?

He considered that for a moment, came up with a logical answer relatively quickly: because they knew that Mercer Senior would never sell the car. The '48 Fleetmaster was Chevy's crown jewel, and its last true wooden-bodied car. Mercer didn't have a large family. The lumber baron's motivation for buying a station wagon as opposed to a smaller car was simple: more space for more wood.

Now, if only the rest could be solved so easily.

And why did it look like his parents had robbed a bank? Another thought came to him: Had they used the woodie? His mind conjured a disturbing image of them dressed like beatniks, brandishing firearms, and fleeing a crime scene in the family car.

Seven

WHEN THE JAR
IS EMPTY
WIFE BEGINS TO SING
"FOR SPICES, JAM & JELLY
THAT JAR IS JUST THE THING"

— Burma-Shave

Sheila jumped up from the computer and gave Jeff a quick hug. "Where have you been? Greer said that you'd be home soon, but he wouldn't even talk about the car."

"Restraint. The sign of a good butler."

"Restraint? What are you talking about?"

Jeff stared absently at the computer screen. "How are the auctions going?"

"That's it? You've waited six months for that car, and this morning you couldn't get out of the house fast enough to go get it. Now, you waltz in here and ask nonchalantly, 'How are the auctions going?' What's gotten into you, Talbot?"

Jeff sat on the Eastlake Victorian rocker

in the corner. He would've slumped into it had there been room, but the diminutive chair with its ornate carvings of larks and flowers had been sized for the female form. With his knees practically at eye level, he felt like the Incredible Hulk bunched up on Miss Muffet's tuffet.

He tucked the manila envelope with its earth-rattling time capsule beside him, squirmed around in a failed effort to find a more comfortable position, and gave up with a sigh.

Sheila sat back down at the computer. "No haircut?"

Jeff's hand instinctively flew to the back of his neck. "Slipped my mind."

"You're Casual Friday's poster boy."

He thought, *It's been anything but.*

She indicated the envelope. "What's that?"

"I'll get to it in a minute."

Sheila had adjusted again to her illness, found her comfort level, and Jeff didn't want to chance upsetting her. He approached the subject carefully, employed the step-by-step method typically used to deliver disturbing news to family members.

When he told the part about nudging the foot, she said, "He was unconscious?"

"Yeah. Permanently."

Sheila sat back.

"Greer threw open the garage doors at the back, and I went through the rest of the place."

Sheila studied his face. "How many, hon?"

Jeff looked up, surprised that she'd suddenly pieced it together. "Four."

"No wonder you haven't been going on about the car." They were silent for a moment. "So, my husband finds four dead people, and Greer doesn't tell me a thing about it."

"I told him not to. Besides, I only found three. He found the first one."

Sheila straightened. "Greer found a dead person? Is he okay?"

"He reminded me that he's trained for all sorts of emergencies."

"I suppose, but he's not like you. You're always stumbling upon this sort of thing." She waved a hand as if Jeff's proclivity for being on the scenes of crimes were nothing. For a moment, she was lost in thought. When she surfaced, she said, "Wasn't that a father-son business?"

"Father and two sons. Both Louie — that's the old man — and Michael were in there, and they both died. But the other son, Tony, wasn't. That's some consolation. At least Marie — that's Louie's wife

71

— still has Tony, not only to help her through this, but to keep the business going."

"You sound as if you know them."

Jeff had never told anyone that Louie had been one of his informants. He'd sworn to take the secret to his grave, and that's what he'd do. *His* grave, not Louie's. The fact that Louie wasn't around didn't change that, except to make it more imperative. The news could put Louie's family in danger.

He didn't like hiding things from Sheila, but sometimes he had no choice. He said, "I *do* know them. Louie was doing maintenance on that woodie long before I was ever allowed to drive it. Grandfather made it clear that no one else was ever to touch it. I've told you how he worshiped that car. Anyway, I usually went with him to Louie's when I was a kid. I practically watched Louie's kids grow up. And Marie used to work in the office, answering phones, bookkeeping, that sort of thing."

"I'm sorry, Jeff. Sometimes your outside world seems pretty one-dimensional to me, and I forget that you know lots of people out there. It's harder when I don't have a face to put with the names."

"It's okay, really."

"You'll be going to visit Tony and Mrs. Stella, right? I'll make something special for you to take along."

Jeff knew that food was a mender in more ways than one. It would likely be more therapeutic for Sheila to prepare something than it would be for the family that received it. Marie Stella was considered one of the best Italian cooks in the region.

Jeff said, "That would be great, if you're sure you have time. It's really about the only thing we *can* do."

"I'll see to it as soon as you tell me about that." She pointed at the envelope.

"Another morning shocker." Jeff sighed, then filled her in on its discovery, and what he had found inside.

While Jeff shared the story, Sheila studied the photos, the postcard, the key.

"So you see?" he concluded, taking the items from her. "There was a mystery this morning, only it wasn't the four deaths. And, until I get a chance to talk to Tony, I can't be sure what's going on with this."

"Where are your snoop skills, Detective? There's plenty you can do. For starters, dig out some old photos of your parents and compare them to these. Look through old clippings, or receipts, or . . . I don't know, but there are *boxes* of stuff stored in the basement and the attic."

"Do you know how long that's going to take?" Jeff watched his wife, practically saw the wheels turning behind her eyes. He stuck the photos and postcard back in the envelope, toyed with the key.

"Tell you what," she said, her voice edged with excitement. "You know that I've been wanting to go through all that stuff. I could begin with the boxes in the basement — that's a summer job, anyway — while you go through old photo albums."

"Don't start, Sheila. I've told you, I don't want to take the time. It's going to be a huge job."

"And I'll do most of the work. All you have to do is walk through and pick out what you want to keep. Listen, it's important that we sustain a steady flow of eBay merchandise, and there's so much stuff in storage. You told me yourself that your aunt never got rid of anything. She was just a more organized pack rat than, well, most pack rats."

"I don't know. It's just too much for me to mess with, especially now that this —" he held up the photos — "has been sprung on me."

"Greer can help me. We'll set up tables, group things according to subject, then you can make a quick pass-through. Greer and I will follow and sort. And, remember, it might actually help solve your mystery. We'll put anything that might pertain to it — documents, old newspaper clippings, ledgers, records — in one segment. It'll be like a real treasure hunt!"

Jeff studied the key, thought about Sheila's proposal. Several times over the years, he'd considered sorting through the boxes. He knew that his grandfather never bothered with anything in the Victorian home, never processed or threw away; he'd left all that up to his daughter, Primrose. Jeff also knew that the woman had never disposed of anything. If she found a different clock for one of the home's several mantels, she stored the discarded one. If she replaced linens or figurines, if she added a new china pattern, the rejects were stored somewhere in the house. She'd never tossed out so much as a magazine.

It was going to be a major undertaking. Finally, though, he said, "Okay. But no selling anything without my okay. And no throwing anything away, either."

"Deal."

He pulled his key ring from his jeans

pocket and strung the key onto it. "I suppose I could call the library in Bakersfield. Or the newspaper. Or both, for that matter, see if I can get copies of articles covering robberies in 1963."

"See? Now you're cooking. I'd tell you to check our local library, too, except for two reasons."

"*Two* reasons?"

"Number one, they're getting ready to close for eight days in order to make budget. I would imagine they're swamped with people trying to get everything done before the shutdown."

"I'd forgotten about that. I wonder if it'll make any difference over the long term?"

"I'm sure it will. The question is: Will it be positive or negative?"

Jeff raised a brow, acknowledging that it was a good question. "What's the second reason?"

"From what you've told me, if your parents were in on something illegal, your grandfather would've pulled some strings — and loosened his purse strings — to keep it out of the local papers."

"You got that right." Jeff slapped his thighs. "Enough about this mess, though. You probably need another batch of something or other to put up for sale."

76

"We have under thirty lots pending, with the promise of another thirty being listed next week. So, yeah, bring me . . ." The last word trailed off as she studied an inventory sheet Jeff had supplied her with earlier, which listed the remaining items from an estate he'd purchased. "Bring me the celluloid boxes, a dozen or so tablecloths, and the jars of marbles."

"How'd the last bunch of tablecloths do?" Jeff only remembered them because they'd been stored in a pristine set of Oshkosh luggage that he kept for his personal collection. Before OshKosh B'Gosh children's clothing made the company name a household word in the eighties, the company had manufactured some of the best-quality luggage around. Even Babe Ruth had carried an Oshkosh suitcase for several years. The last Jeff had heard, someone was trying to buy it from the MCI Sports Museum in D.C.

Sheila's eyes sparked as she flashed a wide smile.

He backtracked his thoughts to the tablecloths. "That well, huh?"

"How does two grand sound?"

"Just from the tablecloths in that set of luggage? Sounds like *you're* the one who robbed a bank."

"Remember, they were all Wilendurs — not Wilendures with the *e,* which was added later — and in new condition. Still had the tags, the bright colors, those great forties graphics. Counting the ones from the trunk, too, I've sold about forty. I kept a few for gifts: one with baskets of strawberries for my friend, Tracy, in Albuquerque, and a couple of luncheon cloths with Mexican pottery and Southwest themes for the old camper that my sister's fixing up."

He grinned. "It wouldn't matter if you weren't making money. You're loving this, aren't you?"

"I really am."

"It's a lot of work. I wouldn't want to wear all the hats you're wearing in this on-line auction business."

"I've got lots of help, actually. Fantastic on-line tools, like automated shipping calculators so the customers can get that info before bidding, and an automated E-mail response that I can preprogram and not have to retype the same basic 'You won!' message every time I make a transaction. There's also automated checkout, and invoice management tools. . . . I could go on and on. And more is being developed all the time. Makes it so much easier, like having employees, and it leaves more time for the photography, posting, packaging, and shipping."

Jeff raised a brow. "I'm impressed. But, even with the conveniences, I had no idea you were doing so much work. I mean, you've been selling on eBay for —" he paused to calculate.

"Three months next week," Sheila said.

"Why didn't you tell me sooner that you were doing so much work?"

"Why? We're in this together, remember?"

He knew that she meant in *everything* together, but still, he didn't want to take up so much of her time. Sure, she'd helped him some over the last few years, keeping an eye on the prices that various antiques were bringing, tracking down and ordering reference books when he'd bought out someone's large collection of something he didn't know too much about. But this auction gig was a whole new ball game.

"If it'll make you feel better, Jeff, look at it this way. It's probably helped me get past what happened last year better than anything else could have. It keeps me busy, it helps me contribute to our bank account, and it's amazing to unpack the boxes you bring home from the warehouse and discover all the treasures that old woman amassed."

Jeff rearranged himself in the chair, but he wasn't any more comfortable than when he started. "Yeah. It was a challenge just wrapping it all up for transport without stopping to check hallmarks, signatures, backstamps, and tags."

"Plus, you had to spend extra time unwrapping, sorting out what to offer to Blanche, then rewrapping the things you brought home for our eBay store."

Blanche Appleby was Jeff's primary buyer and owner of the huge antiques mall called All Things Old that stood practically under the Alaskan Way Viaduct by the downtown piers. Blanche was both friend and business associate and had offered Jeff the use of a vacant warehouse. "No way around it. That caused you more work, though, because I didn't have time to clean anything. You probably cringe every time you open a box of silver."

"Polishing silver is therapeutic, too. And Greer's helped a lot with that. Anyway, I can see why so many people are selling online. It's very lucrative, if you handle it right.

"Matter of fact —" Sheila turned back to the computer, and made a couple of mouse clicks — "let me show you *how* lucrative."

Her antique oak desk came out of a century-old Kansas schoolhouse. To the left of the kneehole, behind a large door, was a slide-out shelf designed for a typewriter. That shelf now held the printer. Sheila opened the door, grabbed the sheets, and sorted them. She handed him a copy. "As you can see, we're doing extremely well."

He skimmed the figures, checked the bottom line, and let out a low whistle. "Is this before or after the huge commission you're going to charge me? I haven't done nearly this well with the things I've taken to Blanche."

"That's part of the appeal of selling online, I suppose. If you've hit on something that's hot — and we've got lots of items that are — you can usually count on making a hefty profit. It was hard for me at first, but I list just about everything with no reserve — even the railroad china."

"No reserve? You're kidding, right? I mean, what if only one person bids, or you sell an eighty-dollar butter pat for three bucks? It's too risky to —"

"Jeff, would you calm down? That hasn't happened. And, I don't know whether others do this, but when I'm about to list several pieces of anything in a particular area of collecting, I E-mail the collectors' clubs and societies tied in to that subject and give them a heads-up.

"Even without all that," she concluded, "we can always count on collector obsession."

Jeff stood, stretched the kinks out of his back. "Well, I can see that I don't have anything to worry about. Before long, you won't need me." He was joking, but she was so fired up over her work that she didn't notice.

"Jeff, the other sellers are also out picking. I can't replenish, so I'm relying on you to do that. And, like you said, Blanche has an obligation to *all* her pickers. She couldn't just buy all that stuff from you at once and, by doing so, have to turn down Lanny, or Tinker, or those retired couples who are trying to supplement their social security checks. This has been perfect for everybody concerned."

Jeff leaned against the doorjamb. "Okay, okay, you've convinced me. Keep working your fingers to the bone."

"So, what's on your schedule for this afternoon?"

"Oh, I don't know. It's too late to mess

with the haircut." He gave her a wink. "What have you got in mind?"

"Sorry, Romeo, but I have work to do. You do, too, if you want to solve The Puzzle of the Perplexing Package."

Eight

WHEN JUNIOR TAKES
YOUR TIES
AND CAR
IT'S TIME TO BUY
AN EXTRA JAR

— Burma-Shave

Downstairs, Jeff grabbed a bottle of Foster's from the refrigerator and headed for the library. Despite the melodramatic spin Sheila had put on things, she had a point. To unravel this mystery, he needed to treat it like any other: Follow each lead, no matter how trivial or fruitless it seemed.

He took the family albums from the barrister case and stacked them on the library table. There were other albums stashed somewhere, albums full of photos that he hadn't looked at in years. Sheila would likely find them while sifting through the items that spelled out the Talbot history.

A fitted leather case that looked like aged tobacco sat at the back of the table. Jeff opened it and chose the ancient magnifying glass with its ivory handle. The set had belonged to a ship's captain, and when Jeff used it, he liked to imagine things along the routes that the captain had sailed. Beside the box that also held a matching telescope, inkwell, pens, and straightedges was an identical case that held a Browning sextant.

The optics of the old glass were impeccable. Jeff set about scrutinizing photos of his parents, recognizing a certain irony that the sea had taken his parents and, according to the provenance of these tools, the sea captain, too, had been swallowed up by the very thing he loved.

The people in the more formal photos looked so different from the snapshots of those on the beach that a casual glance said they weren't even remotely the same. But when Jeff put his training to work, studying the shapes of his subjects' lips, their noses, their eyes, he confirmed it. The two people — wearing carefree smiles, flashing the peace sign at the photographer, standing on a beach in a parallel world of surf, sand, and God knows what else — were his parents.

★ ★ ★

That was easy, Jeff thought. *Unsettling, but easy.* Despite the heat, he shivered slightly. A premonition told him that nothing else about the whole, bizarre discovery would be.

He took the beer with him to his leather club chair near the fireplace and finished it while he considered the clues.

Had his parents met their partner in crime on the beach? Even if they had, the robbery could've taken place anywhere. Apparently, though, the guy who'd written the postcard had lived in the desert.

Jeff pictured unending stretches of parched earth marked with animal skulls picked clean, then bleached by the relentless sun, an occasional isolated cabin, foreboding sounds. Hot *noir.* He'd read short stories that had stuck with him — stories that had drawn a vivid, frightening image of the desert's remoteness, its dangers, its demand for survival instincts: Nancy Pickard's story about how a woman and her child endured, John Lutz's gritty classic about the old man, and Earlene Fowler's that was set in an Arizona diner along Route 66.

Thinking of those made it even more difficult to imagine his mother and father meeting up with a crime partner in the desert. And what if they had? Uncovering the truth probably wouldn't change anything now, if there were any chance he could find the truth.

What did he have? The beach, the desert, hippies, the woodie, surfboards, and a key. And, he reminded himself, the postmark. Was Bakersfield on the beach? He didn't think so, but his California geography wasn't the best.

He pulled an atlas from a shelf on the stand beside him and looked up Bakersfield. No, it wasn't on the beach.

Still, it was in California, so California was where he'd begin.

Greer started past the door, mail in hand, then stopped. "Sir, do you need anything?"

"As a matter of fact, Greer, would you get me the phone number for the newspaper in Bakersfield."

"California, sir?"

"Yeah. Library, too, while you're at it."

"Yes, sir."

Within minutes, Greer returned and handed Jeff a computer printout. "I've included hours of operation, as well."

"Thanks."

Greer bowed slightly before leaving the room.

Jeff skimmed the sheet, amazed at all the information the butler had compiled in such a short amount of time.

The newspaper, the *Bakersfield Californian*, actually employed a librarian. That was promising. And, although the blurb from the Web site mentioned researching microfilm at the town library first, it also stated that the newspaper's librarian would, for a fee, research the archives. Jeff's heart beat a little faster. With any luck at all, he'd have the robbery data before the evening news aired.

He moved to the desk and punched in the phone number.

He was put on hold. While he waited, he pictured CDs spinning in computers, ready to bring forth ancient articles at the stroke of a key. He wondered whether they would want an E-mail address, and if they'd take a credit card number for the charges. He debated tracking down Greer and getting the E-mail address as a measure of saving time when someone picked up on the other end.

"Sorry to keep you waiting," a male voice said. "It's been a little hectic. You know, Friday, summer."

Sounds young, Jeff thought. "I understand. Listen, I need any articles about bank robberies in that area in 1963."

"You're kidding, right?"

Now Jeff *knew* he was young, and probably anxious to get to that Friday summer thing. "No. Don't you have them on computers? You know, CD-rommed, cross-referenced, broadbanded, or whatever it is you do for high speed and quick access?"

"It's enough of a job archiving the week's issues, but you think we can go back to the early sixties just like *that?*"

Jeff heard the snap of fingers. "I'll admit I don't know what it involves, but . . . yeah, I guess that's what I thought."

"We can check back that far, but there's a lot of ground to cover. It's gonna cost some bucks."

"How many bucks?"

"I'd have to check with my boss on Monday. Have you tried the library?"

Jeff glanced at the sheet. "You mean Beale Memorial?"

"Yes."

"No."

"You might get quicker results, digging back that far. I mean, don't they do historic microfilm searches for people all the time?"

"Okay, thanks." Jeff pressed the plunger, punched in the library's number. When someone answered, he said, "Reference desk, please."

"I'm sorry, they just left. We close at six on Fridays." He glanced at the clock on the mantel — it read 5:50 — and was about to point this out when the voice said, "Would you mind calling back on Monday?"

Do I have any choice? he thought. "I suppose not. Thanks."

He rang off. The preliminary steps had been quick, but they had gotten him nowhere.

Were there any other clues that would tell him what his parents had been up to? Anything else he could do till Monday?

He found Greer clicking keys on a laptop computer at the small table in the butler's pantry.

"How long would it take to search online for bank robberies across southern California in nineteen sixty-three?"

"Not long, sir." Greer clicked his cursor on a search engine in a drop-down list, then typed in the keywords. "The next step might, though, depending upon how many hits we get.

"See this? Over thirteen thousand."

"That narrows it down," Jeff said ironically. "It'd be quicker for me to go to Bakersfield."

"No help from the library?"

"Not till Monday."

"Some of these look promising, though."

Jeff hadn't yet told Greer the details of what he'd found in the manila envelope, so he didn't point out that "promising" wasn't the best choice of words. He read over Greer's shoulder as each link was accessed, directed him to move on. Everything that might fit had been solved and, fortunately, his parents' names hadn't been mentioned anywhere.

He thanked Greer, then returned to the library.

What was he going to do now? It wasn't like he could make a weekend trip down there and find answers. He grabbed at the long shot that Sheila might turn up something to narrow the search. In the meantime, he'd have to cool his heels.

Nine

THE ONE HORSE SHAY
HAS HAD ITS DAY
SO HAS THE BRUSH
AND LATHER WAY
USE

— Burma-Shave

The grandfather clock in the foyer chimed as Jeff headed for the den with an after-dinner cup of coffee. He wanted to catch the evening news, see whether KIRO or KOMO would use footage he'd seen them tape at Louie's garage that morning.

Sheila was in the basement, anxious to begin her treasure hunt, and Greer had the evening off.

Jeff waited as a female reporter botched up a report by using *laying* where she should've used *lying,* and tripping over the English language like a pup over its own feet, before announcing melodramatically, "Details of four on the floor —" a pause for effect — "quadruple deaths at a remote auto body shop, when we return."

Four on the floor? Media as entertainment. Nothing new. The St. Valentine's Day Massacre, The Black Dahlia Case, even The Lonely Hearts Murders — all these titles had been coined by the media. He didn't know whether the media's propensity for catchy labels was more common than ever, or whether applied histrionics for the purpose of capitalizing on the misfortune of others only made it seem so. He had to give them credit on this one, though: four bodies, auto shop — four on the floor. Louie would've appreciated it.

The doorbell rang. As Jeff walked toward the front of the house, he pondered the reporter's use of the word *remote.* It irritated him that anything not within the city was considered remote. Didn't news anchors ever venture beyond the daily route from their high-rise, ocean-view apartments to the TV station to a trendy, upscale downtown restaurant before returning to their private cocoons?

As he opened the door, he found himself hoping it was someone he might easily get rid of so that he could get back to the TV. He didn't want to miss the report on the deaths.

Standing on the stoop was an unlikely pair: Chris Fleming, the detective from the morning crime scene, and Gordon Easthope, Jeff's old FBI partner and good friend.

"Get in here, you old scoundrel," Jeff said as he and Gordy exchanged bear hugs and slaps on the back. "Would it have hurt you to pick up a phone?"

"Yeah, yeah." Gordy's booming voice echoed in the foyer. Gordy turned to Fleming, who had followed him inside. "Date 'em once, and they think they own you."

Jeff closed the door. "Don't give me that one-date line. Partners under the badge is more like a marriage than partners under the sheets."

"Yeah, but *you* divorced *me,* remember?"

Jeff let that drop, greeted Fleming, then turned back to his former partner. "Apparently, you heard about Louie."

"The word caught up to me in Florida. Bad deal, that's for sure."

"You're just in time to catch the news report on it." He led the way to the den.

They took seats around the TV set.

Fleming said, "You have a butler, and you answer your own door?"

"Greer has the night off. Either of you

want something to drink, I'll get it during the next commercial."

"Nah, I'm fine," Gordy said.

Fleming echoed him.

The commercial faded, and the network returned to the news. Jeff turned up the volume. The over-the-shoulder graphic behind the news anchor had a deep red ground over which was emblazoned the words, *FOUR ON THE FLOOR*, in a chrome-colored font like diner neon. Below it, the door of a vintage car hung open to reveal the retro-designed dashboard with its round dials and Bakelite knobs. An oversized floor-mount stick shift shot up out of the image with a 3-D effect, its ivory cue-ball grip engraved with a capital *H* and *1 2 3 4* at its four points in black. They'd left out *R* for reverse. Still, Jeff had seen less thought go into the jacket art of many a best-selling novel.

The news anchor resumed the melodramatic air Jeff had witnessed earlier. "What appears to have been a bizarre accident occurred in a *very* remote area southeast of Sea-Tac early this morning. Our own Heather Moore is on the scene. Heather?"

Moore, microphone in hand, stood in front of the now-abandoned auto shop, with its chipped paint and dingy facade counterpointed by the bright yellow tape hanging around its middle like a loosened belt. "That's right, Carrie. As you can see, I'm standing in front of Louie's Retro Resto and Chop Shop in a remote community south of Seattle where four men were found this morning, apparent victims of asphyxiation. Dead are Louis Stella, sixty-two, his son, Michael Stella, twenty-four, both of Rainier Valley; Renton resident Stan Baker, thirty-eight, and, finally, nineteen-year-old Jason VanDyke of rural Black Diamond. It is reported that the building was closed up, and the exhaust fans weren't functioning at the time the four bodies were discovered. The police tell me that they are looking into the deaths, but that they don't suspect foul play.

"However," she continued, "there is a mystery: The whereabouts of a fifth employee — Anthony Stella, who is also the eldest son of Louis Stella — are not known. He was last seen this morning, just before the bodies were discovered." Pause, then, "I'm Heather Moore, reporting live."

"Thank you, Heather."

Carrie and her male anchor exchanged brief comments on the unfortunate accident, then lowered their heads for a slice of a second before looking back up at the camera. They flashed smiles and launched into a report about the annual King County Fair.

Jeff sat back, studied the two men opposite him. "So. Four dead, Tony's who knows where, and you two show up together on my doorstep. What's going on?"

Gordy cleared his throat. "Interstate car theft ring. Louie and I have been working together on this for over a year. Fleming, here, suspects that the deaths weren't an accident. He's agreed to hold off informing the media as much as he can, while I track a few things on the theft angle. As you know, though, when the media makes it sound sinister, Joe Blow Public wants to know whether he's in danger. Bottom line: it just might all be tied in."

"Any proof?"

Fleming sighed heavily. "Not yet. The lab's short-handed — people on vacation, confirmed murders taking priority. They told me to get in line. So there's no telling how long the preliminaries will take. If they can dig up something unusual, we can at least move on to a full toxicological workup."

"GS-MS?" Gordy asked. A gas chromatograph-mass spectrometer was used for detecting chemical poisoning.

"Yeah, but you know how expensive that is? I have to have good reason."

Jeff said, "What's the story on Tony?"

"His mother says he's probably gone down the coast for the weekend. Apparently, it's common for him to take off this time of year, join in on cruise nights, stay with friends, or sack out in cheap motor courts, mom-and-pop joints, like that."

"You don't believe her?"

"It's not that," Fleming said. "I know there are people who take off without any thought to what might happen if there's an emergency. People in our situation — with a housebound loved one, for instance — wouldn't think of being inaccessible."

"What about his cell phone?"

"She said he doesn't have one."

Jeff said to Gordy, "Working with the task force here?"

"Yeah. More than one connection between Seattle and Chicago on this case. When I heard about Louie, I talked the boss into sending me up here."

Jeff had always thought Gordy should be among the top brass, but the longtime agent maintained that he wanted to do field work till it either killed him or he was forced out to pasture.

"Got much to go on?"

Gordy said, "Several threads, but they keep slipping the knots."

"So, Fleming." Jeff drank coffee. "Are you doing anything to locate Tony, or waiting to see if he comes home when the weekend's over?"

"You ask a lot of questions for someone who's no longer on this side of the badge."

"You don't have to answer." Jeff sat back.

Fleming moved a shoulder. "Besides contacting the highway patrol in three states, I had my assistant put out a need-to-locate to all the auto shows and cruise nights she could find scheduled for this weekend. Easy enough with the Internet, put out the word to the clubs that there's been a family emergency, and that he needs to call home."

"You know what he's driving, then?"

"We're assuming, of course, that he's in the car he drove to the bank this morning: nineteen thirty-six Olds that he modified: street rod, checker-cab yellow with flames."

"That shouldn't be too hard to spot."

Fleming said, "On the interstate, no. But get her in with a bunch of other street rods and muscle cars, and it's tougher. You've worked car theft, right?"

Jeff nodded. "Hard enough to train

yourself not to get caught up in the beauty of them. It's the only way to spot something."

Gordy chuckled. "Remember what you used to do?"

"Yeah." Jeff smiled. "I've still got that machine."

"Machine?" Fleming asked. "What is it? Street rod? Muscle car? Stock?"

Gordy coughed. "Wrong gear, Fleming. It's a gum ball machine."

Fleming stared at Jeff.

Jeff filled him in. "I used to sit and stare at gum balls before I had to check a car show for boosted wheels. You'd be surprised how it takes the shine off those bright colors: peacock blue, candy apple red, yellow, orange, green. That way, you go to the show, you're acclimated. Then you're looking at identifying features — grilles, bumpers, headlights, taillights — instead of being distracted by bright, shiny objects like you're a magpie."

"I'll keep that in mind," Fleming said. "Of course, the weekend car trip angle could be a convenience. If you were going to commit a crime, wouldn't you do it when people expected you to be out of town for three days?"

"Good point." Jeff thought about what

else they'd found that morning. "Hey, what about the woman with the check? Did you talk to her?"

"Yeah. Her file had a cell phone number. She's staying in town on some business, not leaving till next week. She picked up her car Friday morning. Question is: Was everyone alive when she left?

"Anyway," Fleming continued, "when I told her there had been an accident at the shop, she asked if everyone was okay. She seemed upset by the news, said she'd see if Marie Stella needed anything."

Jeff waited, but when Fleming didn't add any details about the Tiajuana woman, he decided to see what he could learn about Tony. "You've obviously talked to Louie's bank," Jeff said. "Tony's visit was the usual drill?"

"Right down to his joking with the security guard and telling at least three tellers that he was saving himself for when they left their husbands. He cashed his check, made the shop deposit, was out of there by ten after nine."

The detective seemed okay answering Jeff's questions, so he kept asking them. "Don't you think that if he was planning to go on the lam, he would've kept the shop's money?"

"I thought of that, sure. Then again, *not* keeping it makes him look less suspicious."

Jeff said to Gordy, "You know Marie, right? Are you going to question her?"

Gordy and Fleming exchanged glances, then Gordy said, "That's where we thought you might come in. She'd be more likely to open up to you; might be better for now if she doesn't know that I'm working the car angle."

Jeff looked at Fleming. "And you agreed to this?"

"You think I'd be answering your damned questions if I hadn't?" Fleming glanced at Gordy in a way that told Jeff the detective was letting Gordy call the shots. "I've got a hunch she knows something, but she's not going to open up to the cops. Yet. She said you have to know Tony. He takes off like that, but he'll show up Monday morning at the shop, just like he always does during car season." Fleming shook his head, continued with, "Sounds like it's carved on the calendar, like deer season."

"Might as well be," Gordy said. "These car people take it seriously." He turned to Jeff. "Anyhow, we'd like you to go over to the house, pay your respects, see if you can get a read on the situation."

Jeff glanced at his watch, exhaled. "I planned on going down there anyway. I suppose it won't hurt to see if I can pick up any clues."

"Appreciate it." Gordy slapped his palms on his knees and hoisted himself off the couch. "I'd better find a room."

Fleming followed Gordy's lead, stood.

Jeff jumped up. "Gordy, you're not going anywhere. There's plenty of room here, and Sheila would love the opportunity to cook for somebody else for a change."

"I wouldn't want to put you two out. You weren't expecting company."

"You're not company. Who's driving?"

"I am," Fleming said. "Easthope's rental is down at the station."

"Tell you what," Jeff said. "I'll change clothes, tell Sheila what's up, then drop you off at the station on my way to Marie's." He looked from Gordy to Fleming. "And I'll give you a call after I talk to her. How does that sound?"

"Sounds like a plan," Fleming said.

They walked toward the door, and after Fleming left, Gordy said, "Are you sure I won't be in the way?"

"Positive. You know, I'm surprised Fleming was so agreeable."

"I hear he's bucking for a recommendation. Should give me the leeway we'll need."

"Yeah." Jeff studied Gordy's face. "You're not trying to pull me back into the ranks, are you?"

"Maybe a little."

"It won't work."

"I know. In the meantime, it'll be like the old days."

"Nothing's ever like the old days."

Ten

ALTHO INSURED
REMEMBER, KIDDO
THEY DON'T PAY YOU
THEY PAY
YOUR WIDOW

— Burma-Shave

Rainier Valley. The old neighborhood used to be called Garlic Gulch, back when Remo Borracchini's bakery first opened, and mass was said in Italian at Our Lady of Mount Virgin Church every week. Now, after a bout with gangs and subsequent white flight a few decades earlier, it was cleaning up its act and drawing a fresh population.

Louie Stella, the tough old cob, had refused to be forced out back then. Marie, whose plan was to stay put in one house from "I do" to "Rest in Peace," had proven as stalwart as her husband. They were among a handful who stayed.

Jeff drove the woodie past newer homes

and apartment buildings on his way into town, making his way over to the Stella neighborhood with its clapboard homes, front porches, large shade trees in front, alleys bordered by backyard gardens where dark-eyed women grew vegetables — red, green, and white like their native flag — for sauce recipes long committed to memory.

The curb was lined with cars on both sides, reaching both directions to the cross streets. Several people made their way down the sidewalks, carrying casserole dishes and pie plates as if they were headed to a covered dish supper at church. Jeff inched past the Stella home, then drove around and parked in the alley. He was more than a little protective of the newly restored car and, although there were a couple of cars back there, he saw it as safer than the bumper-car feel of the street. He grabbed the basket containing Sheila's offerings and walked along the fence. The aroma of the sweets in the basket fought with the tomatoes and peppers from Marie's garden. He made his way to the front door.

As he reached up to ring the bell, the door swung open, and a young man brushed past him.

Jeff hadn't seen the man in years. "Hollister?"

The man turned. "Talbot."

"How long have you been out?"

"Long enough to know that I'm never going back. Can you believe it? They kept me longer than they keep pervs, and all I did was boost a few cars. This country needs to work on its priorities."

Jeff knew better than to waste time explaining to Hollister the error of his ways. Most perpetrators had their mind games securely fastened down, always at the ready to justify their actions. Still, he wasn't sure that Hollister was wrong. "I won't argue with you there, Guy. Getting away with murder does seem more likely than walking away from car theft. Of course, stealing a cop car moved you into a different realm."

"Yeah, well, the fool shouldn't have left the keys in it." Guy Hollister leaned against the stair railing, looked up and down the street. "You still driving that woodie? Forty-eight, right?"

"Parked her in the alley. Lots of people here to pay their respects."

"Yeah, most of the neighborhood's gone, but the old-timers have come from all around. Folks are still loyal. To most people, anyway."

"What's wrong? Didn't they welcome you back with open arms?"

"Look, Talbot, I paid my dues. And despite old man Stella's making me stay away from the shop, Marie has always been like a mother to me. I'm truly sorry that she's having to go through this."

Guy Hollister had been to the Stellas what Eddie was to the Cleavers on *Leave It to Beaver.* He'd even looked a little like him, back before prison had taken some of the mischievous glint from his eyes. Until he went from prankster to perpetrator, he was mothered by Marie and tolerated by Louie. He and Tony were the same age, and he used to put up with Michael's tagging along after them a lot more than Tony did.

"I should get inside, pay my respects to Marie and Tony." Jeff started toward the door.

"You'll probably find Marie in the kitchen," Guy said as he descended the stairs. "Tony hasn't showed, though."

Jeff turned back. "No kidding?"

"Nope, and I wanted to take him out for a beer, try to distract him, you know? But nobody's seen him."

Jeff descended the stairs, joined Guy. "When's the last time *you* saw him?"

"If I didn't know better, Talbot, I'd think you're investigating something. Didn't you retire?"

"The only things I investigate nowadays are the dovetailed joints of old furniture and the hallmarks on silver and china." Jeff leaned against the stair railing, tried to appear relaxed. "See, I'm into old stuff, and Tony found some old stuff hidden in my car when he restored it. I'd hoped to talk to him about it."

"Oh, yeah. He mentioned something about that. Showed me some junk — old pictures of some hippies or surfers, something like that."

Jeff bristled, tried not to let it show. He still couldn't wrap his mind around the fact that his parents had gone wild, taken the mother of all joy rides.

When Jeff didn't respond, Hollister said, "Those photos are really eating at you, huh? What's wrong, is it — ?" Hollister paused, then snapped his fingers. "It's your parents, isn't it?"

Jeff tried to maintain his cool. He moved a shoulder. "Could be, I suppose. Did Tony give you any details?"

"From what I could tell, there weren't any details to give. He found an old cigar box wedged inside —"

"Wait, there wasn't a cigar box. Just photos and a postcard."

"Dunno what to tell you. He showed *me* an old cigar box. I only remember it because the label had an old car on it from the thirties, yellow, sort of like his Olds. Can't be worth much — the box, that is. Hell, I recently went on a date with a gal who had a purse made out of one."

Why would Tony keep the cigar box? It could be worth something for the labels, but Jeff wasn't interested in that. It was the stuff that had been found *in* the box that mattered. Now he just had to find out *why* it mattered.

With Hollister, he decided to downplay his curiosity. "Nah, I doubt the box is worth anything. I just want to find out about the stuff that was in it. Which brings me back to Tony. Do you think he'll show up tonight?"

"Search me. I'm surprised he isn't already here. In a way, I think it's harder on his mom than losing Louie and Michael. Don't get me wrong. It's just that dealing with a tragedy face on is one thing; not knowing, that's a tough one to take."

"Yeah."

"She'll call me when he shows. I'll tell him you're looking for him."

Jeff nodded. "He doesn't have a cell phone?"

"Marie has tried to get Tony to carry one, but he says he doesn't need it. Says that if he had one, it would mean that he didn't trust his car to get him from point A to point B, and what would that say about his skills as a mechanic?"

"That makes sense, if you look at it from just the one angle. I only started carrying one a few months ago."

Guy stepped back. "No kidding? *You* have a cell? Welcome to the twenty-first, Talbot."

"Ha, ha," Jeff said flatly. "What are you up to these days, besides staying away from other people's cars?"

"There's where you're wrong, my friend. I might've slipped up and gotten caught, but most car thieves don't, so I'm cashing in on that." He whipped a business card from the breast pocket of his suit coat and presented it to Jeff. "I sell car insurance. Give me a call. I'll beat your current rate on the forty-eight." He flashed a smile, then headed for the sidewalk.

Jeff glanced at the card appreciatively. Where else but in America could an ex–car thief go into business selling car insurance? He couldn't think of a more logical career move.

After Guy left, Jeff considered the things that would keep Tony away when his father and little brother had died that morning. Not knowing about the tragedy, for one thing. It was genuinely possible for Tony to take off for the weekend, with no thought toward the unexpected. It wasn't too long ago that Jeff might've been the same way himself, especially before he'd gotten married. If he were single, he might easily take off looking for antiques and be gone for a few days without feeling the need to check in with anyone or to let someone know where he could be reached.

Jeff ascended the stairs. The steady stream of people going into and out of the Stella home removed the need to ring the bell. Jeff fell in line and went inside. He doubted that he'd have any time alone with Marie, and he wasn't sure what he expected to pick up. Something in her mannerisms, maybe.

Jeff hadn't seen Marie in years. Her hair was wavy, shoulder length, the same style it'd always been, only now the black had given over to gray around her face. She wore a black dress with a double strand of pearls and an apron that looked like it was reserved for Sundays. Her tired eyes were rimmed red.

"Jeffrey!" she called, breaking free of a knot of people.

A young woman took the basket from him and disappeared through a door off the kitchen.

"Marie." He held her. "I'm so sorry."

"It's a sad day, Jeffrey, but look around you. So many people loved my Louie, and my baby Michael." Her voice broke when she spoke her son's name.

Jeff felt helpless. He rubbed her shoulder as he embraced her, allowed her time to compose herself. When she did, he said, "Sheila made her bread pudding with blackberry sauce, and a couple of fruit salads."

"She didn't have to do that."

"She wanted to, said she only wishes she could do more."

"Thank you, Jeffrey. And thank her for me, too. Everyone's done so much," Marie said as she scanned the kitchen.

He followed her gaze. Every perceivable surface was crowded with food.

"Jeffrey, I understand you were there this morning. You found them?"

It surprised him that she brought it up so quickly. "Yes. Yes, our butler and I did. I wish we'd gotten there in time to make a difference."

She gripped his hand tightly. "Did you see my Tony?"

This surprised him even more. He studied her face. "No, Marie, I'm sorry. You haven't heard from him?"

She flapped her hands. "Oh, I'm sure he's at one of his cruises. Guy said he'd go find him for me, if I had any way to narrow it down. But —" she shrugged more elaborately than usual, likely a result of pent-up nerves.

He didn't want her to know he was sort of working with Fleming, so he said, "Do you want the police to do something?"

"Oh, the detective who was here earlier said he'd put out a locator, but who knows whether they really do what they say?"

"I can follow up, if you think it'll help."

"It might." She retrieved a business card from a drawer and handed it to Jeff. "At least it'll remind them to try, and that would give me some peace of mind. A little, anyway."

"Done." Jeff glanced at Detective Fleming's name, then handed the card back to Marie. "Now, do you have someone to stay with you tonight?"

"Oh, sure; people stacked to the rafters, you know. But, I — I'll feel better when my Tony gets here."

"I know. Listen, if you need me to do anything else . . . ?"

"You could let me know if that detective is really trying to find Tony."

"It's a promise." He was cautious with what he said next. "Marie, if he shows up and seems . . . worried, or . . . well, I don't know. But, if he feels threatened or something, call me."

"Do you think — what, Jeffrey? Do you think this maybe wasn't an accident? Did that detective tell you something he didn't tell me?"

"No. At least, I don't think so. But don't you think it's better that he wants to be sure? For everybody's safety?"

"Well, yes, it makes sense that he would. Do you think Tony's in some sort of danger?"

"Remember what you used to say, Marie?" As he recited it, she joined in. "Trust God, but row toward shore."

"Yes, Jeffrey, it's good that they're taking precautions."

"If you think of anything or you need anything, you call me, okay?"

"I will, bambino, I will."

It hadn't been much, yet it had been everything. The desperation in Marie's

115

voice, the urgency in her eyes, the fear, the realization. It told him what he believed Fleming needed to know for now: Marie had no idea where Tony was.

Eleven

SHAVING BRUSH
AND SOAPY SMEAR
WENT OUT OF
STYLE WITH
HOOPS MY DEAR

— Burma-Shave

When Jeff returned from the Stellas, Sheila and Gordy were seated at the refectory table in the kitchen. Gordy was eating dinner leftovers like he hadn't seen a meal in a week.

"The airlines have all but stopped feeding their travelers, and they don't give you enough time between connections to do much more than grab a bag of chips. Besides, how many chances do I get for Sheila's pot roast?"

Sheila beamed. Clearly, it was good for her to have Gordy in the house.

Jeff poured himself a cup of coffee and joined them. "Hon, I know you're busy with the eBay stuff, so don't get carried away with cooking just because Gordy's here."

As Sheila walked to the range, she said, "Anything beyond opening a can classifies as carried away to you." She returned with a duplicate of the bread pudding with blackberry sauce that Jeff had taken to Marie's, and dished it up for the three of them. "Don't worry about me. I've already made a mental menu."

"Jeff's right, though, sweetie," Gordy said. "Most of the time, I'll be in my car."

"Then I'll make takeout."

"I won't turn it down." Gordy mopped up brown gravy with a piece of bread and popped it into his mouth before relinquishing the plate.

"How's Mrs. Stella holding up?" Sheila asked as they started on their dessert.

"Better than I expected, actually. Tony hasn't shown yet, though, and she's more distressed over that than anything."

"I can't even imagine," Sheila said.

The three finished their desserts in silence.

Sheila cleared the table, then came up behind Jeff and gave him a hug. "I'm going to leave you two to catch up with each other."

"I've got your number," he said as he pulled her face to his and gave her a quick kiss. "You just want to do more excavating in the basement."

She held up her hands in mock surrender. "Guilty as charged, Investigator."

Gordy spoke first after Sheila left. "Does Marie know anything?"

"No. I can safely say she hasn't been in contact with Tony."

"Think she'll call when he shows?"

"One can only hope. I'll call and check in with her a time or two this weekend."

"Good."

"Someone else is looking for him, too. Old friend of ours."

Gordy said, "It wouldn't be Hollister, would it?"

"Good work, Agent Easthope. Glad to see that your telepathic skills still work."

"I'm watching him for the car theft ring."

Jeff hadn't seen that coming. "So, you know he's selling car insurance?"

"Only in America," Gordy said flatly.

"I found it admirable. Of course, that was before I knew he was in your sights. Got much on him?"

"Other than Louie dropping his name a few times, no. But I have to consider whether that leopard's spots have changed."

While Jeff wondered the same thing, Gordy said, "Sheila seems excited about some project in the basement. She said you'd probably give me the details."

Jeff filled his friend and former partner in on the time capsule that had been found in the car, and on his concerns.

When he'd finished, Gordy said, "I can put the Bureau on it, you know, check a few files."

"The last thing I want is for the FBI to connect me, a former agent, with Bonnie and Clyde parents."

"Now, that brings up a point. If they really were, don't you think it would've shown up when you were being screened for acceptance?"

"If they'd been caught, sure. Apparently, they weren't. I don't want it added to my file now."

"You're right. No sense in a complication that doesn't mean a damned thing anyway." He gulped coffee.

"It means something to me," Jeff said evenly.

"Don't you think I know that?" Gordy set the mug down hard. "I'm talking about the Bureau. This has nothing to do with your former job, so there's no reason for it to be a monkey on the back of your employment file. I just meant that I could pull some old files on bank jobs."

"If it comes down to that, okay."

"Look, it's no secret that you hate things hanging fire. Right now, though, everything is: Tony's whereabouts, your access to records in California, the funeral for Louie and his kid. Why don't you try to get some sleep for now, then keep yourself busy this weekend? Things will start falling into slots come Monday."

"I hope so." Jeff took his mug to the sink, rinsed it. "What about you? Aren't you going to bed?"

"Time difference has me screwed up. I'll kill an hour or so reviewing what I've got on the car thefts." Gordy stood. "You know . . ." He paused, rubbed the bottom of his lip with his thumb.

Jeff had seen this all too many times during his years working with the man. He braced himself.

"There's a cruise tomorrow night in Puyallup. Why don't you take the woodie over, do a little snooping around? She's the perfect cover."

"I'm not into that scene, and you know it."

Gordy said to the ceiling, "How quickly they forget," then to Jeff, "You've been trained to *fit* into it. You might pick up something. Hell, maybe Tony'll be back in town by then. You're wanting to talk to him, right? So, you can talk to him for all of us."

"You think he'd go to a cruise night after what's happened?"

Gordy shrugged. "Some of these guys are so obsessed with their four-wheeled babies that they're crazy-addicted to the cruise nights and car shows. It might be Tony's way of letting off steam."

Jeff kept quiet.

"C'mon, Jeff, you know what he looks like, you know his mannerisms; the cops don't. Even if they did, they've only got one officer with a car that would fit in, and he's gone on vacation. C'mon, it'll help you kill some time till Monday."

Jeff considered it. There wouldn't be much work involved. The car was spotless. New paint job, too. And he *did* want to ask Tony about the time capsule.

Gordy gave it one last push. "Give me one good reason why you can't do it."

He didn't have one, and they both knew it. "I should've known that asking you to stay here would mean trouble."

Saturday morning, Jeff took Gordy's advice and stayed busy in order to keep his mind off the previous day's events. After hitting a couple of estate sales that yielded nothing spectacular, he returned home, checked on Sheila's progress in the basement, and talked with her about potential storage space for the items still at the warehouse. He didn't want to infringe upon Blanche's generosity any longer than he had to.

After Sheila assured him they had the room, he made a quick phone call to Blanche and scheduled a lunch date for Tuesday. At that time, she would make a final run-through of the warehouse items and determine what else she wanted to buy from Jeff.

He called the Stella home, spoke with a relative who said that Marie was napping — Jeff took that as sedated, since he'd never known the woman to do something so decadent as to take a daytime nap — and that Tony hadn't been located.

After lunch, he and Gordy watched *Bullitt* and *Road to Perdition*. Before leaving for the cruise night, he spent several minutes studying the colored spheres in the vintage gum ball machine he kept in his library.

The driver of a souped-up red pickup slowed, gave Jeff an opening for joining the caravan. Jeff waved. On his wood-paneled door, he kept beat with a song booming from the truck's speakers about a guy who loved his truck.

He made the circle a few times, watching for Tony's yellow Olds, thankful that he'd studied the gum balls. Even people who weren't normally into cars found themselves mesmerized by the bright nostalgia on wheels. He saw a few yellow muscle cars and old trucks, but nothing remotely similar to the gangster car of the thirties with its canary/cab paint job.

He pulled into the fairgrounds parking lot, stopped a short distance behind the people in lawn chairs and on tailgates gathered curbside to admire the participating cars. After pouring coffee into his thermos lid, he got out and leaned against the back of his car and watched the parade of steel and lacquer crawl by.

For his purposes, this made more sense than cruising. Behind the wheel, he'd been limited to seeing only the vehicle in front of him and behind him, and those that he passed on the two-way drag. He'd also had to watch out for pedestrians, and concentrate on the driving, and hope that nothing happened to his newly restored car.

At least the weather was good, and he

assumed that the pleasant evening accounted for the large groups of people flanking the main drag from one end of town to the other.

He drank coffee, relaxed, eventually dropped the woodie's tailgate, and sat down. This had done him good, this participating in a community. He began to understand why people became obsessed with the cruise scene, with their cars as showpieces. Part of it had to be the simple act of escaping to a simpler time. That alone could recharge a person's batteries.

He was about to go up front for more coffee when a Model A that had been crossed with a flamingo rumbled toward him and pulled to a stop.

Guy Hollister climbed out of the driver's seat. "New at this, aren't you, Talbot? Otherwise, you wouldn't be hiding this beauty back here."

Jeff circled the pink car. "Insurance business must be good."

"Sure is."

"Too bad you didn't know that before you got busted for boosting cars."

"Are you sure you're not back on Hoover's payroll, Talbot?"

"Antiques pay better."

Guy eyed the woodie. "I believe that."

"Tony did a great job on her."

"He's one of the best."

"I had hoped I'd run into him, get a chance to thank him personally, but I haven't seen him anywhere. Yellow Olds, right?"

"That's the only one he has running right now. But he's not here."

"Come to think of it, he'd probably be with Marie if he's back in town."

"Yeah. I just came from there. She hasn't heard from him yet."

Jeff nodded, hoped Guy was telling the truth. He indicated the pink car. "Tony do that?"

"Sure did. Michael, too." Guy patted the hood, then whipped a bandana from his back jeans pocket and buffed the spot he'd just touched. "Thirty-one Model A Tudor, chopped six inches, Hemi under the hood, chrome mag wheels. No offense to your Chevy, but Henry *made* the automobile industry."

"Right." Jeff said flatly, slipping easily into the game. " 'Fix-Or-Repair-Daily.' "

"Hey, now." He folded the red paisley square and tucked it away before continuing. "Doesn't matter what you drive, but you have to admire Henry's business sense. Did you know that he despised waste? He even specified that the crates used to ship parts to his factories be made of boards a certain length. Those crates were then dismantled and used for floorboards in the Model Ts."

"I can appreciate that," Jeff said. "My ancestors were in the lumber business."

"Lumber! Did you know that Henry owned four million acres of America, most of it forest? Michigan, Upper Peninsula. Four *million.* That way, he had all the wood he wanted for building his cars: steering wheels, wooden wheel spokes —"

"Wood-paneled." Jeff got a kick out of how Guy said "Henry," as if he were a personal friend of the long-dead auto magnate.

"Right." The guy let a few seconds pass. "Yeah, old Henry hated waste. Did you know that he created charcoal briquettes?"

Jeff raised a brow. *That* he didn't know.

Guy latched on to this show of interest, and Jeff thought how the man's personality was perfect for a salesman.

"Yep," Guy went on. "He had so many ashes left over from the smelters and, true to his character, he didn't want to waste them. So he developed a way to process the stuff, contacted E. G. Kingsford, and struck a deal." He took a deep breath, shook his head. "Henry Ford," he said with reverence, "was the richest man in America. But, you see, he wasn't about the money. He was *genius*."

"Sounds like it," Jeff said. "I have a question for you."

"Shoot."

"If you admire Henry Ford so much, why did you turn one of his cars into a street rod?"

"Hey." Guy stretched the word as he pulled a Fonzie stance. "This is America. Henry had his vision. I have mine."

Guy hopped into his car, gave a wave, and cranked up some retro club mix on his sound system. Jeff had never heard it, but he felt its bass reverberate in his shoes.

As he watched the car glide down the street, he thought about its driver and his unconcerned manner every time Tony's name came up. *Was it unnatural?* Jeff wondered, followed by a question he hadn't before considered: Did Guy Hollister know where Tony was? Or, more to the point, was he protecting Tony from something?

Twelve

COLLEGE CUTIE
PIGSKIN HERO
BRISTLY
KISS
HERO
ZERO

— Burma-Shave

"He's not gonna show." Cookson, who had just returned from a coffee run, distributed the styrofoam cups to Jeff, Gordy, and Fleming, along with his prediction. The foursome had been staked out in front of the auto shop since six Monday morning, had gone through all the coffee in their thermoses, and now had started on the supply from the convenience store a few blocks up the road.

"What do you propose?" Cookson asked Fleming.

"No sense in all of us staying here."

Gordy said, "Talbot and I will check

the cabin I told you about earlier."

Fleming said, "Cookson, if you've got someone who can hang around here for a couple of hours, I'll swing by the lab, see if they have anything new."

"Got 'er covered," Cookson said.

Jeff left first, slowed down after he was out of view. Within a few minutes, Gordy came up behind him. They drove a couple more miles, where Jeff led the way into the busy parking lot of a strip mall.

Gordy parked his nondescript sedan and jumped into the woodie.

Jeff said, "You think Tony's hiding out there?"

"If something's out of whack and Tony's on the lam, that place is as good as any and better than most."

Jeff remembered the last time he'd seen the cabin. When Tony and Guy were teenagers, they'd gotten into some trouble over a prank they'd pulled on the school superintendent and had headed to a cabin the Stellas owned in the hills north of Cle Elum. If the TV reporter thought the auto shop was remote, she'd never find her way out of the wooded area where the cabin was hidden. To Gordy, Jeff said, "You haven't been there yet?"

"Nope. Louie even told me once that

Marie hasn't been out there since the boys were born. If Tony's hiding out there, though, he'll likely stay put for awhile."

"What makes you think he's hiding out? You don't think —"

"That he killed them? No. But I think he knows something, or he would've been back in town by now."

"What are you waiting on?"

"Nothing, now that we know he's under the radar. You drive, I'll give directions."

"Now *that's* like the old days."

Jeff eased the woodie along the dirt road. They had to be on their toes, or they'd miss the path that led down to the cabin. The trees and shrubs were at their height of fullness, which meant the grass was, too.

"Here it is," Jeff said.

"Let me out before you drive in there. I want to check for tire prints."

"If you think I'm pulling this car through that brush, you're nuts."

"Yeah, I don't blame you. If Tony's here, I wonder how he got his baby down there without scratching her up?" Gordy climbed from the car, stooped over, walked through to the other side. He returned, approached Jeff's window. "Somebody's driven in.

Opening's wider than you think, but it's up to you."

He wanted to take care of the car but he wasn't going to be a slave to it. He squeezed through cautiously, waited for Gordy to climb back in.

"I don't know what you were worried about, Talbot. There was enough room left over for a supermodel to walk along beside you."

"Sideways, maybe. Let's hope we don't have to get out of here in a hurry."

As he drove the half-mile stretch down to the cabin, Jeff recalled the last time he'd been out here. It had been almost a decade since he'd met Louie here for info on a car theft ring.

The masterminds had boosted two dozen classics simultaneously one Friday night during football season. They'd hit every high school parking lot in the region, and, although they hadn't gotten many high-dollar wheels compared to what Jeff had seen during Saturday night's cruise, they'd obviously done their homework. In spite of Louie's covert help, it had taken the FBI nearly two years to find the operation that was altering everything from the VINs to the fuzzy dice that hung from the rearview mirrors.

Meanwhile, it was said that the emotional fallout — football players fighting with girlfriends whom they'd allowed to drive said cars to the games, parents dealing with muscle-bound sons who whined because they had to walk to school, and coaches scrambling in futile attempts to keep up team morale (and their own tenure) — had affected the teams enough to spur losing streaks that continued the rest of the season and, consequently, affected college draft choices, upcoming teenage weddings, and the local new car dealerships when graduation rolled around the next spring.

Jeff parked the car. They got out and approached the cabin, Gordy motioning Jeff around to the back.

This is like the old days, Jeff thought. With Gordy's bulk, he'd never liked a foot chase and had always sent Jeff around back. Add to the equation that Gordy was now in his late fifties. He could still chase them down (God help the suspect when Gordy caught him), but he was in heart attack alley, and he knew it.

Jeff waited. Heard the knock on the door. Nothing from inside.

Another knock. Nothing.

He looked around, noted the garage that

stood about fifty feet from the cabin. He was wondering whether it would bring forth anything when he heard someone from inside the cabin walk toward the back door.

Jeff braced himself for the pounce.

The door opened, and Gordy stepped out.

Jeff exhaled. "What'd you do, pick the lock?"

"Louie gave me a key." Gordy turned around, went back inside.

Jeff followed, fell into old patterns, and opened the refrigerator. Inside was a squirt bottle of mustard, a jar of relish, and three cans of Pepsi. "Nothing that couldn't have been left the last time Louie and the boys were here."

Gordy looked around, said, "Let's check out the garage."

Jeff trailed him.

The building was small and dilapidated and looked like it had been painted around the same time as the auto shop. The only door was the lift-up kind, and there was a small window on the side of the building. Gordy peered through the glass.

"I'll be damned." He ran to the door, threw it open.

Parked inside was the yellow Oldsmobile.

"Where do you suppose he is?" Jeff said.

"Search me," Gordy said before searching inside the car, under the car, every square inch of the car, the garage, and, finally, the surrounding woods.

"Okay," he said finally, "we know he was driving this car Friday morning, and we know it's the only car he has. Maybe he stashed this one and took off with someone else."

"Or, could be something as simple as being down the road at a neighbor's place."

Gordy shrugged. "We don't have the time or the manpower to stake out this place for God knows how long. We'll peddle my card, hope somebody calls if they see him."

An hour later, they had cut a wide swath, finding only three people at home, and two employees at a convenience store/Laundromat combo at a nearby crossroad. It reminded Jeff that this was the worst part about being an agent: the seemingly dead-end grunt work that came with following gut instincts and thin leads.

Their best stroke of luck was finding a sheriff's deputy fueling his unit outside the store. He took Gordy's card and, after claiming that he single-handedly patrolled an area the size of Rhode Island, he none-theless promised to keep an eye out.

"If Tony *is* trying to hide," Gordy said to Jeff after they'd started back toward Se-attle, "he's picked the right spot."

"There's always the chance that he or Michael — or even Louie, for that matter — had an old car stashed out here. Wouldn't take much to get one running, if you had the right tools and a few parts."

"It's a possibility, but you know what the trouble is with it?"

"What's that?"

"Anyone who'd know the answer is al-ready dead."

Thirteen

IF HARMONY
IS WHAT
YOU CRAVE
THEN GET
A TUBA

— Burma-Shave

By the time they got home, Jeff was glad he'd asked Sheila to make his calls to Bakersfield. He was in no mood to mess with the phone.

He found her in the basement, surrounded by a couple dozen cartons. "What's with the half-empty boxes?"

She climbed through and kissed him. "Actually, they're half full."

"Not in my world."

"Must mean that you and Gordy didn't have any luck."

"Not enough to tip the scales. Tony never showed."

"I sort of suspected that. Someone who

137

was making calls for the Stella family phoned to say that the funeral's been postponed till Wednesday."

"Really? I wonder what they'll do if Tony isn't heard from by then?"

"Good question."

"What about Bakersfield? Did you find my puzzle piece?"

She looked up from the stack of ledgers she was sorting through. "Not even close, hon. I'm sorry."

"What happened?"

"They're shorthanded, what with summer and all, so it's going to take a while."

"A while like an afternoon, or a while like a week?"

"A while like a week or two. Maybe three. They said it might be easier if you came down and went through the microfilm yourself."

"Not when you're in Seattle."

"That's what I told them." She stood, cocked her head, studied him. "Why *don't* you go down there?"

"You're kidding, right?"

"Think about it." Sheila grabbed an atlas. "I did some checking. See this?" She traced a route with her finger. "You've talked for years about going to the big flea market in Pasadena, and about picking in a different region. And, it couldn't come at a better time. You're meeting Blanche tomorrow, right?"

"Yeah."

"It won't take long to wrap up that project. You said yourself that we're in good shape financially. And I read recently that Pasadena's one of the U.S.'s top ten flea markets. And it's nothing to spot a celebrity there — you might see Diane Keaton!"

"Why would I want to see Diane Keaton?"

"I don't know, but she's been spotted there before. Give me one reason why you can't make that trip."

"Well, for one thing, there's you."

"What's your point?"

"You know what I mean."

"I'm fine, Jeff, and I'm going to be busy with the eBay stuff. I won't even notice you're gone."

"But what about Gordy staying here?"

"That makes it even better, if you think about it. You'll have less to worry about."

"Have you found anything down here?"

"Oh! I can't believe I didn't think to tell you first. You'd better sit down."

"God, Sheila, don't tell me it's that bad."

"I'm not sure, but I found something. I felt strange reading it, like I was breaking a trust or, I don't know, and —"

"Sheila. Would you just tell me what it is?"

"Sorry. It's a diary that your Aunt Primrose kept. I mean, it's one of them. I've found several, but she only recorded the month and day, not the year, so I'm having to skim all of them."

Unable to believe that anything ominous could be found in his old-maid aunt's diaries, Jeff smiled, relaxed. "You know, I'd forgotten all about her doing that."

"She must've taken it to heart. She wrote 'Dear Diary' on every entry, just like a teenage girl would."

"Well, you're wasting your time if you expect to find anything sinister in Auntie Pim's diaries."

"*Au contraire, monsieur.* I think she knew exactly what your father was up to."

"What? Why do you say that?"

Sheila cleared her throat, then recited:

Dear Diary,
  I've decided to help Mercy. He has asked for my help, and I can't find it in myself to turn him down. May God protect me if our father finds out.

"Let me see that."

Sheila handed him the little book, pointed to the passage.

He reread the words. He checked the date: April 1. If he didn't already know that his aunt despised April Fool's jokes, he'd give her credit for this doozy. *This clinches it,* he thought finally as he slumped in his seat. His father had been a . . . what? A bank robber? A fugitive? Had Mercer Senior found out? Found out and bailed out his son somehow? Was all this why the old man had been adamant about Jeff going in to some form of law enforcement?

"Jeff, honey, are you okay? What do you think?"

"I don't know *what* to think. I mean, I keep trying to put a different spin on all this, trying to come up with . . . something. But I can't.

"I'll tell you one thing, though," he continued. "I never realized that Dad and Auntie Pim had such a strong relationship."

"I understand how that is. It doesn't matter how different Karen and I are from each other, we have a sisterly bond that supercedes everything. She knows things about me that even you don't know."

"So now you admit to keeping secrets?"

"Not necessarily. But she and I lived together till she went off to college. A lot happens then, whether parents realize it or not. Sometimes, the stuff seems earth-shattering when you're young."

"Sheila, I know you're busy, so be honest: How long do you think it'll take you to read through the diaries?"

"Gosh, I don't know. They're boxed up with other things: old clothes, linens, books, scrapbooks, albums. I thumbed through three years of diaries before I found this one, and no telling what's in the attic. Don't forget, there's her bedroom to consider, too."

Jeff waved a hand in dismissal. "Anything in her bedroom would've been when she was older, I'm sure."

"You're probably right." She sighed. "I'll go through them until I find everything mentioning your father that sounds questionable."

"At this point, everything sounds questionable."

Sheila thumbed through the diary. "I'll work as quickly as I can, if that's any consolation. I really think, though, that you should consider making that trip."

"No," he said. But the words from "California, Here I Come" started playing involuntarily in his mind.

Fourteen

CAUTIOUS RIDER
TO HER
RECKLESS DEAR
LET'S HAVE LESS BULL
AND LOTS MORE STEER

— Burma-Shave

Blanche Appleby's copper-red hair was the shape and height of a bee skep, adding eight inches to her four-foot-seven body. Under the hair was a brain with more business sense, and a body with more energy, than any woman half her age could claim. She ran All Things Old with equal parts passion and grit. She had a keen eye for antiques, an uncanny knack for snapping up what would sell, and a mind like a calculator.

"Clear as mud, Jeffrey?"

"Got it," he said, more than a little grateful for the removable stickers and roll of curling ribbon he'd brought along for identifying the items Blanche wished to purchase.

He'd arrived at the warehouse a couple of hours early in order to unwrap and categorize the stuff for Blanche to look through. It was a bonus for the future, too. Anything left over could be boxed and labeled according to category, making it easier for Sheila on the Internet end of things.

Then he'd frantically tied and labeled, noted and calculated, while Blanche floated through the displays, choosing figurines, furniture, textiles, and accessories with her Midas touch.

"I'm famished, Jeffrey, and I'm sure you are, too. Why don't we walk down to Bell Street Diner and have lunch? After that, I'll send the boys over to load up my stuff."

"Sounds great."

They strolled silently down the boardwalk toward Pier 66, enjoying the breeze off the Sound, the welcome sun.

After being seated, and giving their drink orders to the hostess (tea for Blanche, coffee for Jeff) Blanche opened the menu and said, "I've been *craving* their crab cakes."

Before the server returned with the coffeepot, Jeff automatically turned over his saucer and checked the backstamp.

"You aren't thinking of slipping that into your pocket, are you, Jeffrey? It's not worth more than a few dollars."

Jeff shook his head at himself. "I've never been this bad, Blanche. As you know, there was so much restaurant china in all that stuff. Since Sheila's been selling a lot of it on eBay, I've learned more than I ever cared to about dishes."

"And, yet, I'll grant you, it's not a drop in the bucket. You're a picker, Jeffrey, and, believe it or not, there are still people out there getting rid of valuable pieces just because they don't want to spend the time, or don't have the time, to find out what they have. And don't forget those who have inherited a house-load, and the job is too overwhelm—" she interrupted herself. "Well, I don't have to tell you that. You just experienced it firsthand."

"You're right, Blanche. I'm partly joking. And, it *is* overwhelming. Heck, I use a jeweler's loupe just to make sure flaws are fleabites and not nicks, or straw marks and not cracks. Then there's the whole challenge of identifying the patterns used by the railroads."

Blanche shook her head. "Tell me about it! I've had many an argument with my pickers over what is and what isn't china from the SP&S glory days."

"The dogwood patterns." Jeff had come across several pieces that he thought had once been used by the Spokane, Pacific, and Seattle Railway. "Those are hard to tell apart."

"It's no wonder. Lord knows how many different dogwood patterns exist. Sure, some were used by the railroads, but who even knows how many were used by restaurants and diners over the years?"

The server approached with their drinks and to take their orders. Blanche requested the Dungeness crab cakes with two sauces: ginger plum and beurre blanc. Jeff ordered the salmon. Both ordered house salads with bleu cheese dressing. After the server left, Jeff thought he'd finish up the china conversation. "Anyway, that's why I carry a small library with me, just to try to avoid getting burned."

"A small library of big books."

"Yeah. Barbara Conroy's second volume on restaurant china is nearly three hundred pages longer than the first. Then there's Luckin's guide, and that other guy . . ."

"McIntyre."

"Right. I'd hate to be doing this without them. It's too much of a challenge keeping up with the railroad china market. Too many variables: Was the pattern exclusive to one line, like the Milwaukee Road's peacock pattern? Or was it a stock pattern used by restaurants and hotels, too, like Roxbury?"

"I love that pattern; still haven't discovered whether the pieces with the red band were used only on the Kansas City Southern, and those without the band were used in restaurants *and* on the trains, or whether all of it was used by both. At least with the peacock, it was custom — as long as you know that Syracuse used the same peacock decal in the center of some other pieces, but the design and color on the rim is different."

"There again," Jeff said, "you have to know which was which. Some beginners head to the flea markets, see something with a peacock on it, and think they've hit the jackpot."

"Now, a piece from private car stock, like The Turquoise Room? *That's* hitting the jackpot."

Their server returned with their salads. After she'd left, Jeff said, "Sheila saw one of those Turquoise Room plates sell online; brought four figures." Jeff shook his head. "*Four* figures. Wouldn't you like to find a few of those buried in a box some-where?"

"How do you think I made the down payment on my town car?"

Jeff swallowed the salad he'd been chewing. "I bow to you, Blanche Appleby."

She raised her teacup. "Accepted."

"Sheila also discovered a bed-and-breakfast somewhere that actually uses the Milwaukee Road Peacock pattern for serving breakfast."

"The value of that stuff's nothing to sneeze at! I'd die if I were using it in my tearoom and someone broke a piece."

"Me? I see it as an invitation for a break-in. Think how easy it would be to call up to book a room, and learn that the place was closed for a week while the proprietors went on vacation."

"Jeff, you've got too much cop blood in you."

"Occupational hazard, even when you leave the occupation, I guess. Anyway, it's crazy to watch how much the railroad china goes for on eBay. Of course, a fellow picker told me that when a railroad announced it was going to change china, the dining car employees were told to get rid of the old stuff. Many times, they'd just dump it along the tracks. I suppose that's part of what drove up the value."

Blanche said, "It makes me sick to think about that. You know, there are several clubs for those of us who collect china. Maybe there should be an organization for those who become addicted?" She grinned. "China Anonymous, perhaps?"

"Sure. At the annual banquet, they eat off paper plates."

Blanche smiled impishly. "Pretty *dish*-functional, don't you think?"

After they'd laughed at the puns, Jeff turned serious. "If it weren't for them — dishfunctional and otherwise — you and I would be out on the streets."

"That's for sure."

"We're all dishfunctional, Blanche. You've got your eighteenth-century porcelain, Sheila has her yellow ware, and her group of friends in the Restaurantware Collector's Network — she recently got hooked on butter pats and creamers. And you know me: I'll never be able to sell off any of Auntie Pim's dishes that have a primrose pattern."

Until he mentioned his aunt's name, Jeff had managed to keep his personal puzzle tucked away in the dark recesses of his thoughts. He was glad to see the server approaching with their lunch, and hoped that Blanche wouldn't notice his change in mood.

Blanche announced that she'd been away from the store long enough, so their walk back to the warehouse was more purposeful.

"Give Sheila my love," she said as she and Jeff exchanged hugs. "And, if you need to talk about whatever's going on in there —" she lightly tapped his forehead — "you know where I can be reached."

He smiled. He should have known better than to think he'd pulled something over on her. "I'll keep that in mind."

Fifteen

IT'S NOT
HOW FAST OR SLOW
YOU DRIVE
THE QUESTION IS
HOW YOU ARRIVE

— Burma-Shave

Jeff stood in the church foyer Wednesday morning and listened to the services for Louie and Michael Stella. He'd arrived two hours early, as Detective Fleming had requested, in order to help watch for Tony.

The detective, who had gotten the lay of the place the day before, had given Jeff the cook's tour. The floor of the massive sanctuary had a gradual decline leading to the pulpit, and Jeff wondered if this provided extra momentum to those contemplating heeding the call. Downhill was always a faster trip. The elevated stage held a large oak pulpit, behind which were dark red draperies concealing the baptismal. A

151

choir loft, and piano and organ completed the stage scene. Doors to either side of the platform led to small rooms that held metal folding chairs and clothes racks. White robes hung there like ghosts, and open staircases led up to the baptismal chamber. Two rest rooms were back there, too, and Fleming checked both, despite the protests of a church secretary who was overseeing the whole procedure. She argued strongly against locking the exit door at the back, but finally acquiesced.

Gordy, who didn't doubt the possibility of foul play and the likelihood that it tied into his theft ring case, had commandeered three agents from the local office to help keep an eye out for Tony.

Besides the obvious task of watching for the errant man, Jeff's main assignment was to visit with Marie, try to learn whether she'd heard from her son. Jeff wasn't keen on deceiving her, and he wasn't sure that he could tell Fleming if she did admit to knowing his whereabouts. But he hoped that, if she admitted to having heard from him, he could persuade her to get him to come forward.

Jeff gained admittance to the family waiting area about a half hour before the service was scheduled to start. Several knots of people were scattered around, chatting about how long it had been since they'd seen one another, and lamenting over the circumstances that had reunited them. Four children sat on a couch, quietly talking among themselves. A knot untied, and Jeff saw Marie then, seated in a wing chair, staring at the handkerchief she held in her hands.

"Marie?"

"Jeffrey." She smiled, clasped his hand, and held it. "How good of you to come."

"How are you doing, Marie? Hanging in there?"

"No choice but." She patted his hand.

He studied her eyes. The pain and desperation he'd seen at her home Friday night were obviously masked with something to numb her, a sedative, to help her get through the trial of the moment.

"Marie, I'm so sorry that we haven't been able to find Tony." He wasn't lying, wasn't trying to set her up. He truly hated seeing her put through this, and, whether Tony knew something or not, whether he was guilty of something or not, she needed him right now.

She gave Jeff a direct look and smiled. Did she know her son's whereabouts? Or was the gaze a result of extra effort needed simply to keep her eyes open against the tranquil effects of the drug? He couldn't be sure, but at least either answer meant she was better equipped to cope with the task at hand.

A clergyman entered, began laying out guidelines. Jeff kissed Marie's hand, then hugged her before taking his leave.

Fleming was waiting for him outside the door. "Does she know anything?"

"Detective, a little compassion for the woman wouldn't hurt. She's going through hell right now."

"You think I don't recognize that? At the same time, we have twenty minutes before everyone scatters. If he's going to show up at all, this is it. This is our window."

"I realize that, and you've asked for my help because I know the family. So excuse me if it ticks me off to be in the middle. I don't like seeing her go through this. Besides, you have nothing yet to indicate that the deaths weren't an accident."

"You mean other than four dead — two of them from one family — and another employee-slash-relative who's gone missing? Granted, I don't have much, but I know this: You have a reputation for following your gut. Easthope respects the hell out of you, says that you'll do what's right, no matter who's involved."

Jeff exhaled. "Yeah. But it doesn't mean I have to like it." He paused. "I can't answer your question. She's obviously sedated, but not enough that she doesn't have her faculties."

"Any number of things they can give her. Adavan's usually the choice for the initial blow, because it's the fastest acting."

"You know a lot about drugs?"

"My share, I suppose."

"If there *was* foul play at the shop, somebody could've given them something, I don't know, drugs? Poison? Should show up easily enough in a tox test."

"You think I haven't thought of that? *Should* isn't the problem. Getting the case moved up is. But the ME promised he'd have a preliminary report for me by Monday."

"Monday? Why not Friday? You know, end of the week, wrap up the quick business?"

"Because the Mariners tickets I'm giving him are for Tuesday's game."

"They on the road this weekend?"

"Yeah."

"You're convinced, then, huh?"

"Yeah."

The door to the family area opened, and the clergyman Jeff saw earlier led a stoic Marie across the foyer and into the sanctuary. They were followed single file by the rest of the family.

"Stay alert, Talbot," Fleming said before heading up the stairs that led to the balcony.

Jeff glanced out the double glass doors at a few stragglers who hurried up the sidewalk. He watched as a woman checked her reflection before entering. Earlier, he'd entered those very doors and had found it odd that they were mirrored on the street side. Now, they made his spy job easier.

He scanned the parking lot across the street, watched as Guy Hollister climbed from a car and started toward the church.

Just then, a striking woman dressed all in black — fitted suit, hat, gloves, and sunglasses — climbed from her car and called to Hollister. When he paused, she caught up to him and the two started what appeared to be a heated discussion. According to the woman's body language, she was beseeching him; she was clearly upset about something. Hollister shrugged a time or two, as if to say, *Can't help it,* or *Can't be changed,* something like that. They continued in this manner as they walked toward the church. When they neared the door, and the woman faced it full on, Jeff noticed that her red lipstick was the same shade as her car. He looked more closely at the vehicle. It was a red Nomad.

He disappeared through a door off the foyer as Hollister reached for the handle on the entry.

At least now, he thought, *I have something to give Fleming.* If the detective knew that Hollister and the Tiajuana woman had some connection, he hadn't said anything about it. Maybe this news would get the detective's mind off interrogating Marie Stella for awhile.

Jeff found Detective Fleming in the balcony.

After he'd reported what he'd seen, Fleming said, "That's a pair I didn't figure on. I'll ask them to come in this afternoon."

Jeff glanced over the railing. "I'll tell you one thing: If Tony's here, he's found one heck of a place to hide."

"Right," said Fleming, "and it's bad news no matter which way you slice it — whether he's guilty of something big, or whether he's in a hell of a lot of danger."

Sixteen

THIS WILL NEVER
COME TO PASS
A BACKSEAT
DRIVER
OUT OF GAS

— Burma-Shave

Detective Chris Fleming's office was like thousands of others across the country: cheap off-white paint, framed certificates hanging off-plumb, putty-colored slab of a desk with matching credenza, both stacked with precariously balanced file folders, manuals, and papers.

After Jeff and Gordy entered, Fleming shut the door, and the wall frames flapped. Fleming sighed, then closed the bowed window blinds before seating himself on the business side of his desk. He pulled a package of gum from his breast pocket, cracked it open, and set furiously to work on a stick of the stuff. Both Jeff and Gordy declined Fleming's gum offer. Jeff, surprised at the detective's indulgence in the habit, wondered whether the guy had recently given up smoking.

Gordy wobbled the stick chairs positioned in front of the desk. "Will this pretend furniture hold me?"

"Sorry. New ones are on order. Here —" Fleming started to shuttle boxes from a love seat that looked as if it were trying to swallow them. "I haven't had time to do more than hang my shingle out since I transferred here."

"Don't mess with it," Gordy said. "You'd have to call reinforcements to wedge me out of the damn thing."

Fleming remained standing, as well. "Good timing. We finished questioning Hollister about ten minutes ago."

"Yeah," Gordy said. "We watched him pull out before we came up. Get anything out of him?"

"Nothing you don't already have," Fleming said. "I sent a tech team out to that cabin where you found Tony Stella's car."

"They find anything?"

"It was wiped clean."

"Surprise."

"The Tiajuana woman's in front of the

mirror now. You two want to observe?"

"Damn straight," Gordy said. "I could use a break on the theft ring, and you never know where it's gonna come from."

Fleming plucked the wad of gum from his mouth and anchored a flimsy picture frame to the wall, then led the way down the corridor. He showed the pair which door to enter before moving on to an identical, adjacent one.

They stepped inside and allowed their eyes to adjust to the dim light. Jeff studied the woman through the glass.

She had changed into khaki slacks, red sandals, and a sleeveless red knit top that revealed sculpted arms. Her thick, wavy hair looked as if it'd never been pressed under a hat. She seemed nervous, but not to the point of paranoia.

"These are more like it," Gordy said as he lowered himself into a large, cushioned chair.

Jeff followed suit. "Yeah, just like going to the theater."

"Let's hope the show's worth it."

When Fleming addressed the woman, Jeff reached over and adjusted the speaker volume.

"Miss Tiajuana, thanks for coming in."

"Of course. But I still don't understand."

"You said yourself that you're leaving soon. We're just covering all bases." Fleming seated himself opposite the woman before continuing. "Now, you stated initially that you left the shop a little after nine. You're sure about the time?"

"Positive, Detective. I remember being pleased that the cab ride down was faster than I expected. After visiting a few minutes with Louie, I went to the ladies' room. When I returned to his office, he wasn't there, which isn't unusual for Louie. He wasn't one to sit behind a desk much. Anyway, I put my check on the desk, grabbed the Nomad's keys from the key box, and left."

"No one else around, no other vehicles parked outside?"

"I told you, no. Don't you get tired of having to ask everyone the same questions over and over? Must be like working on an assembly line."

Fleming ignored the comment. "Go over it again. Everything."

"Why? I thought the deaths were accidental."

"You want to help us if they weren't, don't you, Miss Tiajuana?"

"Or prove my innocence, isn't that what you're saying?"

"Just cooperate, please. Answer the question."

She exhaled, closed her eyes. "Cab pulled up, let me out at the front door." Opened her eyes to add: "I always do it that way if I have to leave a car at Louie's for very long, take the train up, then a cab to the shop." She closed her eyes, continued. "I went straight to Louie's office, small talk for a minute, asked how much the damage was, he handed me the work order. I had to go to the rest room, so I took it with me, filled out the check while I was in there. Took the check back, got the keys." She opened her eyes.

"I don't think I asked before: How long were you in the rest room?"

"That's getting kind of personal, don't you think?"

"How long?"

She dropped her head, thinking. Finally, she shrugged. "I don't know, twenty minutes maybe? I took my time. I'd slept in, so I changed clothes, applied makeup, touched up my hair at the shop. I had my bags with me, of course, and I had a ten o'clock meeting scheduled at the Edgewater, and you're lucky if you can check in before three."

"Why didn't you stay there your first night in town?"

"Like I said, I couldn't get a room."

"Anything about your meeting that we should know about?"

She shrugged. "No, just business."

"While you were in the rest room, did you hear anything unusual going on in the shop?"

"Typical sounds — doors sliding, hoses spewing. There was a radio in the rest room. I had it playing, so I wasn't really paying attention."

"What happened after you got your keys?"

She shrugged. "I left."

"Go on."

She exhaled again, making no effort to hide her irritation. "I put my luggage in the back of the car. You know, I remember noticing that the fumes in the place were stronger, but I thought at the time it was because I'd just applied my perfume. The contrast. Anyway, I slid open one of the back doors, pulled the Nomad out, got out, and closed the door, then looped around the delivery van, drove around the build—"

"Wait." Fleming stood. "What delivery van?"

"The one that's —" her eyes widened briefly before she shut them and slumped into the chair — "always there." Seconds later, she said, straightforward, "I missed it, didn't I? Damn it!" She stood, slamming the table with her palm, and paced. "How'd I *do* that?"

"We deal with it more than anything else, the inclination to overlook the invisible, the thing that's constant." Fleming studied her. "If you're telling us the truth, Miss Tiajuana, you were likely on the premises with the murderer."

"My God. But . . ." She sat back down, looked at Fleming. "Don't you think he would've killed me, too?"

"Did you see the van's driver?"

Thinking, again. "No. No one in the driver's seat. I like to see who drives what, like a game. Business vehicles don't usually count, but my habit to look is the same." She leaned forward. "Do you think I'm in any danger?"

"Hard to say." Pause. "We can put someone on you."

"I don't have to stay here, do I?" She was up again. "I told you, I have to be in Monterey for the Concours d' Elegance."

"Have to be? Isn't that a race?"

"Among other things, yes."

"You're racing?"

"Me? Not anymore. I've hired a driver

for my vintage race car. After the race, that car's being auctioned off. This is big: champagne at the auction Sunday night, celebrities, both from the race car world and from film and television. I've got a lot at stake, Detective. Not only with the car, but also with my career. I can make a lot of promising contacts with the film industry people."

"When's the race?"

"End of next week."

"Why the rush? You can make Monterey in a couple of days, easy, right?"

"I have business on the way back down, then I have to pick up my driver at LAX. From there, he'll haul the race car up to Pebble Beach while I drive one of my street cars."

"Where's he flying in from?"

"Funny you should ask. Sea-Tac."

Jeff and Gordy exchanged glances.

"He lives up here?" Fleming said. "Why doesn't he just ride back down with you?"

"Several reasons. I have no tolerance for backseat drivers and, besides, I prefer my alone time in my cars. My fill-in driver is a salesman working on commission, so he doesn't want to take too much time off."

"What does he sell?"

"Car insurance."

Jeff shot out of his chair. "C'mon, Fleming. Don't let that opening get away."

Gordy leaned forward. "Think it's our boy?"

Jeff thought Fleming's next move would be to ask her for the name. Instead, he said it himself. "Guy Hollister."

"Why ask the questions, Detective, if you know the answers?"

"It's our boy," Gordy said.

"That was a shot in the dark," Fleming said. "I just heard the voices in the room before anybody knew I had a gun." Fleming broke away, walked. "Did Tony Stella recommend him to you?"

"Yes, several years ago. Last week, my driver broke his arm, so I called Tony. He hooked me up with Guy, and I doled out money. It's what you do when you own vintage cars."

Jeff smiled. That *was* what you did when you owned a vintage car. He glanced at Gordy, who raised his brows hopefully and nodded. This twist — Hollister's name dropping — definitely interested the G-man, since he was looking at the former con for a theft ring tie-in.

Fleming told her to wait, then walked out of the room and into the one where Jeff and Gordy were.

Jeff said, "Does what she said jibe with Hollister's story?"

"Right down to the spark plugs." Fleming turned to Gordy. "Easthope, anything you want to ask her?"

"Rain check."

Fleming nodded.

Jeff checked his watch. "I've got to get going." He extended his hand. "Detective, thanks for the listen. Gordy, I'll see you later at the house."

Seventeen

DON'T PASS CARS
ON CURVE OR HILL
IF THE COPS
DON'T GET YOU
MORTICIANS WILL

— Burma-Shave

Jeff sat at his desk in the library that evening, updating business ledgers, squaring away bills, sorting through mail.

He'd felt out of sorts after the funeral and subsequent interrogation, had wandered the house from top to bottom, had bugged Sheila a hundred times about whether she'd found any more pieces to his puzzle, until finally after dinner she'd said, "Go to California already!" and he'd said, "Fine, I will!" and that was that. It was a done deal.

Sheila had stopped cold, as if wondering whether she'd heard him wrong, then had told him she'd be upstairs sorting through his clothes in search of something that might work for the beach/desert combo.

He'd finished estimating how much money to take along and was juggling funds by way of filling out withdrawal and deposit slips on three different accounts, when Greer entered with a tray that held a coffee carafe and a mug. Jeff leaned back in the leather desk chair, kneaded the back of his neck. "Greer, you're a lifesaver."

"Thank you, sir." Greer poured coffee for his employer. "Sir, I'd like to discuss something with you whenever you have a moment."

"Sure, have a seat."

"It doesn't have to be now. I understand that you're busy."

"Nah, a break would do me good. Besides, it'll be hard to squeeze out any time later." He glanced at the mantel clock. "Gordy'll be back in an hour or so, and Sheila will probably be through with the packing by then."

"Thank you, sir." Greer perched on the leather club chair, his posture ramrod straight, his hands clasped atop his knees.

"What's on your mind?"

"Well, sir." The butler cleared his throat, began to fidget, then stopped himself.

Jeff leaned forward. A sudden disquiet

sent a cold chill up his spine. "You're not tendering a resignation, are you, man?"

"No, sir!"

"Thank God. There's nothing to be nervous about, then." Jeff sat back again. "Out with it."

"Yes, sir. When my grandfather was in service, he was particularly fond of one of the vehicles owned by his employer. It was the least elaborate of the fleet, one that Mr. Chandler kept as a backup. The year my grandfather married my grandmother, and she began serving the household as well, the employer purchased a new vehicle. He gave the older one to my grandparents as a wedding gift."

Jeff nodded appreciatively. "Generous."

"Yes, sir."

"Are you trying to tell me that you want the PT Cruiser?"

"No, sir," Greer said quickly. "That never crossed my mind. What I'm trying to say is, well, that car was stolen when my grandparents took me to the theater to see *The Muppet Movie*. I'm surprised more vehicles aren't stolen from movie theater parking lots. It's quite easy to see someone go into the cinema and know that they'll be in another world for a couple of hours. To this day, I've never been able to view that movie again." Greer took a deep breath. "Anyway, sir, she's been found."

"Found? You mean that you found the same model, right?"

"No, sir." Greer smiled broadly. "It's *her*. She's a 1937 Cadillac, with suicide doors, chrome-trimmed running boards, and free-standing headlights that look like torpedoes. She still has the blanket rope that I used to hang on to while I was riding in the backseat. My grandfather kept all the papers — records that prove owner-ship, as well as a copy of the police report. The officials have verified the vehicle iden-tification number, and it's the very same car that I rode in as a child."

"That's incredible. I mean, the thing was over forty years old when it was stolen, right?"

"Yes, sir. Obviously, the thieves were carried away with her beauty; they didn't think ahead enough to realize that they couldn't drive her anywhere. Apparently, to avoid prosecution, they stowed her in an old outbuilding almost thirty years ago. There was so much junk piled on top of her that no one realized she was there. The owners recently passed away, and the benefactors were preparing for an auction when the car was discovered. Since no title could be located, they called a friend in law enforcement who ran a check on the VIN."

"Incredible," Jeff said again. He shuffled through things on his desk, not even sure why. He flipped past the check stubs in his business checkbook with its oversized checks, three to a sheet. "What do you need? A loan, or time off to go get her?"

"Thank you, sir, no. I have the money. I'm not sure, however . . . well, you see, sir, the car is in somewhat of a state of disrepair."

"It's a good thing, though, that the thieves put her in a building."

"Absolutely. She's not in great shape, but it could have been much worse. Since she wasn't exposed to the elements, there was no oxidation of the paint, no fading."

Jeff said, "I don't understand. Are you looking for an auto shop recommendation? I'll have to give that some thought, since Louie was the only one I —"

"No, sir, that's not it." Greer sighed elaborately. "I have no place to put her, and I was wondering if I might utilize a portion of the carriage house?"

"Is that all you need? I don't care about that. Lord knows, I'm not going to 'add to my fleet,' as it were. Matter of fact, I've been considering selling the Cruiser — that is, unless you'd rather drive it, instead of the Jimmy."

"No, sir, thank you. Robbie, however, is quite taken with the Cruiser."

Robbie, a butler who worked for a family over on Capitol Hill, was Greer's dearest friend.

"I'll give him a good deal," Jeff said. "But, back to your Caddy. Take all the room you need. I can tell you from experience, though: It'll be months before you get her back from a restorer."

"That won't be a problem, sir. I can do all the work myself."

Jeff stared at the young man seated before him. Greer had been the Talbots' butler for going on eight years. He ran the household fastidiously, could do everything from — well, Jeff wasn't quite sure what all the man did, but he knew that everything was tended to with such care and finesse that neither Jeff nor Sheila had to worry about a thing. He recognized that his butler had a social life. Typically, he took only one night a week off work, but during the theater season, both Greer and Robbie worked even harder in their employers' respective homes so they could take time off to attend two or three events a week.

Jeff wasn't one to stereotype, but the last thing he'd expected his butler to know how to do was restore a whole car.

"You're pulling my leg, right?"

"Of course not, sir."

Greer looked injured, and Jeff suspected he'd hurt his butler's feelings. He hadn't intended to appear surprised at the butler's ability to do guy stuff. Jeff sighed. "Greer, I'm only surprised because you've never shared your interest in restoring old cars."

"The Chandlers, whom my grandparents worked for, had a grandson who was quite the shade-tree mechanic. He taught me everything from rebuilding an engine to replacing a headliner. As far as sharing my ability with you, there was never reason to. When you employed me, you said that Mr. Stella's establishment had always seen to the woodie.

"My restoration of the Cadillac will be in my spare time, and Robbie's willing to assist. I assure you, it won't interfere with my duties."

"I'm not worried about that, and you know it. I apologize if I was thoughtless."

"Thank you, sir."

"It might be fun, actually, to watch you transform that car. When I was with the Bureau, I knew enough about cars to get by. I've discovered lately that I've forgotten what little I knew. Part of it back then was that I didn't allow myself to get hooked, for fear I'd become obsessed."

"Yes, sir. That thought crossed my mind about the Cadillac. But, what else am I going to do with my money?"

The sound of the front door opening and closing was followed by Gordy's booming voice.

Greer said, "I'll tell him you're in here."

"Thanks, Greer."

After a moment, Gordy walked in and dropped an accordion folder as thick as Portland's phone book on the desk. "We checked the Tiajuana woman's files after you left today."

Jeff swallowed. "You're kidding? *That's* her FBI file?"

"No, this is from Louie's." Gordy removed the rubber bands from around the creased and stained folder. From it, he took a stack of spiral notebooks. "I never noticed it before, of course I wasn't in his shop that much. Somebody color-coded the file folders for every vehicle they ever worked on: antique, muscle, classic, flivver, flame-painted, two-tone, you name it. All of them. Look at this."

"Yeah, I think Marie started that about a

hundred years ago. I don't know whether she kept it up, or whether one of the boys was doing it."

Flipping open the cover of a black one, Gordy said, "We might ask her. Some of the more artistic ones are signed MS, but that could stand for Marie *or* Michael."

Jeff looked inside the notebook. Taped to the inside cover were two photos — one front view and one rear view — of a black Thunderbird convertible. It had a hood scoop, bumper-mounted spare, and round, shiplike porthole. He skimmed the notes on the first sheet, which told, in addition to make, model, year (1956), and VIN, such statistics as engine and tire sizes, interior and exterior color identification numbers, record of service and restoration, and the vanity plate: BLKBRD. "So, she's got two classics, in addition to the race car."

Gordy slapped down a red folder, then flipped open the cover. Inside was the red Chevy Nomad, 1955.

Jeff said, "That's the one she picked up."

On top of that folder, Gordy dropped a red-and-white-checked folder that looked like a speedway flag, opened it to reveal a '58 Chevy Corvette convertible — red and white. Next, he flipped open the light blue one: '65 GTO two-door.

Gold metallic folder: 1957 Studebaker Golden Hawk. Someone had written "RARE" above the photo.

Dark blue folder: 1941 Graham Hollywood. Another "RARE."

"The woman's a car *nut,*" Gordy concluded. "It set me to wondering how she could afford all of them. I assumed she was married to somebody who'd earned a twenty-four-karat gold jacket from a national real estate chain — do you know what they're asking for Malibu beachfront? — so I ran a more detailed background on her than the prelim that Fleming did."

"And?"

"Not married. Never has been. Doesn't look like she inherited it, either. She has a Hollywood connection, though, so that must be it."

"Yeah?"

"Yeah. She's a prop contact of some sort. Goes around finding anything and everything that might be of use in period films. Then, when some director needs a specific antique or some retro clothes or whatever for a project they're directing, who do they call?"

"Donna Tiajuana?"

"Donna Tiajuana. If she doesn't have it

on hand, she tracks it down. Sort of like what you do, I suppose."

Jeff smiled. Gordy had had a hard time wrapping his mind around the fact that Jeff had left the FBI — and him as a partner — to dig through junk. "Between the cars and the props, this Tiajuana woman must have some impressive property for the storage alone."

"She does." Gordy slid a piece of paper across the desk.

Jeff skimmed it. "Wow."

"*Wow* ain't the half of it. The place on Malibu, and the storage unit with twenty-four-seven security. Pretty smart, when you think about it. More security while she's out buying up more stuff."

"That'll require more security."

"Right."

"Sounds a little too close to the rat race, if you ask me."

The doorbell rang. Greer shot past the library's pocket doors, returned momentarily. "Mr. Easthope, sir, Detective Fleming would like to see you."

Gordy nodded to Jeff, who told Greer to show the man in. When he did so, Jeff asked the butler to bring in more coffee and some extra mugs.

"With this house," Fleming said upon

178

entering, "it'd be a shame not to have a butler. Antiques must pay a hell of a lot better than law enforcement."

Before Jeff could respond, the detective went on, "Matter of fact, I know they do after reading up on this Tiajuana woman."

Gordy said, "We were just doing the same thing."

"You guys have a seat," Jeff said.

Fleming sat in one of the armchairs across from Jeff while Gordy fiddled with the notebooks. "If my mother had a butler, she'd probably never try to leave her home."

Jeff had never thought of it that way. Was he being an enabler, as opposed to a provider? "*Tries* to leave?"

"Tries a lot. Succeeds every now and then, with the help of her therapist and God knows how much medication."

"Yeah, Sheila never had much luck with pills, so —"

"What are you two talking about?" Gordy dropped the fat folder with a thud before doing the same with himself, only into the chair beside Fleming.

"Oh, nothing," Jeff said, suspecting that his buddy (aware that Sheila's agoraphobia was a touchy subject for the Talbots) had interrupted on purpose.

Fleming didn't seem to notice. "The Tiajuana woman's story checks out about that delivery truck. The company reported a truck stolen the morning of the murders. It was found abandoned before noon that same day."

"Wiped cleaner than Greer's pantry, I'll bet," Gordy added.

"Owner said it was cleaner than he'd seen it in some time." Fleming cocked his head, studied Jeff.

"You were right, Easthope, it's the hair. Takes the agent look right off him."

Gordy reached across the desk and grabbed a lock of Jeff's hair at the neckline.

Jeff jerked away and batted at Gordy's hand.

Gordy shrugged. "Yeah, if he tousles it some, stays away from the barber's chair, stops shaving for awhile, it should work."

The detective studied Jeff. "He'd have to do something about the clothes. But that could be taken care of when he's down there."

Jeff eyed both of the men warily. "What are you two up to?"

"We want you to reconsider going down to California."

Greer returned with the coffee.

180

"Matter of fact," Jeff said, "I decided a couple hours ago that I am going. Why?"

"Perfect." Fleming accepted a cup of coffee from Greer. "Can you leave tomorrow?"

"Gordy," Jeff said, "have you been talking to Sheila?"

"No, why?"

"Never mind."

"Look." Fleming again. "Donna Tiajuana lives in L.A. She decided to leave this afternoon, right after we finished questioning her."

"So? What's that got to do with me?"

"Simple." Fleming set down his cup, then stood, moved around. "We want you to, you know, bump into her, watch her, see what she's up to. She's spending a few days in San Francisco, so you can catch up with her there. You're both into antiques and old cars. You've got the perfect cover, and you've had the training. Should be a cinch.

"Here," Fleming continued, pulling a sheet of paper from his pocket. "I've got her itinerary. She's leaving Frisco on Saturday, so she can go to some flea market in Pasadena on Sunday."

"The one at the Rose Bowl?"

"That's the one. Is that where you're going?"

"I'd considered it."

"Well, there you go."

"Do you have any reason to believe she's guilty of something?"

"Statistically, the opposite is probably true. I mean, felons come up with a lot of cockamamie stories, but being in the bathroom while four people are murdered and not noticing anything when you come out? I'd just like it if someone was watching her moves, and you're the best man for the job."

Gordy broke in. "Doesn't mean you should let your guard down, but it might give us something."

"Do you know how much extra time this is going to take? I've got . . . stuff to do in southern California, and I'm not sure how long I can be gone."

"Where were you planning on going after Pasadena?"

"Bakersfield. Why?"

"Maybe by Pasadena, you'll know something. Might even have an in with her, who knows?"

"Wait a minute, you said she left today. What makes you think I can get to Frisco before she leaves?"

"For one thing, she's staying there till Friday. For another, she's not taking I-Five;

told us that it would be a perfectly good waste of her newly restored car. She's hugging the coast all the way to L.A., wind in her hair, sunsets on the ocean, unrivaled views, all that. She claims it keeps her young."

Jeff thought about the woman he'd seen at the funeral and in Fleming's interrogation room. "It's working. How old is she, anyway?"

"Fifty-seven. It's damn near like looking at Raquel Welch, isn't it? Must be the Latino blood."

"She's got Latino blood?" Gordy asked.

"She said a little, but that if she cut herself she'd probably lose it."

"She's seen my car," Jeff said. "Don't you think she'll remember?"

Gordy laughed. "She didn't notice four bodies. What makes you think she noticed your car?"

Fleming took a more serious tack. "That could help, if she starts talking about the auto shop. And if it doesn't help? That's where the picking comes in. You both have the antiques connection. As far as she's concerned, you're doing nothing more than making a trip for loot."

Gordy: "Are you still a member of the National Woodie Club?"

"Yeah, why?"

"If she gets curious, show her your membership card. Tell her you're visiting some of the California clubs' summer events. Like I said, grow some scruff to match that hair, get a few of those loud Hawaiian shirts, some deck shoes or whatever, a surfboard, hell, I don't know. Figure out what they wear once you get there, and then do the same. You'll fit right in."

Jeff stared at Gordy. "You have to be kidding."

"Come on. You used to be one of the best we had for climbing into the skin of a different type of character. That's all you'll be doing now."

"Gordy, I swear, if I didn't owe you so much already . . ."

"You don't owe me anything. Walk away from this if you want to, and I won't mention it again."

Jeff thought about it. The antiques and old cars were a primo cover. The Tiajuana woman would have no reason to question his showing up at the same haunts. Also, he knew that what Gordy said was true. He could walk away from it. But he wouldn't. He knew he wouldn't. Gordy probably knew it, too.

"I suppose I might as well."

"Good deal." Fleming handed Jeff the

itinerary. "Jot down what you need from this."

Jeff glanced through the dates and events. "I won't be down there this long, but I should be able to cover a week or so."

When Jeff was through, he returned the schedule to the detective.

"Thanks, Talbot." Fleming folded the paper, returned it to his pocket. "Why'd you say you're going down there?"

"I didn't."

Fleming paused, as if considering whether or not to push it. At length, he said, "You're the same as sworn in, know what I'm saying? Keep me posted."

Eighteen

IF YOU DON'T KNOW
WHOSE SIGNS THESE ARE,
YOU HAVEN'T DRIVEN
VERY FAR

— Burma-Shave

It was one of the harder things to train
yourself to do: sit reading in a lobby — or,
in this case, a parlor — as if you don't expect to run into anyone you know, all the
while hoping that the person you're tar-
geting walks in, or walks through, or walks
by, and just happens to glance your way.
Meanwhile, you're *willing* it to occur and, if
you're on your game, your eyes connect
(not for too long — you don't want to appear threatening — but long enough so as
not to seem indifferent). You flash a signal
— recognition — and hope the other
person reciprocates.

If, however, those telepathic skills fail
you, you reach up your sleeve, quick as a

cardsharp, and grab an ace. Distract? Advance? Flank? It depends.

In Jeff's current situation, both advance and flank were questionable. What would prevent her thinking that he'd followed her in off the street? At least, if he had to distract her as she strolled by, she'd recognize right off that he was already a fixture. He was obviously a guest of the place, since he was comfortably ensconced in one of the parlor chairs, reading the paper like any educated gentleman might.

He double-checked that he wasn't holding the newspaper upside down.

The eye contact maneuver had worked for Jeff more times than he could remember — and he had no reason to believe it wouldn't work now — but he'd never felt confident in it, never believed he approached it quite right, never thought he was nonchalant enough to pull it off.

Ideally, the current situation called for eye contact, because he had come face-to-face with his mark earlier that afternoon.

He'd lucked out after pushing himself on Thursday in order to put most of the drive to San Francisco behind him. He'd made Frisco by Friday afternoon. According to the itinerary Fleming had given him, Donna Tiajuana was spending Frisco afternoons

187

at an antiques mall south of downtown. If she hadn't lied to the detective, Jeff was in luck.

It was almost four when he found her in the antiques mall. She wore linen slacks, a sable-brown knit top, and a wide-brimmed straw hat with an animal-print scarf tied around it. She seemed taller when she wasn't behind glass.

Poring over a display of vintage gloves, she chose first one pair and then another, examining the stitching, the trim, the labels, before either returning them to the table or placing them atop the burgeoning stack of textiles in her arm.

Jeff had ambled over to the other side of the table, where he'd spotted a pair of particularly striking gauntlets that he believed were women's gloves from the early automobile days. The gauntlets, with their sturdier fabric and protective cuffs, were a must to help keep road dust off one's clothes. He reached for the pair, and instead grabbed the Tiajuana woman's hand.

He let go. "Sorry about that."

She held up the gloves, smiled an infectious smile, and shrugged slightly. "Nine-tenths of the law, right?"

"Absolutely." He turned, started toward

the next booth. *Play it cool.* He didn't want her to think he was a threat.

"What about these?" she called.

He looked over his shoulder.

She was holding up a pair of opera gloves with tiny pearl buttons at the wrists. "I have plenty like this, and I can assure you that this pair is easily worth four times what they're asking."

The helpful sort, Jeff thought. *Good to know.* He faced her, took the gloves. "Thanks. I have a friend who's recently begun collecting them, so I'm not likely to duplicate something she has."

The woman started to respond when Mozart notes sounded from her purse. "Excuse me, but I have to take this call."

Jeff held up the gloves, said, "Thanks again," then rounded the corner and started down the next aisle. Out of sight, but not out of earshot. Oftentimes, it amazed him at the conversations he heard people having in adjacent aisles of antiques venues. Even if the booths were constructed of sheetrock instead of lattice, they were typically open on top, and most shoppers seemed unaware that they were compromising their own privacy.

The Tiajuana woman spoke quietly, but Jeff picked up a few words: "Are you sure?" Pause. "Okay, the Tivoli."

He hurried to the register, paid for the gloves, and returned to the woodie. Once inside, he called Sheila and asked her to check the word on the Internet.

In the time it takes to say "Tivoli," she'd found it, the Chateau Tivoli in Alamo Square, and had started to give him a bunch of details about the place. He'd interrupted, told her he didn't have time for all that, just "Call, please, book me a room for the night, and I'll call you later."

He'd had a hard time dragging himself from the rows and rows of promising antiques booths, but it had paid off. He'd found the Square on his city map, then the building. When he went inside, he learned that it was a bed-and-breakfast. As much as he liked Victoriana, he wasn't much for B and Bs. But his mark was headed here, so he checked in, stashed his luggage in his ornately decorated room on the second floor (complete with a taxidermied peacock, no less), and settled into the parlor before the woman arrived.

Now, with peripheral vision to rival a fish-eye lens, he saw her slender form, the linen and brown outfit, the hat. She was carrying red luggage.

She turned her head toward the sitting

area. Only then did he look directly at her.

Flash. Recognition. Smile. Approach.

"You're the man with the gloves! From this afternoon?"

He smiled, stood, and bowed slightly. "Guilty as charged."

"You drive an old woodie, right?"

"That's right." He was beginning to think that *she* was spying on *him*. "How'd you know that?"

"Oh, I'd taken my armload of loot up to the register so I could shop some more, and your car caught my eye as you pulled out of the parking lot."

He indicated the cases. "Shouldn't someone have helped you with those?"

"They're small." She set down the matching vintage pieces: a hatbox and an overnighter in red leather with ivory calf-skin trim. "It's part of my stay-young regimen: Never pack more than you can schlep yourself."

"Smart." He extended his hand. "Jeff Talbot."

She shook his hand. "Donna Tiajuana."

He should offer her a seat, but he wanted to see if she continued closing the gap.

"I'm always amazed by coincidence, Mr. Talbot, and —"

"Jeff."

"Jeff," she said, nodding, "and afraid to ignore it lest it's fate. I usually stay at the Red Victorian on Haight — they have funky decor, rooms with names like Summer of Love — but the inn is full, as it were." She looked around, then said, "May I join you?"

"Of course. Forgive me for not offering." He indicated the tufted chair situated at a right angle to his own.

He smiled. "This is my first time here. It's quite comfortable. Reminds me of home."

"Your home is Victorian?"

"Right down to the Eastlake furniture and the Oriental rugs." He studied the ornate woodwork, said conspiratorially, "This place might even have hidden passageways and staircases."

"Your home has them? How exciting!" Her dark eyes glinted.

"It does. I discovered them when I was a kid."

"You must've had a blast, traveling behind walls, resurfacing on a different floor or in a locked room." She was leaning forward, practically begging him to provide a mystery story.

He'd never thought of his childhood as "a blast," and he hadn't been allowed to play in the secret corridors. He needed to change the subject.

Be accommodating. "Say, would you like something to drink? The innkeeper mentioned that some things are set up in the dining room."

"Red wine would be perfect, thanks."

"Be right back." In the dining room, he poured Shiraz for them both and considered how trusting she was. Weren't women supposed to keep their drink glasses in sight? Had investigative work made him paranoid?

You struck up conversations, you accepted the offer of a drink, or a cup of coffee. It was the ultimate social bridge. Take camping, for instance. You wouldn't accept a cup of coffee from a guy on the street corner, or in a parking lot. But, say, you're walking back from the bathrooms, following the road around to your campsite, and a fellow camper chats you up. Before you know it, he's offered a mug of hot coffee — smells good, brisk morning — and you've accepted. What was it that made us trust strangers in those settings?

"Sir?"

Jeff snapped back to the present, moved out of the way for an older woman who was waiting for access to the sideboard.

Back in the parlor, he handed the wineglass to Donna before taking his seat.

She took a sip. "Very nice."

He got the conversation back on track. "So you're a glove collector?"

"Sort of. They're for my work."

"Vintage gloves for work?"

She laughed, her eyes glittering, and Jeff found this as infectious as the smile he'd seen earlier at the mall. In addition, it revealed a genuineness. It wasn't one of those fake laughs that never reaches the eyes. This one started at the soul, filled the face.

She said, "Sounds crazy, doesn't it?"

"Actually, one or two professions come to mind," Jeff said, taking care not to tip his hand. "Museum designer, or community theater, maybe."

"You're close. I provide props for the film industry."

"As in *the* film industry? Hollywood?"

"That's right. I freelance for all the big production companies."

"Fascinating. I apologize for thinking small-scale." It was easy for him to pretend he didn't know anything about her, because he really was interested in her line of work. "So, if someone's producing, say, a Victorian-era film, they contact you, and . . ."

"Usually, it's the wardrobe designers and set designers who contact me — if I'm not serving in one of those capacities myself. They have many items at their disposal in the studio vaults, but they also have a lot of specific ideas and requests."

"I've heard that those vaults are like museums, in and of themselves."

"You heard right. It's amazing."

"Do the performers actually wear valuable antiques?"

"Typically, a valuable piece is used as a pattern, then several are produced because of the inordinate amount of wear and tear they take on the set. It's nothing for an actor to go through, say, three or four jackets.

"What about you?" she continued. "What work are you in?"

"Plain and simple. I'm a picker."

"We're the same, then. We find treasures for others and hope we can make a living doing so."

"Right, except that I don't have the Hollywood connection."

"Granted, I've been fortunate, but I've worked hard, too. I attended design school when I was young, where I learned the history of textiles. When I realized that I could parlay my penchant for stalking garage and estate sales into a lucrative business, I decided to go where the big money was."

"Or where the big money's lost."

"True. Gotta be gutsy, though. Anyway, I'm always excited when news comes down the pike that a period film is in the works, whether it's set in the thirties, like *Road to Perdition*, or during the Victorian and Edwardian eras, like *The Age of Innocence* or even in the fifties, like *Peggy Sue Got Married*."

"All favorites of my wife and mine. I'll bet she's watched *The Age of Innocence* fifty times."

They drank in silence for a few moments, watched people move in and out of the sitting area, couples meeting up with each other, tourists returning with shopping bags and worn-out kids. Three women checked in, boisterous and openly excited about their shopping weekend.

When the Tiajuana woman finished her wine, she said, "Listen, would you like to have dinner together tonight — Dutch, of course. I love my time alone when I'm at home, but dining alone in restaurants gets old."

"I'd love to, actually, but only if it's my treat. You'd be rescuing me from a dull evening of ordering takeout and surfing channels."

"That would be a waste of a beautiful Frisco evening. I know a fun French place near here, the Absinthe Brasserie."

"Sounds great."

"Meet here, say, six forty-five?"

"Done."

Nineteen

THE PLACE TO PASS
ON CURVES
YOU KNOW
IS ONLY AT
A BEAUTY SHOW

— Burma-Shave

After the exchange with the Tiajuana woman, Jeff went up to his room and called home.

"Talbot Travel, may I help you?" Sheila answered. She loved Caller ID.

"I'm in a bed-and-breakfast."

"Hey, you're the one who didn't have time to hear the details. You're lucky they'd had a cancellation."

"That wouldn't have mattered, because my mark is staying here. At any rate, it worked. I'm having dinner with her tonight."

"I always knew you were a fast operator. Listen, Gordy asked to talk to you when you called in, and I've got a ton of work to do. Okay if we visit later?"

"Sure, hon. Is he there?"

"Somewhere. Let me find him. Oh, and enjoy the ruffles. Love you."

"Love you, too," he said, but he suspected she'd already put down the receiver.

"So" — Gordy's voice — "how's it going with your female version of Jay Leno?"

"He'd have to add to his fleet to catch up to her, wouldn't he?"

"Probably."

"She's very charming, forthcoming, and we're having dinner together this evening."

"Good work. Anything yet that we can use?"

"Not really, unless you want to know that I'd be surprised if she's guilty of anything, other than spending Hollywood money. What about you? Anything from your angle?"

"No, and it's got me wondering what the hell's going on."

"What do you mean?"

"Well, every lead I got from Louie has run me into brick walls and bridge abutments."

Jeff, who was untying his shoes while Gordy talked, stopped midstream. "That's not like Louie."

"You're telling me it's not."

"Any of those leads take you in the direction of Hollister?"

"Nope. Surprising, huh?"

"Yeah, actually. Are you still looking at him for this?"

"Sure, but I haven't linked him to the boosted cars. You know something else, though? There hasn't been a single boost since I got here. You'd think I had FBI tattooed on my face."

"You do, Gordy. Didn't anybody tell you?"

"Right."

"What about Fleming? He turn up anything?"

"He hasn't called, so I'm assuming he hasn't."

"You know, Gordy, I think you might hit it off with this Tiajuana woman. You should've tailed her, instead of sending me."

"She's *way* outta my league. And don't forget why you're buddying up to her. She just might be our killer."

"I doubt it. I mean, she doesn't seem the least bit cautious. Aren't women supposed to be careful nowadays?"

"You talking about something specific, or just lamenting the loss of innocence?"

Something wedged itself in Jeff's thoughts.

He examined it. It was no more than an idea, a long shot, to be sure, but, actually, the continuation of an earlier idea. He was working it loose when he heard Gordy's voice.

"Jeff? You still there?"

"I'm here. Gordy, something happened with Donna Tiajuana, and it got me to thinking about an idea I mentioned to Fleming at the funeral. I got wine for us this evening, went to a different room to get it. I could've put anything in her glass, and she wouldn't have known it."

"Yeah, that's why GHB's called the date-rape drug."

"Exactly. So, what if the deaths at the auto shop were helped along? What if GHB was put in their coffee?"

Gordy picked it up. "And whoever did it closed up the place, waited for the fumes to finish them off. It's possible. And you gotta admit: The whole incident has a stink on it."

"Maybe Fleming's gut instinct is right."

"Maybe the lab rats aren't thinking how easy it'd be to use the date-rape drug when it's not a date, you know?"

"I'll call Fleming," Gordy said, "and talk to you later."

"Okay, later." Jeff cradled the phone.

The more he thought about it, the more it seemed possible. If there had been foul play, it was a hard thing to pull off with four people. Four people in four different rooms. Different rooms, yet connected. A challenge, all right, for somebody who wanted to take them out of the picture.

Something else was bothering Jeff, and it took a minute for him to land on it. It was the bit Gordy had said before about Louie's dead leads. As an informant, he'd never been wrong before.

After changing into black slacks and shoes, a charcoal rayon shirt, and silvery silk sports jacket, Jeff stepped out his door and started toward the staircase.

Donna Tiajuana stepped out of the room at the end of the hall and walked toward him. She was wearing a long yet simple black dress and strappy sandals. Folded into a triangle and knotted at her hip was an exquisite paisley shawl (vintage, no doubt) woven in colors to match her iridescent peacock feather earrings: emerald, royal blue, teal, coppery bronze, black.

"Nice outfit," he said as they descended the stairs. "Are you the only peacock in your room?"

"What?"

"Oh, there's actually a stuffed peacock in my room. I just wondered if every room had one."

"Not mine. Should I feel slighted?"

"I don't think so. I'll probably have to face him away from the bed tonight so I don't feel as if I'm being stared at."

Outside, she led the way to her Nomad. "You don't mind if we go in Bacall, do you?"

"What?"

"I name all my cars after movie stars. This is Lauren Bacall: tough, beautiful, and still going strong."

"Don't mind at all." Jeff held the door for her. "Is this permitted, or am I crossing some equal rights line?"

She laughed and shook her head.

After he climbed into the passenger seat and admired the car, he prompted with, "You said *all* your cars?"

She explained as she drove. "I collected them along the way, before most people knew they were going to be valuable. For instance, I bought this baby —" she patted the steering wheel — "for four hundred dollars. Some guy had blown the engine, taken her in for repair, then didn't have the money to bail her out."

"Do you know how many people pay that much a *month* for a car payment?"

"Exactly. My Graham Hollywood is Greta Garbo — rare and mysterious. Marlene Deitrich is the seductive Alfa Romeo — that's my race car. The black T-bird is Audrey Hepburn, sophisticated and fun. And Kate Hepburn is my Golden Hawk, similar to the T-bird, but with a longer body and subtle coloring. Funny, I didn't even think of the same last names when I did that. Grace Kelly is the '58 Corvette convertible — all-American with style enough to take her anywhere. And, finally, my baby-blue GTO is Ginger Rogers — power to move, and always ready to dance."

"You must have one heck of garage."

"I stack them."

He couldn't tell if she was joking, and he didn't want to look stupid, so he let it slide. "What about your place? Historical? Contemporary?"

"A little of both, I guess. The house is older, but it's been kept up to date, has lots of windows for the view, with furnishings and decor inspired by Hollywood's glamour days."

She appeared to have no warning bells at all inside her head. For all she knew, he could be a serial killer. He wondered whether she was truly naive, or whether she was villain enough not to feel threatened by anyone. Recalling Gordy's info about her property, Jeff pushed the envelope. "Sounds like something you might find on Malibu with an ancient movie star living in it."

"It is! The Malibu part, anyway. It was never owned by a celebrity, and I'm certainly not a movie star."

"You're not ancient, either."

"Kind of you to say." She maneuvered a turn, then continued talking. "I'd die if I couldn't live on sand and water. It's so soothing, running on the beach every morning, listening to waves every night as I fall asleep. I like to travel, too, but there's no place like home."

"Yes, Dorothy."

"You mean Donna," she corrected, but the realization hit her instantly, and she laughed. "I have so many movie lines in my brain that sometimes I forget I'm quoting them."

"It's an easy habit to fall into."

"Here we are," she said, pulling up to the curb.

After she'd given her keys to the valet, Jeff said, "Doesn't it bother you to hand over the keys to *that* car?"

"I only do it at places I know I can trust."

The staff recognized Donna and immediately led her and her guest into the dining room. Jeff took in the place, with its deep red walls, atmospheric lighting, and unusual art while they walked to their table.

After they'd been seated and had ordered drinks, they spent a few moments perusing the menu before Jeff said, "So the gloves are for work, but — besides the cars — what do you collect for yourself? Is there anything that you won't turn over to just any old celebrity?"

"Sure. Anything from the twenties that fits my decor and reflects the light off the Pacific: etched mirrors, crystal. Oh, and I have a collection of mourning jewelry."

"Victorian hair jewelry, right?"

"You're familiar with it?"

"A little. It was popular to make it from the hair of a departed loved one, and when photography gave mourners a much better memento — an actual image — mourning jewelry fell out of favor." He sipped his water. "That's valuable stuff. What if someone wants it for a film?"

"Actually, that's happened, but we send photographs of my pieces to an artist, and commission copies. There's a society working to preserve the techniques and history of hairwork."

"Which also means that we have to watch out for reproductions."

"True."

Their server returned with their drinks and a bread basket. "May I take your orders?"

"Sure," Donna said. "I'll have a Caesar salad and the roasted quail."

"Caesar salad for me, as well, and the rib-eye, medium."

After she'd gone, Donna said, "I used to collect fairings, too, but I've slowed down on those. I find them more challenging to display."

"Fairings?" He tried to figure what fairings were, but he came up empty-handed. "I must confess, that's a new one on me."

"Souvenirs from fairs. You name a World's Fair, I have tchotchkes — Paris, New York, Chicago, Seattle —"

"I should've known what fairings are." Jeff grimaced. "I grew up practically at the foot of the Space Needle."

"You're a little older than the Needle, though, aren't you?"

"About a year. I was born in sixty-three." He smiled. "You should guess people's ages for a living."

"Sorry," Donna stammered. "When you

work in Hollywood, you catch the local obsession."

Jeff chuckled. "It isn't exclusive to Hollywood. I'm ten years older than my wife, and I think about it more than she does."

She raised a well-shaped brow but didn't comment. When she spoke again, she said, "I'm fifty-seven. And a half, if you want to get technical."

"Wow." Jeff's eyes widened, partly for her benefit, since he already knew this about her, but partly because it was even harder to believe, now that he'd spent time with the energetic, exotic woman. For the first time, he understood the attraction younger men had for certain older women. He wasn't attracted to her that way, but he admired her self-confidence, her apparent hunger for life, her — what was it? — self-contentment, perhaps.

Few women realized that if they would embrace their good qualities, improve what they want to improve, and stop constantly voicing disappointment in their bodies, their jobs, and their lives, they'd be much like the woman now sitting before him. Instead, they burned daylight instead of calories, fought the coworkers instead of the problems, dwelled on imperfections instead of dwelling in possibility.

If he could find a way to bottle it, he'd make a fortune.

"Did you ever marry? Have kids?"

"My cars are my kids. I pour money into them like I'm bankrolling college funds."

Perfect opening. Jeff turned the conversation toward his reason for being with this woman in the first place. "I can relate. I got the woodie out of hock recently, after six months in the restoration shop. When you expect artistry, you have to be willing to pay for it. I suppose it's a good thing I'm not having to save for kids' college funds, either."

"You and your wife don't have any children?"

Damn. She'd taken it another direction. "No, no kids." He fiddled with the paper coaster, drummed up a way to bring up Louie's shop. "You obviously keep your own steel artist busy. Are there many good ones around where you live?"

"Probably, but I've never used them. I take my cars up to a place near you. I did, anyway. My restorer recently died."

"Yeah?" He sat up, played the game. He wanted to see if she'd be the first to say the name. "So did mine. You don't suppose . . . ?"

"Louie Stella?"

Jeff nodded emphatically. "He's the one. Of course, Louie's son, Tony, did all the woodwork on my Chevy." He shook his head. "Bizarre, isn't it?"

"How they died? Yes. They were professionals. Why on earth would they work among all those fumes and not turn on the vents?"

Their server returned with their salads, disappeared again.

Donna raised a forkful of salad, then stopped before putting it in her mouth. "Is there any chance . . . ?" She shook her head.

"Any chance what?"

She seemed to be looking through him. "Your car was at the Stella shop last week, wasn't it?"

Jeff nearly choked on a crouton. He took a drink. "How'd you know that?"

"I remember seeing it, now. Mine was, too. I still can't get over what happened."

He nodded. "Horrible tragedy, isn't it?"

"It is. I don't know how Marie's handling it."

"You know the family?"

"I've known them most of my life, actually. Louie's the one who rebuilt Bacall's engine. He and Marie are why I got into classic cars, and we had a deal going. He gave me some fantastic discounts, and I gave him a lot of Hollywood business. He could find any model of vintage vehicle I needed for a movie. It was well worth my doing business so far from home. I don't know whether I got that through the detective's thick head or not."

"He's just got a job to do."

Her back stiffened. "Are you defending him? You almost sound like a cop."

Jeff looked up. If he didn't come clean now, he might lose her trust down the road, if and when she found out. He shrugged, said nonchalantly, "I used to be FBI, but that was years ago. Believe me, I'm glad to be out of it."

She watched him for a long time, then went back to eating.

Jeff suspected that she was replaying their conversations, asking herself if she'd revealed anything she shouldn't have. He wondered whether she trusted him less now that she knew his background, instead of when she knew almost nothing at all.

Finally, she spoke. "Okay, so you've had training. Do you believe they were murdered?"

He wiped his mouth with his napkin. "Honestly, Donna, I don't know. I was trained to investigate thefts, museum heists, stuff like that. Not murder."

"Have they questioned you?"

"Sure."

"See? I suppose you're calm because you've been in on so many interrogations. You probably have total recall. I was a nervous wreck."

"You didn't —"

Their server approached again, this time with their entrées — fortunately for Jeff, because he'd almost said, *You didn't look it.* As he watched her arrange their plates, he came up with a different ending to his sentence.

After she'd left, Donna said, "I didn't what?"

"You didn't have a lawyer with you?"

"No. It never crossed my mind. I mean, I haven't done anything wrong. Stupid, maybe, but not wrong."

"Why do you say stupid?"

She fluttered a hand. "They think I was actually in the building when it happened. And, they — the detective, anyway — thinks it was murder. I can't even fathom it, frankly."

"That they were murdered, or that you were in the building?"

"Both, now that you mention it. If I'd

known something was going on, I'm not sure I could've helped. And I've convinced myself that the killer — if there was one — didn't know I was there, or I wouldn't be here, if you know what I mean."

"You're probably right." Something flitted through his mind as he talked to her, reminding him that all this could be an act. But, then, so was his angle. "If someone came in to kill four people, what was to prevent him — or her — from killing five? I say don't worry about it. The cops are grabbing at straws."

"Do you really think so? I mean, coming from you, since you were there, since you've been in law enforcement . . . well, it would put my mind at ease, if you mean it."

He didn't want to mislead her, but he knew that if he didn't reassure her, he might not learn anything else about her. After all, what did the cops have? Nothing.

He could always say later that he'd reconsidered the situation. For now, though, he looked her square in the eye, and said, "I really think so."

Twenty

THE MINUTES
SOME FOLKS
SAVE THROUGH SPEED
THEY NEVER EVEN
LIVE TO NEED

— Burma-Shave

"So," Donna said Saturday morning after they'd been served a breakfast of smoked salmon omelets, fresh fruit, and an assortment of pastries, "where to from here?"

"L.A. I've got some business in the area."

"You're kidding. You should try to squeeze in some time at the flea market in Pasadena tomorrow."

"It's already on my list, since my business dealings aren't till Monday. I've never been there."

"Never? I'm going there, too. Tell you what: Why don't you find me? I'll be there all day. Then, afterward, you could come out to the house for dinner." Her tone switched from excited to apologetic. "I assumed you wanted company, and I shouldn't have."

"No, it sounds great."

"I'd take you to a nice restaurant or something tonight, but I already have plans."

"Thanks, but there's no need to baby-sit me. I thought tonight I'd check in on one of the woodie club gatherings."

"Sounds fun."

"I have to admit that I've never been to a woodie event, and you can lay odds that my grandfather never took the car to one. Now, my father? Who knows what Mercy —"

"Mercy?"

"I know, it's a weird nickname that I think his sister gave him."

"You called him that, too?"

"No." *Did I? I don't remember.* "I don't think so. My parents died when I was eight, and I recently learned some things that have me thinking about them more than usual. I'm probably boring you, though."

"Not at all. You've learned more about them?"

He wasn't about to tell her that they'd been criminals. "I guess they went through a sort of rebellious phase. It shouldn't surprise me that I never knew: my grandfather

— who raised me — was so old-school that he obviously made sure I didn't know that my father, *his* son, had strayed from convention. That would've been completely unacceptable in his eyes."

"A true patriarch?"

"He was."

"Was he good to you growing up?"

"Oh, sure. Stricter than most, I suppose. But my aunt tried to make sure I had a normal childhood, even though she was more like a grandmother; several years older than my father.

"I see now," Jeff continued, "that it must've been extremely difficult for my grandfather to watch his only son — whom he'd raised to carry on the Talbot name — stray so far from convention."

"You're pretty open about it."

"I'm sorry, I'm probably making you uncomfortable." He'd used it as a tactic to get her to open up, without realizing that he must've needed to put his thoughts into words.

"Not at all. It's rather intriguing. I just meant that you obviously need to talk about it. How is it that you only recently found out about this 'phase' they went through?"

"My car was wrecked, and while Tony

was restoring her, he found a sort of time capsule." Jeff chose the photo from his wallet and handed it to the woman. "This was in the door panel."

She glanced at the photo, seemed to stifle a gasp by clamping her hand over her mouth. She looked out the window where their cars were parked.

Jeff recalled the waitress at the diner who had recognized the woodie just as quickly. Why, he wondered, had it been so hard for him to see? "Yeah," he said to the woman seated across from him, "it's the same car."

She looked at him, or at least he thought so until he realized that she was looking through him. The gaze told him she was a million miles and a hundred years away. "Donna? Are you on your own trip down memory lane?"

She smiled, dropped back in her chair. "I got caught up in a sort of hippie movement myself for awhile. That was so long ago, experimentation, sexual revolution, breaking away from convention. It took Kent State to snap us back to reality. Most of us, anyway. By then, we'd 'sown our wild oats' — as our parents would say — and, if we were able to live with the consequences, we settled down to an accepted way of living."

"Consequences? Sounds as if you did

some things you aren't proud of."

"We all did." She laid the picture on the table. "Some things were worse than others. Personally, though? I don't regret any of my choices."

"My hat's off to you, then. Not many people can say that."

He picked up the snapshot. "I haven't seen many photos of my mother and father. I really only remember their wedding photo, but it was removed from the mantel after they were killed." Jeff snapped the photo with a flick of his finger. "I'm still having trouble buying it, believing that these are my parents."

"Oh, that's your parents, all right."

"What makes you say that?"

She looked from Jeff's face to the photo and back again. "You look just like them."

He started to disagree, then remembered that he'd allowed his hair to grow. He supposed he did resemble the scruffy-looking man in the photo.

She looked out the window again. "How long have you been driving that car?"

"Almost fifteen years." Jeff shook his head. "Blows my mind that something so mysterious, so cryptic, was in it and I didn't know it."

"The strangest thing I ever found in a

car I bought was a pair of dentures wrapped in a tissue." She smiled, then glanced at her watch. "I'd better go. I've got a wrap party to go to tonight. It's for a swashbuckler that's coming out next year."

"Oh, yeah? I'm always up for a good pirate movie."

"I guarantee this one will be. Stars Johnny Depp. And here's a kicker: A friend's son is putting together a band, and they couldn't come up with a name. After I'd mentioned something for the film, they latched onto it."

"Really? What is it?"

"Prop Monkey Stand-In."

"Actually, that's not bad. Tell them to come on up to the grunge capital. They'd probably get along great with Pretty Girls Make Graves."

"Are you into grunge?"

"No, but Seattle is. I remembered that band's name from something I saw in the paper."

"Then the name's working."

They finished breakfast and started up the stairs to the second floor.

"Oh, I need to give you directions." She strolled down the corridor toward her room.

He seemed to have no choice, so he followed her.

"Where are you staying?"

"The Argyle. My wife says I'll love it."

"She's right. It's a fabulous Art Deco. You'll be able to see it for miles before you get there." She entered the room, quickly jotted succinct rows on a tablet on the desk, flipped up the sheet, and did the same on a second page. Tearing them from the pad, she said, "I've put my phone numbers here, too — home and cell — just in case. The first sheet has directions from your hotel to the Rose Bowl, second sheet is to my home."

"Great." He took the papers, then took a card from his pocket and handed it to her. "Here's my cell phone number. Just in case *your* plans change. And, thanks again."

"I'm looking forward to it." She looked around her room. "Okay, I'm on the road."

She started to reach for her luggage, but Jeff grabbed it. "Allow me, just this one time, okay?"

"You have your own luggage to carry."

"Yeah, but I have to make a couple of phone calls. I'd like to see you to your car first."

When she seemed hesitant, he added, "You can spend the time telling me about your great luggage. I don't have any like this in my collection."

"Do you really collect luggage, or is that a ploy?"

"I really do. If you want proof, we'll stop by my room, and you can see my most recent acquisition: Oshkosh Chief, tan with red-and-black-striped design, black calf-skin trim."

"That was proof enough," she said, her tone revealing that she'd been thwarted. "I have the same set."

She led the way downstairs, where she dropped her room key in a basket on an antique desk before going outside.

Once they'd loaded the suitcases into the red Nomad, Donna approached the woodie. "May I?"

"You don't have to ask." He unlocked the door, opened it.

"You're not into the auto show circuit, I take it."

It took him a second to realize what she meant. "Oh, I get it, the signs. I saw one last week: Unless You're Naked, Don't Lean on This Car. Do you use one?"

"A sign? Definitely. It reads: Fine Cars Are Like Husbands. If It's Not Yours, Don't Play With It."

She climbed into the driver's seat, held

the wheel, scrutinized the dash, the seats, the slat-and-canvas headliner.

It was clear that the woman truly loved cars.

"Thanks," she said, climbing out of the car. "She's a real beauty. Now, if I'm going to make it back in time for that wrap party, I'd better get going."

Twenty-one

PROPER DISTANCE
TO HIM WAS BUNK
THEY PULLED HIM OUT
OF SOME GUY'S TRUNK

— Burma-Shave

Rising early for the breakfast portion of B and B had given Jeff a jump on the drive toward L.A. He'd decided to take the coastal highway, but he knew Donna was way ahead of him. He wasn't used to the cliffs, the view, the curves, and had to take it slower in the woodie. Early on in the drive, he pulled over at scenic lookouts, clearly making the tailgaters happy as they soared past him. Eventually, though, he grew anxious to move, to skirt the cliffs. He rolled down the front windows, let the sea breeze wash his brain, and began to understand Donna Tiajuana's reasons for this rejuvenating solitude.

Before leaving San Francisco, he'd filed

a brief report with Detective Fleming. Much to the detective's dismay, Jeff couldn't very well trail after the woman, particularly with the woodie. So what had been a good "in" was worthless when it came down to surveillance. The detective seemed appeased, though, when Jeff shared Sunday's plans.

Then he'd called Sheila. After the usual small talk, she'd said, "Greer found information about a woodie event being held in Santa Barbara this weekend. I'm looking at the Web site now. We think you should go."

"Why?"

"What, you've got something else planned today?"

"Other than driving, no, but —"

"Since you're driving anyway, and you're going right through Santa Barbara, you might as well. It's mostly people from the National Woodie Club, I think. Let me check. . . ." She dragged out the last word, effectively holding the floor. "Yeah, looks like the Santa Cruz and San Diego clubs join the one in Santa Barbara, but it's open to anybody with a wooden-bodied car."

"What do they do?"

"Looks like mostly, they gather and schmooze, show off the cars, hold raffles. I don't know how much you can catch, but this month there'll be hula dancers and a couple of surfing legends. Won't hurt to drop by this afternoon and check it out."

"Okay, might be fun."

"Really? You're going to do it?"

"I can be spontaneous. If you give me enough time."

"Ha, ha," she said flatly. "Well, I can't wait to hear what this event's like."

"Sounds like you've already got it nailed."

"I don't know. It'll be cool for you to see that many cars similar to yours, all in one place."

"How many?"

Pause, then, "Wow. Around a hundred."

"Okay. Got directions?"

After their conversation, he'd clipped the Santa Barbara info to the sheet she'd sent along with him about his L.A. hotel. On Sheila's insistence, he'd be staying at The Argyle for two nights. She'd seen an article about an upcoming film — something Jamie Lee Curtis was working on — that had used the Art Deco hotel in a few scenes. He'd like the decor, Sheila had assured, and, besides, she had to have its stationery for her collection. It wouldn't do him any good to go to Bakersfield till

Monday morning, anyway, so he'd agreed.

Now, several hours later, he arrived in Santa Barbara. He exited the highway, consulted Sheila's directions, then headed toward the wharf and the beach.

Woodies were everywhere, mostly dark ones — blues, reds, blacks, greens — but a few light ones, too. He drove down the rows of backed-in cars, looking and being looked at.

He'd never seen so many whitewall tires in one place. Although he'd always kept whitewalls on his woodie, he'd never considered how fitting they looked. He'd simply done it that way because his grandfather always had.

He spotted a hole next to a car identical to his own (except for the surfboard on top), backed in like the others, and climbed out of the car.

The man next to him strolled over. "She's a looker."

"Thanks. Looks like we both have good taste."

"I'll buy that. I'm Hal, by the way."

"Jeff."

They shook hands.

"You aren't looking to sell her, are you?"

"The woodie? No. That's one thing I *won't* be doing."

226

Hal seemed relieved. "I'm glad to hear it. The wife jumped up and took off looking for you when you pulled in. She's decided we need twins, so that our twin daughters don't fight over this one when we're gone."

"Will your wife win out?"

"Probably. Say, I haven't seen you at any of the meets. Is this your first time here?"

"Yeah. Down from Seattle on business."

The man nodded. "You go to Willamette?"

Jeff was only vaguely aware of that one, having read about it in *Woodie Times*. "I've never taken the time to get into the auto events. I figure once it's in your blood, you don't get much else done."

"True enough. My wife finally got into it, just so she wouldn't be a wheel widow every weekend. She's hooked now."

Lots of people strolled through, admiring the cars, paying compliments. The two men smiled, acknowledged. Jeff said, "Your wife on her way back yet?"

"Not yet. She's probably picking up some hot dogs for supper."

Jeff rubbed his stomach. "Think I'll do the same. Catch up with you in a few?"

"Sure thing."

Jeff drifted, glad for the chance to stretch his legs after driving all day. The atmosphere was part beach party, part company picnic, with lots of chatter, Beach Boys music, camaraderie. Everyone was laughing, having a good time. He bought a hot dog and a Coke and took them down by the water to eat. He wasn't sure what had pulled his parents to this place long ago, but now he could relate to their happiness, evident in the discovered photos.

He watched a volleyball match while he ate, then made a wide loop back through the cars, slowly circling toward his own ride.

Hal was talking with three other people. They broke into two pairs, one bidding Hal and the petite woman beside him good-bye. The woman's pants legs were rolled to midcalf, and she wore white socks with saddle oxfords. The retro effect stopped there. Her T-shirt had a large photo on it of their car, with a caption that read, I'm Not Getting Older, Just More Collectible.

Jeff thought the caption might fit both the car and the woman.

Hal spotted Jeff then, and said, "Hey, here he comes."

"Hey, Hal," Jeff said, falling into the easygoing mind-set that everyone else seemed to have.

"Linda, this is Jeff, the guy I was telling you about."

Linda shook his hand. "I was hoping you'd abandoned this one, so I could adopt her."

"You'll be the first to know."

"Linda!" A woman called as she drove a depot hack past them.

"I'll be right back," Linda said, sprinting away.

"Well," Hal said, "we've had a heck of a good time today. What'd you think of it?"

"Great stuff. Do you attend every month?"

"With the woodie, since last summer — see the stickers?" He pointed to the side glass at the back of the wagon.

Jeff read a few of the dozen or so — Wavecrest, Encinitas, several on the subject of surfing.

"I used to have a Packard," Hal went on, "thirty-four, but the wife talked me into switching over."

"Switching over?"

"You know, sell the Pack, buy a woodie, join the National Woodie Club, and start wearing Aloha shirts." The guy shook his head. "I agreed, and before I knew it, she'd loaded up the truck and pulled a Clampett. Only thing she hasn't done is glue my feet to a surfboard."

Jeff toyed with the idea of strapping one

to the top of his car. It'd be fun now, but what would he do with it once he returned to the real world? "Looks like you've got a perfectly good one, though, if she decides to."

"No joke, it'd better be good," said Hal. "Dang thing set me back three hundred bucks. But," he said with a shrug, "we woodie owners are into our props." He seemed to notice for the first time that Jeff's woodie wasn't wearing props. "Where's your longboard?"

"I didn't want to mess with it. Drove down on business."

"Ah," he said. "Your wife doesn't travel with you?"

Jeff wasn't going there. "No."

"Tell you what really hooked mine: scrapbooking."

Jeff knew about this latest craze from Sheila. She wasn't into it, but she liked the variety of supplies for making greeting cards. "Why scrapbooking?"

"Linda's a scrapbooker, so she asked if she could be in charge of the build book." He said "build book" with grave reverence, as if it were the Holy Bible. "Wanna see it? She's proud of it, and, I gotta admit, she did a heck of a job."

Jeff didn't know what a build book was, so he said, "Sure."

Linda was on her way back over, so Hal said, "Honey, show Jeff the build book."

"Gladly." She pulled it from the backseat and set it on the tailgate.

The cover matched the blue of the car, with the words *BUILD BOOK, 1948 WOODIE*, in gold. Jeff flipped page after page that documented the restoration of the car: detailed photos, well-penned notes, dates, statistics. He'd have to ask Greer if he was going to make one for the Cadillac.

"This is great. *Very* professional."

"Thanks." Linda's wide grin belied her obvious pride. "Some judged venues require a build book, you know."

Jeff looked at her wide-eyed, a bit surprised that she didn't squint against the high-watt bulb that had turned on in his brain. If he were to give the light a name, it would be *evidence.*

Twenty-two

IT GAVE MCDONALD
THAT NEEDED CHARM
HELLO HOLLYWOOD
GOOD-BY FARM

— Burma-Shave

Donna said, "Sure. Sugar."

Jeff's astonishment must've come through loud and clear. He'd asked Donna if she'd ever seen anything like the item he was inspecting, and she'd called him . . . sugar?

"Not *you*, sugar," Donna said, laughing. "*It*, sugar. It's a sugar chest. This dealer is from Nashville."

Jeff could think of several Nashville-related collectibles: guitars, guitar picks, even Hatch Co. show posters, and anything by Manuel, who'd been designing rhinestone-studded clothes for country and rock stars since back when cars started growing fins. But this well-crafted piece of furniture before him was new. New to him, anyway.

He'd been among the crowds at Sunday's flea market for three hours before he'd found Donna Tiajuana. During that time, he'd found several items that could be turned for a decent profit, and had stashed them in the car. After having lunch, the two covered the rest of the place together.

"A sugar chest?"

"Right."

As he inspected the item — built like a hinged box with a locking drawer underneath it and four turned legs under that — Donna explained.

"A necessity, really, in the eighteenth- and nineteenth-century South. You've heard, of course, about tea caddies, used to keep valuable leaves under lock and key, mostly from the servants. Many people don't realize that it was the same with sugar down South, mostly Tennessee and Kentucky. Sugar was in cones — not loose, like we're used to — and it was an extremely valuable and treasured commodity. Sugar nippers and a ledger were kept in the drawer, and any withdrawal was recorded."

"Amazing." Jeff stooped, inspected the legs. "What's with the discoloration?"

"Actually, that's from oil. People often

stood the legs in tin cans filled with oil to keep ants out of the sugar."

"Would you buy this one?"

"Yes, even though I just bought three of them from a friend in Nashville who has a wonderful antiques shop *full* of American primitives, and Southern furniture like Prudence Mallard."

"I have some Prudence Mallard, a couple of bedroom suites."

"Gorgeous stuff. Cindy's house is full of Mallard pieces, too."

"Cindy?"

"Cindy Silberblatt. The one with the Nashville shop."

Jeff nodded. One thing was for sure: Donna Tiajuana knew her antiques.

A couple of women came up beside them, and one said to the other, "Claire, isn't that one of those sugar chests you've been looking for?"

Jeff and Donna exchanged a look of mild panic and grabbed the piece before the woman named Claire had a chance to respond.

"Sold," Donna said, as they carted it past the women.

Jeff paid for his find, then proceeded to purchase smalls, which he stowed in the handy little chest.

Donna was prepared. She pulled an upright, wheeled cart to haul her finds, that had a side pouch for a bottle of water. Also attached to the cart was a condensed version of the picker's toolbox Jeff carried in his car. Donna's was a rectangular makeup case, with compartments holding small notebooks, pens and pencils, a tape measure, a jeweler's loupe, a tube of Simichrome (great for polishing most metals), and a Ziploc bag with a white cloth. There were also a couple of trail mix bars ("In case I'm on the south forty and the eats are too far away"). Today, she wore a black tank top and dance tights under a white oversize shirt. When she found a forties suit — olive, fitted, with a flounce at the waist that she called a peplum, Bakelite buttons, and a long, kick-pleated skirt — she dropped the overshirt and slipped on the suit.

Smart, Jeff thought.

After she paid for the suit, they made the trek toward the parking lot, reflecting on the day's successes, and making specific plans for the evening.

As Jeff drove back to his hotel, he thought about the last couple of days. He felt as if he'd known the Tiajuana woman for years. He couldn't believe she was involved in the theft ring, let alone the four deaths. And, if she wasn't? No reason that Gordy shouldn't strike up a social relationship with her. Jeff smiled, wondered whether to give Cupid an arrow from his quiver.

He showered, dressed in dark taupe slacks and an off-white and taupe retrostyled shirt. He wasn't sure where Sheila had dug up his wardrobe for the trip, but it seemed to work.

He survived the drive from Sunset Boulevard to Malibu, and that said it all. He arrived at Donna's place only ten minutes late.

The driveway wound around, strategically designed to offer a glimpse of rear decks and open staircases descending toward the beach and ocean beyond, before ending at two garage doors: one double, one single.

The home, large and tall, was painted the same shade as the sand, providing a canvas for palm trees fronted by shrubbery and bright, tropical flowerbeds.

He parked the woodie and, as soon as he stepped from the car, he felt transformed. The ocean's surging resonance, a background for seagull cries and distant, nondescript sounds, was healing.

He rang the bell, and she appeared instantly, dressed all in soft ivory: slacks, a lightweight sweater, and flats that looked like ballerina slippers. "You're right on time."

"And you're too kind. I'm afraid the woodie doesn't know what to make of the edgy pace."

"It takes some getting used to." She stepped aside and invited him in with a sweep of her hand.

"I can see why you live out here. It's healing."

"Yes. I'm fortunate."

She seemed different to him, older, more settled than she'd been along the trip. Her magnetic presence was still evident, but he guessed that she had slipped into her home like one would sink into the soft comfort of a broken-in robe.

He gave her a bottle of wine, which he'd brought from the hotel, then took in the large, luxurious living room. Its far wall of windows gave over to the Pacific as if the structure had been sheared and adjoined to the water. "This is phenomenal."

"Thanks. I'll give you a tour after dinner. Now, make yourself at home. There's Chablis chilling over on the credenza. Can I bother you to open it and bring a couple of glasses to the kitchen?"

"Sure." He uncorked the bottle, poured two glasses. Before joining his hostess in the kitchen, Jeff looked again at the room.

Donna's decorating sense was impeccable, and Jeff saw why she'd been such a success with props and set design. Everything was in cream, champagne, and gold, with the etched glass and crystal she'd mentioned collecting for its reflective qualities. Vintage hotel silver, heavy and with a warmer patina than silverplate, glinted in displays grouped to rival any gallery. Large-scale paintings featured women during the era of Hollywood glamour, posed beside luxury cars from the twenties, thirties, and forties. She'd somehow created an oasis that felt warm and cool at the same time. Inviting, yet not cloistering.

He was inspecting a pair of vintage armchairs — open design, in ivory Naugahyde and old gold with a small yet regal crown on the back of each — when she leaned through the doorway, "Those are from the Fairmont in San Francisco. They renovated a few years ago, and I latched onto several things."

"They're amazing; all of it is. I can see why you've been so successful in the film industry. You have an impeccable eye."

"Thank you." She bowed slightly. "Everyone expects more color, but this is my quiet side — away from the car shows, the races, the rat race, the search for all those different colors and styles and graphics needed to help capture an era. This is my serenity, my luxury."

He nodded appreciatively. "You didn't mention the hotel silver."

"I didn't even think about it. I rarely buy more pieces for that collection since it's such a bear to keep polished. Follow me, I'll let you in on a little secret."

She led the way down a corridor off the kitchen toward the back of the house. In a room lined with built-ins, she opened four huge cabinet doors, revealing row upon row of gleaming hotel silver, all encased in Ziploc bags.

"At one time," she said, "I was totally obsessed with this collection. Now, a couple of times a year, I switch out the pieces and create new displays. It helps keep the eye sharp where graphic lines are concerned."

"My wife uses those bags, too. She says it's just as good as investing in silver cloth, and you can see what you have."

"Exactly." Donna closed the doors.

Back in the kitchen, she removed a tray from the refrigerator. "Something to snack on while I throw dinner together."

Jeff seated himself at the island bar, chose an appetizer, and popped it into his mouth. "These are great. Sheila would love the recipe — unless it's a secret."

Donna laughed. "I love sharing recipes, and this one's easy." She stepped over to a desk with a computer, made a few keystrokes, and handed him the printout.

"Talk about service. I'm impressed." He glanced at the ingredient list: shrimp, cream cheese, raspberry salsa, a few spices. *That's it? Must be the combination. Or, maybe, the setting.*

"It's how you get things done. In the moment."

He ate another canapé, watched as she performed an expert range-top juggling act. He thought of a question that might tell him a lot about her character. "Did you ever want to be an actress?"

She glanced at him, shook her head, and said, "I know my limitations," then returned to the steaming, simmering, and sautéing. "I truly admire actors; it's an extremely challenging thing to do, crawling into the skin of someone else."

She plated the food quickly and creatively. "I thought we'd sit on the deck, if that's okay with you."

"I'd love it." At least, he *thought* he would. At home, of course, they never ate outside.

She handed him a tray, grabbed one for herself, and led the way. At the patio table, she unwrapped a basket of bread, un-corked a bottle of red, and poured. She toasted, "To newfound friends," and they spent the next few moments savoring the meal.

"Wonderful food," Jeff said sincerely.

"Thanks. Cooking is therapeutic. You're so in the moment when you're slicing and dicing."

He hadn't thought about it that way and made a mental note to ask Sheila if she felt the same.

The kitchen phone rang, and Donna waved it off. "I'll let the machine get it. It's probably Guy again."

Twenty-three

SHE PUT A BULLET THROUGH HIS HAT BUT HE'S HAD CLOSER SHAVES THAN THAT WITH

— Burma-Shave

Jeff froze. The bite of beef medallion he'd taken nearly choked him. He washed it down with wine. "Guy?"

Fortunately, Donna didn't seem to notice Jeff's reaction. She finished breaking a morsel of bread from the slice on her plate, and buttered it as she spoke. "Oh, he's the young man who's driving my race car this week. I hate to say it, but what he's driving is me nuts with the phone calls."

Jeff knew about the race car, but he couldn't believe Donna was so forthcoming with the news. It wasn't a trait of the guilty. He was scrambling for a way to get her to elaborate, when she paused and looked at him. "He's from Seattle. Maybe you know him."

Don't appear anxious. "Seattle's a big place."

"That *did* sound silly, didn't it? I mean, he's into cars, so you might have seen him around. Guy Hollister?"

"Are you talking about the reformed Guy Hollister?"

"That's what I'm told." She sat back. "Don't kid yourself, I had my concerns. But Tony Stella assured me that Guy would *not* be a threat."

This news surprised Jeff. "Was that recently?"

"Uh-huh, a few weeks ago. I'm picking him up Tuesday at LAX, then we go to Pebble Beach."

Jeff would call Gordy about Tony's role in all this first thing. Now, though, he needed a conversational approach. "I ran into Guy at a cruise night last weekend. We got to talking about car history, and I was amazed at how much he knows about Ford history."

"That's reassuring." Donna visibly relaxed. "Henry Ford had a profound impact on the industry, on so many things that are taken for granted today. As with any revolutionary enterprise, a lot of people

243

jumped into automobiles — literally and figuratively. If you'd lived back then, would you have invested in Henry Ford, who had failed twice before?"

"Not when you look at it from that angle."

"Compare the early auto industry to the Internet: There were *hundreds* of start-up companies at the onset. Now, look at what's left."

"Obviously, people trusted the man."

"The Model T — or the Flivver, as it was nicknamed — was *the* car from 1906 to 1927. The company became so big that when Henry shut down production in the late twenties to retool and design a new car, he caused a major depression. The Model A was the new Ford. Other car makers shot for the higher-end market, but Ford went for the regular guy, the average Joe."

"Smart," Jeff said. "But, what about his ad? 'You can get any color you want, as long as it's black.' Shouldn't the average Joe have a choice?"

"Supply and demand. The choice was to own a car. Demand was incredible. Ford discovered that Japan black lacquer dried fifteen minutes faster than color, which meant he could roll that many more off the assembly line — which, by the way, was another one of his inventions."

"Why don't you own one of those early cars?"

"Not my style, even though the twenties is my favorite decade. So many exotic looks came in then, after the excavation of King Tut's tomb. That resulted in Hollywood making *The Sheik*, which, in turn, influenced fashion — not only clothing, but also interior design of homes and cars. Think beaded curtains."

"Your knowledge of history is remarkable."

"More like a curse, probably."

She gathered a forkful of salad. "Another genius I admire was Tucker. If you haven't seen it, watch the movie starring Jeff Bridges."

Jeff shook his head. "That Cyclops of a headlight was too out there for me."

"Preston Tucker was a forward thinker, though; politics killed his chances in the industry. Oh, Bridges is in a film coming out next year called *Seabiscuit*. It opens with his character in an automobile factory in the early 1900s, and he goes on to be instrumental in the industry. The film is *loaded* with great old cars."

"Based on the book, right? I thought it was about horses."

"Horses, *and* horsepower."

"I can't get over how much you know about cars. Aren't you a rarity?"

"In the minority, maybe, but not rare. Heck, the executive editor of *The Classic Car* is a woman — and an automotive historian."

"Okay, okay. I'm not a male chauvinist."

"And I haven't felt like burning a bra in forty years. I like what I do, I do what I like."

Jeff lifted his glass in salute. "Nothing wrong with that."

They carried their trays inside, and Donna set about making French-pressed coffee. "How about I show you where I work before we have dessert?"

"Sounds good."

They walked to a lower level of the house, and she paused before a closed door. "I'll warn you, my office isn't as serene as the rest of the house."

They stepped inside.

"Organized chaos," she announced, and Jeff made a circle, taking in the bookshelves crammed with volumes on the film industry, vintage fashion and accessories, cars, American history, and culture. Collaged project boards covered one wall, while photos from movie sets finished out the rest. And, below all those were sugar chests: some small ones stacked on larger ones that were draped with protective scarves.

Donna said, "Each drawer has an inventory journal in it, which tells me what's stored in that unit."

"I'll remember that, when I decide what to use mine for."

He moved to a project board labeled Speculation. It was covered with photos of Edsels. "Now, there's a Ford I recognize. Leave it to me to know the duds."

"The car might have been, but I don't think a movie would be. Rob Reiner's looking at a crime novel about that one, so I'm doing my homework, tracking down contact info on Edsel owners.

"Lots of producers still do it that way: start production on a script, then hunt down the vehicles needed. Also, there's another approach — scripts being written around specific cars. And some major motor companies are partnering with major production companies — the movies get their cars, and the cars get promoted."

"Like product placement?"

"Exactly. Hopefully, it doesn't get in the way of a good story."

"I'm seeing lots of these on the road lately." Jeff pointed to a photo of Charlize Theron folded inside a tiny car.

"The MINI Cooper. That's from the set of *The Italian Job*. She did most of her own stunt driving in that one."

"Wow. I just saw that movie." He scanned the photos — Cage and Duvall in *Gone in 60 Seconds*, Mitchum in *Thunder Road*, even Aidan Quinn in *Benny and Joon* — and stopped at one of Steve McQueen as Bullitt in the '67 Mustang. "Just saw that one, too."

"Ford put the pony to pasture and brought out big-gun muscle with that fastback.

"Speaking of cars," she continued, "do you want to see what's in the garage with my Nomad?"

"Love to."

Now he understood what she'd meant by stacking the cars. In the garage were two bunk bed–type setups — hydraulic lifts, she said — with the vintage race car above the T-bird, and the Golden Hawk above the old Corvette.

In front of the single garage door was the Nomad. On the wall was a set of Burma-Shave signs that read:

HER CHARIOT
RACED 80 PER
THEY HAULED AWAY
WHAT HAD BEN HER

— Burma-Shave

"Are these original?"

She nodded. "I practically hyperventilated when I saw them from a distance in an antiques mall. I was shaking by the time I reached them. You know the feeling."

"Sure do. You feel like you're sending out some sort of signal that everybody else in the place picks up on their radar."

"Right! Like it's flashing, 'treasure located!' over and over. Anyway, that set reminds me to be careful when I hit the road."

She led the way back to the kitchen, saying, "Cars — pickups, too — *are* American culture. Just look at the collectibles that are a direct result: those roadside Burma-Shave signs, old gas pumps, hood ornaments, license plates, road maps, advertising, even pedal cars and Hot Wheels and anything Route 66."

Jeff sat at the bar, while his hostess sliced a dense chocolate cake and topped it with fresh orange ice cream. She talked while she worked. "You can follow the history of America by the cars. Look at us now, watching what the foreign car manufacturers are going to do. In the sixties, *we* were the leaders, *we* were the muscle that the world watched: just like the muscle cars of the time."

Donna set the coffee and desserts on the bar and sat across from him.

"That reminds me of some car history I learned at Quantico," Jeff said. "Cars are the reason for a national fingerprint repository, because they made it so easy for crooks to leave town. Before that, fingerprints were only kept locally."

"Fascinating. That would've been early twenties, I'll bet."

Jeff chuckled. "Is there anything you don't know?"

"Sorry. I'm an obsessed collector *and* historian, I suppose. I'm afraid I've talked your ear off."

"Don't apologize. It's been an entertaining evening, and the food is first-rate. I've enjoyed it very much."

They finished their desserts in silence, then rose. He gave the place a final look as they walked to the door.

Donna said, "It's been so nice to visit with someone who shares the same love of, and knowledge about, antiques and cars."

"Antiques, yes, but I've never met anyone who knows as much as you do about auto history." *Except maybe Guy Hollister,* he thought.

They hugged briefly, and Jeff walked toward his car.

"Have a safe trip to Bakersfield," she called as he opened his car door.

He smiled and waved, then headed back to L.A.

Twenty-four

DROWSY?
JUST REMEMBER, PARD
THAT MARBLE SLAB
IS DOGGONE
HARD

— Burma-Shave

"Gordy and his shadow just came in," Sheila said. It sounded like her hand was cupping the mouthpiece of the phone.

She and Jeff had finally made some time for catching up, and had been talking for twenty minutes. "I'm sorry, hon. Are they underfoot?"

"Not at all. I just find it funny that Fleming seems to be 'following the master,' you know? Actually, he's been quite pleasant. He told me about his mother."

"I hope he didn't make you uncomfortable."

"No, nothing like that. It's cool."

"Hi, you two," she said, away from the

phone. "I have a lonely quasi-agent on the phone, says he's up to his chin in volleyball nets and palm trees."

To Jeff, she said, "Bye, hon," then Gordy was on the phone.

"Got something?"

"Maybe."

Jeff heard someone pick up another phone, then Fleming said, "I've got the cordless. How're you doing, Talbot?"

"Good, thanks." Pleasantries aside, Jeff gave them the news.

When he'd finished, Gordy said, "So, Tony vouched for Guy, huh?"

"Interesting," Fleming said. "And the Tiajuana woman sure is a player in all this. Think she had something going with one of the guys? That could lead to a motive."

"Anything's possible, I suppose," Jeff said. "But she's not the type to say something like, 'Leave her, or you'll be sorry.' "

"How would you know that?"

"She has a live-and-let-live attitude. Don't tie anything or anyone down. She's a free-spirited, self-made woman, confident, independent." Jeff was searching for words. Now, he had something the men would relate to. "Picture Katharine Hepburn's independence in Raquel Welch's body."

"Easthope," Fleming said, "I don't like

the look on your face. Don't start dating a suspect."

"Give an old man the right to remember better days." Gordy cleared his throat. "Solve your case, and I'll know whether she's free and clear."

Jeff said, "It's a school night, girls. Some of us have work to do tomorrow."

Fleming said, "What was it you said you were doing tomorrow?"

"Didn't." Jeff hung up the phone and turned in.

He overslept. He'd failed to leave a wake-up call, so his came in the form of a housekeeper turning on a vacuum cleaner in the next room. The more he tried to make up for lost time, the more time he lost. He ripped the coffee filter, spilled the water, finally succeeded in brewing a pot, only to spill the first cup he poured. He was grateful that he'd stopped shaving for this trip. Factor in Los Angeles and Monday morning traffic, and he didn't arrive in Bakersfield till one in the afternoon.

He grabbed lunch, checked into a chain motel on the strip, and decided to forgo the newspaper for the relative privacy and quiet of the library's microfilm bays.

He stayed till they closed that night at

nine, left with nothing more than bloodshot eyes and old headlines crowding his brain.

He picked up takeout on his way back to the motel, started a movie while he wolfed down the food, and fell asleep two bucks into the eight ninety-five he'd been charged.

His cell phone rang, and he popped awake as if he'd had a power nap.

Gordy said, "Hey, buddy, call us from a land line, okay?"

"Okay."

He did, and Fleming said, "Your hunch was right, Talbot. Lab found GHB in the coffee, both in the pot and the mugs. So I'm thinking Tony Stella's looking better and better. Spike the coffeepot with GHB, knowing that everyone goes to his own corner for a break — grab the bank deposit, and disappear."

Give Fleming credit, Jeff thought, *for acting on a hunch that this wasn't an accident.* Jeff had been thinking about the GHB angle ever since San Francisco. "Tasteless, fast-acting. Were there four mugs?"

Away from the mouthpiece, the detective said, "Easthope, you were right. He hasn't forgotten his training."

Back in Jeff's ear, Fleming said, "Only three. Michael Stella never drank coffee."

"Which means —" Gordy's voice — "there's something in the bodies that hasn't shown up yet."

"Oh, it'll show up," Fleming said. "This new development lit a fire under the lab rats. They're running all kinds of tests."

Jeff said, "Yeah, but if something was used that would kill them, why put a sedative in the coffee? Rather, how did the murderer use whatever it was to get to Michael, if he *wasn't* sedated?"

"That's the question. One of them, anyway. I have to think that Michael didn't feel threatened."

"And the rest did?" Jeff said. "Does that make sense?"

"If Michael were in on something," Gordy said.

Jeff said, "So you think his partner took him out of the picture as part of a cleanup?"

"Remains to be seen," Fleming said. "One thing's for certain, though. Whoever did it knew the morning routine around there — whether he learned it from Michael, or from frequenting the place himself."

"You're right." This from Gordy. "I'm

afraid Tony's looking good for it."

Fleming said, "Maybe it was Tony's job to sedate them, then be out of the picture for the worse stuff."

"Wait," Jeff said. "Don't you think Tony would've known that his brother didn't drink coffee?"

"You'd think so," Gordy said.

Jeff said, "It could've been anyone who's been around there much."

"Like the Tiajuana woman?" Fleming said. "Wouldn't be the first time a female did a multiple."

Gordy said, "Has Guy Hollister been a regular there since his release from prison?"

"From what I've been told, Louie wouldn't let him come around," Fleming said. "That doesn't mean he didn't. Being a regular isn't enough, though. I've got a long list of those."

"Maybe Hollister knows where Tony is," Jeff offered.

"Says he doesn't." Gordy's voice. "Also says he's looking for him, too. For Mrs. Stella's sake."

"Motive, gentlemen," Fleming said. "We need to find the motive."

"I thought I had it," Gordy said. "But Hollister keeps coming up clean. Nothing, and I mean *nothing,* hooks him to the theft ring."

Jeff said, "I haven't found anything remotely like a motive where Donna Tiajuana is concerned, either. She said she's happily poured a fortune into Louie's coffers for years, said the place was as trustworthy a place as anyone could hope for. She seems genuinely distraught over the deaths."

Fleming cleared his throat. "When's the next time you're going to see her?"

"Hard to say. She's picking up Hollister tomorrow, and they leave Wednesday for Pebble Beach. I don't see how I can watch both of them when they know my car. And she'd said they would be busy getting ready for several different events. You can only do so much spying if you're not part of the inner circle."

"Maybe you could call her," Fleming said, "try to get an invite to join them for dinner tomorrow night."

"I don't know," Gordy said. "If those two are in on something together, you're throwing Jeff in the wolves' den. Hell, he's not even carrying."

"You're right. I forgot he's not an agent."

"Believe me," Gordy said to Fleming, "I've been guilty of that a time or two."

"Why'd he leave the stellar ranks of law enforcement, anyway?"

"I'm still *here*," Jeff said into the phone.

"Right," both of the men in Jeff's library said.

Jeff wished he were there with them, instead of in a chain motel following a chain of dead ends on his own search. "Any chance Louie and the other three had been working all night?"

"We've already checked," Fleming said. "All the guys went home, got about six hours' sleep before they showed back up at the shop. And, before you ask it, I've checked out the other two vics. No red flags."

"How long do you think it'll be before you get your puzzle piece?" Lately, Jeff was fixated on puzzle pieces.

"Actual cause of death?" Fleming said. "No telling. Meanwhile, I'm not giving this to the media just yet. If you can use it as a litmus on the Tiajuana woman, do it. Be careful, though. And, Talbot?"

"I know, keep you posted."

"Okay, I'm out of here."

Jeff heard a click, followed by a moment of dead air before Gordy was back in his ear. "Jeff, you doing okay down there?"

"Yeah, just tired of coming up empty-handed. Nothing I haven't dealt with before." Jeff shifted on the bed, stuffed another pillow behind his back. "Gordy, have you given any more thought to the dead leads?"

"I've got an idea, yeah. The way things are stacking up, I'm wondering if one of the Stella boys was in on the theft ring, and Louie found out about it. Reason enough for him to feed me false information as a stall, while he tried to figure out a way to protect his sons."

"Meanwhile, whichever one it is panics, tells an outside partner, never realizing that the partner's going to take drastic steps."

Gordy coughed. "I'll go back to some of Michael's buddies tomorrow. Tony's, too. God knows I haven't been able to crack Hollister."

"Maybe he learned his lesson in lockup."

"Could have. The MO on the current theft ring is completely different from Guy's when he was convicted. I questioned him yesterday. He was adamant about his innocence, enough that I'm beginning to wonder if he *is* clean."

"Your theory about Louie covering for his kids might be a sound one." Jeff exhaled. "I'll try to drop by Pebble Beach on my way home. *If* I can make some headway on my own puzzle."

"You being straight with Fleming? You really think the Tiajuana woman's innocent?"

"I think so."

"Yeah, but what if she's picked up some real acting tips along the way?"

"I keep thinking about her letting me bring drinks from another room. Wouldn't you expect someone with a sinister streak to think ahead about that sort of thing?"

"Big deal, you fixed her drinks. Last night, she fixed you dinner. Did you ever stop to think that you're lucky to be alive?"

"Every day, Gordy. Every day."

Twenty-five

SUBSTITUTES
CAN LET YOU DOWN
QUICKER
THAN A
STRAPLESS GOWN

— Burma-Shave

Tuesday morning started out better than its predecessor.

Jeff rose early and checked out of the motel with no thought to where he'd stay the night. Everything depended on what happened. Would he find something? Have to go somewhere else? Would a phone call change everything, like last night's had? Could he find what he needed, so that he might stop at the Concours on his way home and see how Guy Hollister and Donna Tiajuana acted?

He was waiting at the library when they opened for business at ten, picked up where he'd left off with September. He

262

moved through reels of film, scanning for headlines that might give him the information he needed. He found plenty of crime, but only one lead: a bank heist and subsequent murder of a young CHP officer. Further reading told him that all three criminals had been apprehended. Dead end.

He had needed the alone time, enough so that any notions of asking for assistance went unheeded.

His cell phone rang, and he jumped. He answered before the second ring, not wanting to be booted from the facility for breaking the *Shhhh!* law.

"Jeff, it's Donna. Am I interrupting anything?"

"No, I'm due for a break." He rolled his shoulders, worked the kinks out. "Everything okay?"

"Actually, no."

Had she already heard about the GHB? "What's wrong?"

"Guy called this morning and canceled on me for the Concours, so I have to rearrange everything."

"I hope he had a good reason."

"I suppose so. His boss was called away on a family emergency, and he can't leave the office."

Easy to verify, Jeff thought.

"The thing is, he was supposed to come out to the house for dinner. I wondered if you'd like to join me? The menu's planned, the groceries are bought — that is, if you can get away from business commitments."

"Well, I'm not making any headway here." He would enjoy it, actually, and Fleming would be thrilled at the prospect of gaining more information about the situation between the woman and Hollister. "Maybe the break away from microfilm would help me plan my next approach."

"I'm glad. See you around seven?"

"Sounds good."

Jeff arrived at the Malibu home on time.

Donna answered the door, and the first thing he noticed was the cut over her right eye, held together by three butterfly bandages.

"What on earth happened to you?"

"I think someone tried to kill me."

"Come sit down." Jeff closed and locked the door, then led her to the living room. "Can I get you anything? Do anything?"

"Thanks, no. It just shook me up. Some jerk ran me off the highway."

Jeff didn't know which question to ask first. "Any other injuries?"

"Grace Kelly's bumper will need some work."

Jeff hesitated, then smiled. "Oh, the Corvette. I meant to *you*."

"Oh. No, just this." She gingerly touched her forehead. "I used to do a little racing, so I'm pretty good at high speeds."

"Did you get a look at who it was? A tag number?"

"The driver had on a big hat. The car was some new white thing — they all look alike to me.

"I wouldn't have hit the shoulder at all," she said, "except that the other driver was so crazy, so relentless, that I was afraid someone else on the road might get hurt."

Jeff said, "You sacrificed your own safety?"

"It's not a big deal. You would've done the same thing."

If she was telling the truth, it *was* a big deal. Jeff said, "What's your plan now?"

"Short term, dinner. Long term? I suppose I'll hire a transport for the race car, since it's already listed in Sunday night's auction."

"I can help with the short term."

"Good. If you'll get the wine going, I'll check on dinner."

He uncorked the bottle of Merlot on the credenza, just like before, only this time he thought about Gordy's warning. He poured two glasses, then hurried to the kitchen.

Donna was taking a dish of lasagna from the oven. "I hope you don't mind a simpler meal tonight. What with the ER, and filing a police report, I lost the entire afternoon. I had to rethink dinner."

"This looks like anything but simple." *And it's all in one pan.* That thought was followed immediately by irritation with Gordy for planting suspicions in his head. If Donna Tiajuana had wanted to poison him, she could easily have done it before now.

Nonetheless, he insisted that she sit at the bar while he assembled the salad and made garlic toast.

"This is nice," she said while he worked. "Why don't we eat right here?"

"Works for me." Jeff dished food onto two plates and set them at the bar. "You sure you're okay?"

"I'll be fine. A day like today just takes some of the wind out of your sails, you know?"

"I know."

Jeff debated whether to tell her about the GHB. On the one hand, seeing her first-hand reaction might prove helpful. On the other, she'd already had a stressful day.

"Donna, I'm afraid I have something to tell you. I thought about waiting, but if the media gets hold of it, and you hear while you're alone, or driving? Well —"

"It's Tony, isn't it? Oh, God." She held her napkin over her mouth. Tears welled in her eyes.

Jeff touched her arm. "No, no. Tony's still alive. I mean, I think so. They haven't found him yet."

She exhaled, dabbed her eyes with the napkin. "Thank God. Marie's a strong woman, but I don't think she'd survive that, too."

She looked at him. "It's about the deaths, though, isn't it? Your news?"

"Yeah. They were drugged."

"Drugged? That sounds like something out of *Arsenic and Old Lace*. Who drugs people nowadays and expects to get away with it? Technology is so advanced."

She seemed sincere. He didn't explain that Michael hadn't been. "True, but so are criminals' minds, apparently. GHB was found in the coffee."

"Where'd you get that? It wasn't on the news."

Uh-oh. "Not nationally, I guess, but my wife said they'd reported it locally."

"Isn't that the date-rape drug? I don't

guess I realized it could kill you."

"It didn't, in this case. There wasn't enough in their systems to have done the job."

She frowned, then winced and touched the bandage on her forehead. "None of this bizarre, senseless tragedy is making any sense. Why aren't the police working faster? What about that detective, oh, what was his name?" She studied her plate, as if she'd find it written in the dressing. "Fleming! Is he on this?"

"I'm sure he is." Sunday night, he'd paid attention as she talked about cars. Her admiration for them wasn't fake, and he'd noted her facial expressions, her mannerisms. Now, he compared those mannerisms to the ones she displayed while talking about the murders. They were the same.

"In the meantime," he added, "you should be more careful."

She touched the bandage again. "So you agree? The accident today might not have been an accident? Or . . . oh." The word came out and dropped with a thud. "Maybe the murderer *did* see me at the shop."

There was no mistaking the fear in her eyes.

"In all likelihood," Jeff said, "he

would've tied up loose ends right there. Just be aware. Contact some friends to watch your back, if it'll make you feel better. When I said be careful, I meant about letting men pour your drinks."

She seemed to ponder that advice for a long time.

Dessert was a repeat of Sunday, served with more apologies.

Jeff waved her off. "I've wanted second helpings since I first tasted it." After a few bites, he said, "There's a big auto show next month up in Snohomish. Are you entering?"

"I hadn't planned on it, but Guy talked me into it. I haven't participated in that show for a few years. After everything that's happened, though, I don't know if I want to make the trip."

Likely, Donna would arrive in Washington a day or two before the Snohomish show. "I hope you'll let me know if you decide to."

"Okay."

When they'd finished, Donna put the plates in the sink. "I'm not the only one who seems distracted tonight. Didn't your trip to Bakersfield pan out?"

"What I'm trying to find wasn't in Bakersfield."

"If it's a rare antique you're after, perhaps I beat you to it." With a sweep of her hand, she said, "Have you looked around?"

Over the course of the evening, he'd felt increasingly silly for suspecting her. Now, he decided to share more about his odyssey. "You remember the photos I showed you? The ones of my parents?"

"Sure I remember. Why?"

"Well, something else was found with those photos." He stood. "I'll be just a sec; it's in the car."

"This is a Fred Harvey card."

"Yeah, a generic one," Jeff said. "I've seen others that show scenes of Southwest life local to the town: Santa Fe, Taos."

"These train routes all over the Southwest sure bring back memories." She studied the postcard again, read the message aloud:

" 'The treasure is in the vault. Next step: the caper. Meet me at my home in the desert. Will let you know when.' "

"Wow." She looked at him and smiled for the first time all evening. Her eyes glinted with excitement, just as they had when he'd mentioned hidden passageways.

"That explains my edginess. My parents were involved in a heist, or a bank robbery, or something. And I don't want just any-body to know about this."

"I won't break your confidence." Donna flipped the card over. "Bakersfield post-mark. Okay, so that didn't yield anything. Why don't you go to the home in the desert?"

"I would if I knew what it meant."

"You didn't show them this at the li-brary? I'm sure they would've known." She smiled. "Casa del Desierto."

Jeff stared blankly at Donna for a split second before the translation hit him. *Casa: home. Desierto: desert.* "Are you telling me that this is the name of one of Fred Harvey's hotels?"

She nodded. "He used Spanish names for some, as part of the draw to the South-west. The El Tovar was in Arizona's Grand Canyon, The Alvarado in New Mexico; might still be, I'm not sure. In California, El Garces, and this one."

"The Casa del Desierto." Jeff took the card. "Do you know what town?"

"Sure. Barstow."

"I wonder if it's still there?"

She smiled again. "One way to find out."

Twenty-six

WHEN THE STORK
DELIVERS A BOY
OUR WHOLE
DARN FACTORY
JUMPS FOR JOY

— Burma-Shave

Route 66. America's Main Street. The Mother Road.

Donna had encouraged him to take the historic byway, to trust serendipity to provide a place with character to stay at along the way. It went against just about everything he'd been taught: prepare, anticipate, prepare some more. Finally, though, he'd thought: *If a nearly sixty-year-old woman can live on the edge, it's not going to hurt me to try.*

He felt like the Joads in *The Grapes of Wrath.*

She had mapped him a route to Victorville, telling him that between the world wars around two hundred films were shot in the area.

At Victorville, he exited and found the old route. He wasn't sure how long he'd driven the big nowhere before he saw the lonely, flickering neon of a motel sign, then the outline of an old motor court. He stopped, rented a room from an old hippie behind the counter.

The room was simple and clean. Jeff stowed his luggage, then grabbed the ice bucket and walked outside. From the car's ice chest — the ice had long since melted — he chose a soda and made his way toward the ice machine he spotted at the end of the long building. It was enough like a scene from *The Grifters* that he found himself nervously glancing over his shoulder for Angelica Huston.

Back in the room, he double-latched the door.

Surprisingly, there was a phone on the nightstand, and it reminded him that his cell phone hadn't rung since Donna's call that morning. Where was it? He played back his time spent in the library. The briefcase. He'd thrown it in there before he left. He retrieved it now, and checked the battery indicator. Dead. He called Sheila on the land line.

She choked off the first ring. "Jeff?"

"Yeah?"

"I've been worried sick. I've tried your cell phone a hund—"

"Sheila, I'm sorry. I forgot to charge it." He drank some soda. "I need to tell Gordy something real quick, okay? Just take a sec."

"Okay, but don't you dare hang up before I get back on the phone."

"Promise."

Momentarily, Gordy said, "What's up, pup?"

"Hollister bailed on Donna for the race, put her in a bind. That was this morning. So she invited me to dinner. When I got there, she said she'd been run off the road this afternoon."

"Do you believe her?"

"She has a butterfly bandage on her face, and she talked about filing a police report."

"Thanks, I'll give this to Fleming. He can verify with the department down there. Here's your wife."

Sheila said, "Where are you?"

"I'm not sure. Somewhere between L.A. and Barstow."

"Barstow?"

"Home of 'home in the desert.' Casa del

274

Desierto. It's a hotel. Used to be, anyway."

"You mean, you found your clue? That's the place from the postcard?"

"I hope so. Donna implied that any Californian could've told me that, had I asked."

He heard clicking, then Sheila said, "There's quite a bit of info about it on the net. It's a Route 66 museum now, and home for Amtrak and Greyhound. According to this, it was once a lavish hotel and restaurant on the Santa Fe Railway route." Silence, then, "Jeff. It was owned by Fred Harvey."

"That's what Donna said."

Sheila was quiet for a moment. "What a history," she said, finally. "When rail travel fell out of favor, it shut down and was abandoned for several years; vandalized during that time, most of the furniture and architectural elements were looted. When it was announced that the building was to be demolished, preservationists squawked. Somebody started to renovate. Then an earthquake in 1992 set them back a million dollars, but they forged on. From the looks of all this, it was a lavish place." She took a deep breath, exhaled. "What do you think you'll find?"

"I don't know. Maybe nothing, maybe everything. Since it's being restored and there's a museum in it, maybe they've got some old ledgers or records. If not, I'll check the town library, go through archived newspapers. If you don't mind getting me addresses and phone numbers of those in the morning, I'll call you when I wake up. For now, though, I'm beat."

"Sure thing," Sheila said. "Maybe the person who wrote the postcard worked there."

"Or maybe this is the mother of all coincidences. Maybe this guy really did have a place somewhere in the desert. It's not unheard of. And maybe my parents already knew where it was, but no one else did."

"Why?"

"Because he was a loner? Or he didn't have any family?"

"Or he didn't want anyone to know where to find him."

"Yeah, I know."

"Will it bother you if you find out that your parents were in on some bank job or something?"

"I don't know. But I'll promise you one thing."

"What's that?"

"If I find out they were, Seattle will think it's having another earthquake when my grandfather turns in his grave."

★ ★ ★

The racetrack looked like asphalt, but the woodie circled it, plodding along like it was struggling through mud. Jeff white-knuckled the wheel, leaned forward, urged his car onward, floored the gas pedal, cursed. Nothing helped.

Everyone whizzed past him. They laughed, then shook their heads in pity before they escalated to blaring horns and yelling at him to get out of the way.

Eventually, the number of racers dwindled, the spectators dispersed, until, finally, he was left alone to finish the race.

The finish line bell jangled, and he pressed the accelerator, but he couldn't gain rpms. He checked the needle on the fuel dial, thinking he'd run out of gas. It registered a full tank.

It jangled again. He tried to yell, but he couldn't make a sound. He needed to make them stop. *Stop ringing!* His mind cried. *It doesn't matter anymore!*

His flailing woke him. The phone rang again.

"Yeah?" His tongue felt like a rolled-up sock.

"Jeff! Jeff, wake up! I found it!"

Jeff groaned, squinted, glanced at the window. Blue neon flashed, rimming the curtains, telling him where he was. He mumbled, "Is it morning already?"

"Almost. Listen, I found some more of your aunt's diaries, and couldn't stop reading. Then there was nothing. It threw me off that she didn't write anything for a few weeks. But, boy, when she did! Jeff, are you listening? Come on, you have to hear this."

"Can't it wait till morning? I'm asleep." He rolled over, pulled the sheet over his head.

"Jeff, just listen, okay? You don't have to open your eyes to listen." She cleared her throat:

Dear Diary,
It's a boy!
Mercy just called, and I can hardly contain my excitement!
A boy. We would've taken a girl, of course, accepted her into the family; but the fact that it's a boy will help to make Father more accepting, I think.
Mercy reported that all is going well, and that he foresees no problem with the arrangement. He also said that Ellen's ecstatic, and that you'd think she had given birth to the child herself.

Jeff had roused himself as she read, swung his legs around, sat on the edge of the bed, switched on the dim lamp. Emotions cloaked him gradually, beginning with a contagious excitement. He was the only child born into the family and, thus, this entry must be about him. Then the last line sank in. How could Ellen *not* have given birth to him? She was his mother. Or —

He swallowed against the lump in his throat. "When did she write that?"

"Oh, sorry. Your aunt was so frugal. Many times, she didn't even skip one line when she made a new entry, so I've gotten used to skimming until I find the words, 'Dear Diary.' This particular entry continues onto the inside back cover, like she hadn't gotten around to buying a new —"

"*When,* Sheila?"

"Here it is, November tenth."

Jeff breathed a sigh of relief. "Didn't you check the date first, Sheila? That baby's not me."

"Jeff, I'm sorry. I didn't even think." Silence, then, "Wait, could it have been a child for Pim? Remember, you weren't hers to raise then, and she had no prospects of being a wife and mother."

"I don't know." He stood, paced.

"What'd they do —" He pulled the phone off the table, cursed, picked it up. "What'd they do, just leave me behind with Auntie Pim while they went gallivanting off? What if they were doing another bank job?"

Sheila gasped.

"What now?"

"Oh, Jeff. What if they weren't bank robbers? What if they were *kidnappers?*"

"Sheila, for God's sake."

"Well?" Her voice was high-pitched. "Got a better answer?"

"No, but we're going to find one." *Easy to say.* For all of Jeff's investigative training, he couldn't think where to begin. He cast about till he snagged it. *Take the next step, of course.*

"Do you have the next diary?"

"Not exactly." Her voice was almost normal again. "I mean, there are several more cartons in the basement. What I've been doing is opening boxes until I find what promises to be the next sequence, then I check the first pages of the diaries and put them in some sort of order. When that's done, I start reading."

"Greer's been helping you, right?"

"Yes."

"Okay. I'll check the angle down here

when things open. You wake up Greer, tell him what we're looking for. We need all the help we can get."

Twenty-seven

HE SAW
THE TRAIN
AND TRIED TO DUCK IT
KICKED FIRST THE GAS
AND THEN THE BUCKET

— Burma-Shave

Casa Del Desierto was a fortress of white stucco and red brick, with rows of archways framing the piazza at ground level and the balconies above. What looked like cupola-crowned sentry towers anchored its corners.

Jeff walked past the towering gooseneck streetlamps toward the entrance. He swallowed against the lump of adrenaline in his throat, not sure whether it was a result of anticipation or dread.

He stepped inside.

Business was just getting under way. A couple stood at the Amtrak counter, discussing schedules with a clerk, while a uniformed man — Jeff assumed he was one of the Greyhound drivers — drank coffee and talked to a group of people wearing name badges.

The neo-Southwestern architecture continued here, with a large lobby flanked by two magnificent staircases leading to an open expanse.

In the Route 66 "Mother Road" Museum, a man rolled a short display rack of souvenir T-shirts to a position near the entrance.

A tall woman with ramrod-straight posture and gray hair cut into a contemporary bob approached him. She wore a turquoise pantsuit with a brass name bar pinned above the pocket. Engraved on it in black block letters was JOANN.

"May I direct you somewhere, young man?"

"I understand you have a guided tour?" Although it would take more time — as well as patience, and a dose of cordiality — he suspected it was the best way to get answers.

"That's right. I'm Joann, from our local historical society." She tapped the name bar with a fingernail polished coral. "I'd be happy to show you our Casa."

"That'd be great. Thank you."

As she led the way up one of the staircases, she said, "You can see, of course, that the first floor is still the subject of travel, but quite different from the Casa's heyday. Now this —" she stepped aside and swept her arms wide — "reveals the grandeur that was Casa del Desierto."

The ballroom floor was like a sea. Light turquoise ceramic tiles shimmered like waves flowing to walled boundaries.

"The floor is original," Joann exclaimed. "Imagine you are from Chicago, and you're traveling the rails for a glimpse of the Southwest. You arrive after a long day at this glorious lodge, settle into your well-appointed room, dine on first-rate Southwestern cuisine, then dance away the stiffness from the train in a lively ballroom."

Jeff watched Joann as she spoke. She was clearly lost in the moment.

He gave her a second, then said, "Did you do that? Take a train here, dance with your husband, fall in love with the place, and stay on?"

She smiled wistfully. "No, son. I worked here as a waitress. I was a Harvey Girl."

"You mean, the black dresses and long, white pinafore aprons? You can't be that old."

"Do I *look* like Judy Garland?" She fluttered a hand, then gazed fifty years across the room. "No, I was here just before cars left train travel forever in their dust."

"Have you been here ever since? I mean, in the Barstow area?"

"Sure have."

She broke away, led him a little way down a corridor, and showed him a guest room with a velvet rope across the open door. "I watched this place go from an oasis in the desert to run-down hippie commune to wrecking ball. Did you know that one segment was demolished before we finally got enough people behind us to rescue her? The earthquake of ninety-two set us back, but we persevered. Eventually, we'll have her back to her glory days. Well, never like that, really, but she won't ever be in tatters again."

She fluttered again. "Forgive me. I'm not doing my job very well, am I?"

"On the contrary. I'm an antiques buff, so I admire any and all efforts to preserve history."

"Antiques? I'll bet you'd like to see the basement storage area. It's not prepared yet for the public eye, but I think you'd appreciate what's down there."

The cook's tour. Jeff wasn't about to turn that down. "I'd love to."

He followed her to the ground floor, then through a corridor toward the back of the building. She opened a door and flipped a switch, then started down the dimly lit staircase. "There isn't much left after all the vandalism, of course, but I think these steps were gone at one point, so that slowed down the thieves."

It looked like the back rooms he'd seen at some rundown flea markets, where iron headboards, chests with drawers missing, and grimy pedestal sinks with chipped finishes skirted the room. A long, narrow alcove, lighted by one naked bulb, held segments of metal lockers shoved end to end, yet not plumb with one another. A quick mental tally told him that there were well over a hundred separate units. He wondered how it was decided who got the upper ones. Seniority, like in high school?

"You're right," Jeff said. "Lots of potential here, isn't there?"

"Sure is. We have volunteers working to repair and paint furniture. Then we'll continue to restore the guest rooms and the employee quarters on the third floor."

She walked to the alcove, grabbed the rectangular latch on one of the lockers, and jiggled it up and down. "This one was mine. Lord knows what happened to the keys to the old things." She started back toward Jeff, saying, "I'm always curious as to what's inside, *if* the vagrants left anything behind, that is."

Jeff jingled the keys in his pocket. "You have time for a little story, Joann?"

She nodded, and he told her about the time capsule that had prompted his trip, the false leads, even his suspicions, his concerns. He mentioned the beach photos of his parents, the old postcard with its puzzling message, and the tiny envelope containing a plain little key.

When he finished talking, he took the keys from his pocket and held them up.

Joann rubbed her hands together. "Get started already!"

He spent three-quarters of an hour inching along the rows, with Joann at his heels. He inserted the key into one locker after another, in a knee-bend pattern of upper, lower, upper, lower.

He felt like the prince with the glass slipper, not missing a single maiden's foot, yet growing more and more doubtful as he moved toward the last plat of land in the kingdom.

As he wondered whether the small key's

wards would even withstand all this action, he heard it. A tiny sound, but unmistakable.

Click.

He opened the locker.

Twenty-eight

AT SCHOOL ZONES
HEED INSTRUCTIONS!
PROTECT
OUR LITTLE
TAX DEDUCTIONS

— Burma-Shave

Jeff stood with his arms wrapped around himself, hands gripping biceps, as if he could physically contain the inner storm that threatened to rip him to scraps.

By some miracle, he'd held it together in front of Joann at the museum, and had driven from Barstow to Monterey in a surreal fog.

"Why didn't you just tell me?"

Fortunately, Donna had been easy to locate at the racetrack. She said, "You found something."

"Two somethings. First, that you'd been admitted to the hospital."

"I didn't want to be, but there were

289

complications. The second thing?"

"My birth certificate — my *real* birth certificate, I take it — stored in an old locker at the Casa, along with the newspaper clipping of hospital admissions with your name on it. I spent all morning there, trying that key in those lockers."

"I'm impressed."

"I wasted a lot of time, when all you had to do was tell me. Why didn't you?"

"Let's go someplace where we can talk." She led the way to a concession area with a dozen or so picnic table/bench combos under a large canopy. Several people were seated there, eating and visiting. Donna walked to an isolated table a short distance from the crowd. Jeff followed.

He sat across from her, jaw clenched, arms still gripped across his chest.

"When I showed you the photos, I thought you looked out the window because you'd recognized that the car in them was the same one I was driving. But that wasn't it. You recognized *that* car. *And* my parents. You'd seen it before, when they first came down here."

"Jeff, please don't be angry."

"I'm not angry. I don't think. Who knows? Maybe I am angry, as if I'd recognize it in here with all the shock and confusion, and whatever all else I've got going on. My insides haven't stopped shaking since I opened that locker." He exhaled, rubbed his hands over his face, then clenched them together on the table. "Why didn't you just tell me?"

"For one thing, I wanted to know if you were a good investigator. I wasn't being facetious when I said I was impressed. For another, I wanted you to take the journey, see the place where you were born. I doubt you've had much adventure, considering the thumb your grandfather kept on you. And you said yourself that you rarely venture far from home. I wanted to help give you that adventure, add to the story that is your life."

"That story's been fiction up till now."

"You don't really believe that, do you?"

"I don't know what I believe. You can count on one hand the real blows I've dealt with in my life. That probably makes me lucky; no doubt there are plenty others who have lost count. That doesn't make them easier to endure, though."

"I wanted to let you find the truth on your own, have some time alone with your discovery. As time passes, I hope you understand that decision.

"And," she concluded, "I hope you enjoyed the journey."

He stared at his hands, didn't respond.

She reached toward him, but hesitated, then withdrew. "Jeff, did you?"

He thought back over the last couple of days, the open-windowed flight down Route 66, the motor court, the broad stretches, the remoteness of it all. He remembered the thrill when the key opened the lock, how he felt a little like he was searching for buried treasure.

"Yeah," he said, finally, still staring at his hands. "Yeah, I did."

She exhaled.

"I'm glad," she said. "You see, I don't have an ounce of motherly instinct — that's why the deal worked — but after I met you, I became curious. Not about being your mother. Believe me when I say that *no one* could've been the mother to you that Ellen was. I was curious about *you*. I really like you, Jeff. I'm amazed that we have so much in common, and I wanted to help bring some more of that side of you to the surface. A DNA nerd would have a field day with us."

After a moment's silence, she said, "Did you think your parents were in on a heist?"

Jeff looked up.

Donna smiled that smile, so open, so genuine.

He couldn't resist smiling, too. "Yeah, I did."

"That was all your dad's idea, to make the postcard sound like that."

"Why?"

"They — Mercy and Ellen — tried to think of everything — ways to cover our tracks till after you were born, ways to make sure I was taken care of. That's why the postcard was sent general delivery, to avoid any chance that Mercer Senior might see it. I was the true bohemian, living in that deserted hotel. Your parents had no idea it was deserted, bless their hearts. They were so naive. Yet they wanted a baby more than anyone I've ever known. Not because of the pressure Mercy's father had put on them, but because of — well, whatever it is that makes people want to be parents. Ironic, isn't it? If your grandfather hadn't applied all that pressure, your parents never would've taken off for California. I never would've met them."

"And I never would've existed."

"That's right." Donna glanced away for a moment, then turned to him. "Jeff, don't judge them because of all this. They loved you. They loved you fiercely. So did Mercy's sister. And even his father." She shook her head. "I really felt sorry for

Ellen. Her biggest worry was that Mr. Patriarch wouldn't accept you because she wasn't the woman who'd given birth to you. It dawned on him rather quickly, though, that you were Talbot blood. It didn't matter to him *who* your biological mother was, as long as Mercy had fathered you. I think that hurt Ellen more than anything."

"So you and my father . . . ?"

She shrugged. "Didn't have in vitro back then."

He shifted on the bench.

"So you stayed in touch with them?" he asked.

"It was the other way around. Your grandfather wanted to pay me to stay out of the picture, and to secure my silence. You see, he never understood. I wanted nothing more than to help two friends."

Jeff considered what she'd done. He wasn't sure if he would ever wrap his mind around all he'd learned, but it wasn't lost on him that she seemed more concerned about his attitude toward his parents, instead of worrying about what he thought of her. He'd gotten to know Donna Tiajuana enough to believe that what she said was true. "You should've taken the money, even if it doesn't mean anything legally."

"Oh, I did, finally, but only to get your grandfather off my back. And off your parents' backs. Jeez, talk about relentless. No wonder he made a fortune in the lumber industry. I was still free-spirited, but I had learned one thing: I wanted a life independent of people. I didn't want to marry and end up compromising my time, my beliefs, my *self.*

"It wasn't a huge amount by today's standards, but it turns out I had a real knack for finance. I invested a little, then used the rest for college. I studied American culture, fashion, and film, then started working in Hollywood. I'd always admired the history behind things, and had always been a bit of a pack rat. It became one big circle: the knowledge, the interest, the knack for finding old stuff. Before I knew it, I was one of the top names in Magic Town's Rolodex.

"I wasn't a bum, Jeff, or a freeloader, or even a gold digger. The money gave me choices, secured the independence I wanted. I hope you can understand that."

"I'm trying. Remember, though, I was raised by Mr. Patriarch. This long hair, the sandals — they're not me." He shook his head at himself.

She cocked her head and studied him.

"Oh, I don't know. I've watched you grow into them over the last week or so. It never hurts to try on something new.

"Jeff, I'd love to continue being friends, but I won't push. The rest is on your terms." She stood. "Now, Garbo needs her nose powdered for the competition."

Jeff stood, too, hesitant to let her go, yet a little uncomfortable in her presence. Only time would tell whether he could accept her offer of friendship. "So the secret died with my aunt sixteen years ago?"

"Well, no. There were two other people who knew, but I don't think either your aunt or your grandfather was aware of that."

"Do you mind telling me who they were?"

She studied his face a moment. "I don't guess it matters now, in light of everything. And if you can get her to talk about it, she might shed more light on that end of it, the Seattle end."

"She? At first, you said 'they.' "

"Half of the 'they' is gone. I'm talking about Louie and Marie Stella."

Jeff left Pebble Beach, worked his way over to the interstate, headed north. He thought about the events that had brought him to the place, the murders that had thrown him into contact with a woman who had made a profound difference in his life. The news that Donna Tiajuana was his biological mother would take a while digesting.

But what if she was in on the auto shop killings? What if the shock of his discovery was clouding his judgment? He counseled himself to look at the crime through professional eyes. When he did that, the needle swung far in favor of her innocence. But what if he'd lost his knack? What if his instincts were wrong? Did he have the genes of a murderer?

You're thinking too much, a voice inside him cautioned. He rolled down his window, punched the gas, and shifted mental gears.

He thought about the things Sheila had told him before dawn that morning; thought about his aunt and her secluded life. He believed it had been a good life, as he couldn't recall any unhappiness in her. She was a gentle, compassionate soul, with few friends, and even fewer hobbies. She gave everything, though, to the small number of people in her life, and she didn't neglect the scheduled hobbies that she took comfort in.

She didn't neglect her hobbies.

The cell phone rang, and he glanced at the screen. Sheila wasn't the only one who could take advantage of Caller ID. He hit Talk, and said, "She transposed the numbers. It was supposed to be ten-eleven, not eleven-ten. October eleventh, my birthday."

There was a pause, then his wife's voice. "How'd you know?"

"Before she began spending all her time raising me, Auntie Pim's diaries were her closest confidants. Remember when you said you'd been thrown off by the weeks of silence? I realized that she wouldn't have stayed away from her diaries that long."

"You're right. I fou . . . nex . . . di . . ."

"Sheila, you're cutting out. Can you hear me? I'm on my way home."

He heard enough of "okay" before the call was dropped to tell him that she understood.

He was anxious to tell Sheila what he'd learned, but it was a story that needed time, patience, physical interaction. It couldn't be done in an impersonal phone call.

As he gripped the steering wheel, he thought for the first time about his father's hands on that same wheel, driving that same route up from California. This car tied him to his parents, to his past, even to Donna. He wasn't sure yet how he felt about that, or about his grandfather. He knew what his aunt would say, because she had a knack for going to the core of things:

"You were loved, Jeffrey Mercer Talbot, and love's never wasted."

Twenty-nine

TO KISS
A MUG
THAT'S LIKE A CACTUS
TAKES MORE NERVE
THAN IT DOES PRACTICE

— Burma-Shave

They embraced.

Jeff held his wife, not willing to let go, not sure if he could put into words all that had transpired over the last ten days.

When they broke free of each other, she said, "You look so different. If I didn't know better, I'd say you've been gone the entire summer. You've got a rugged, tanned, Pierce Brosnan thing going."

"More like a weathered, tired Redford."

"And wiser? That always adds character to the face."

"It's been character-building, all right."

He retrieved his birth certificate from the Wells Fargo safe in the basement, showed it to her along with the one he'd found in the locker at the Casa del Desierto — his *real* birth certificate. While she read them, he shared with her the meaning of the cryptic postcard message.

"You're telling me that 'treasure in the vault' was like 'a bun in the oven'?"

"Right."

"And, the caper?"

"The trip to pick me up."

Over the next several hours, Jeff filled Sheila in on everything he'd learned about his family's past, and everything he could think of about the woman who had given birth to him. He told her about all he'd seen and done while he was away. They shared relief that his parents hadn't been bank robbers or kidnappers, and acknowledged that the truth, although shocking, could be enveloped.

Sheila was his kiln, his proofing fire. She helped shape his emotions, burn away impurities, cleanse the spirit, and then glaze the surface, so that he might withstand the flames that were sure to graze him while he cured from within.

They moved from one stage to another, from exhausting explanations and revelations, to circumspect discussion, to ordinary household subjects and a quiet dinner. Sheila had gradually brought him to the foundation that was his life.

"I had Greer put your phone messages on your dresser. We didn't want to leave them in the library, since Gordy and Detective Fleming are using it. Blanche has called a few times. I didn't tell her much."

"I don't know when I'll feel like returning calls."

"Do you want me to fill her in a little?"

"Thanks, hon. She'll understand, give me some space."

"I thought you'd like to have this, for whenever you're ready to read it." She handed him a small journal. "I've marked the passage."

He gripped it, not wanting to open it yet, not sure that he wanted Sheila to watch him read it. She knew what it said, but he had no clue how he might react.

She kissed him, said she had some sales to box up, and that she'd see him in their room in a couple of hours.

He sat there for a long time after she went upstairs, at the old refectory table in the kitchen. There was something about a relationship that stood the test of a kitchen. Occasionally, camaraderie was achieved around a dining room table, but the crux of a relationship was usually fed here, where nourishment started. He'd felt comfortable in Donna's kitchen, and he wondered whether he'd ever be in that place again.

He surfaced, discovered he was still gripping the diary to his chest. He wanted to read it, and he knew where he needed to be. It seemed fitting; a little silly, too, perhaps, but he didn't care. Weren't there moments when every man needed the security of childhood again?

He climbed the back staircase, turned left on the landing, and walked to the end of the corridor. Although certain the door was locked, he tried it anyway.

As he tried to recall where the key might be, he heard someone coming down from the third floor, then saw Greer at the linen closet just off the landing.

"Greer?"

The butler jerked almost imperceptibly, then turned. "Sir?"

Jeff walked toward him. "Sorry, didn't mean to startle you."

"Quite all right, sir. I'm not accustomed to anyone being in that wing at night."

"I can't think where the key is."

Greer reached inside the closet, opened a small door, and chose an old skeleton key. "Allow me, sir."

"I haven't spent any time in here in years. No telling what shape it's in."

"Actually, sir, I have the housekeepers air and clean the room once a month."

"Oh. Good idea, Greer. Thanks."

Greer unlocked the door and opened it. "Let me know if you need anything else, sir."

Jeff nodded.

Primrose Talbot's room smelled of her in spite of the regular cleanings. The scent of rose perfume held its own against the liniments used in later years to combat the effects of arthritis. He smelled lemon, too, and thought of Pim's daily lemon tea, although he supposed this came from the furniture polish.

The bed, the armoire, the dressing table with its white marble top were Prudent Mallard, fashioned from rosewood and carved ornately in the Rococo Revival style. A spinet writing desk stood near one of the windows, its top closed. Jeff had only seen it open on a few occasions when he'd dropped by the room to visit with his aunt. She'd tended to most of her correspondence in the early morning hours while she sat at the desk with her lemon tea. Her diary entries were recorded at night, just before retiring.

It had been fifteen years since he'd last seen her seated there. He shut the door, walked over to the desk. It was locked, no surprise.

His aunt hadn't had much privacy. She'd lived under her father's thumb, in his house, all her life. Jeff had never breached that privacy, and he wasn't doing so now. He simply needed to feel her presence.

He went to the bed, unscrewed the finial that covered the secret compartment, and retrieved the key to the desk. Odd, that he'd go to it without conscious thought, after missing a beat with the room key. He sat in the chair where she'd sat thousands of times, opened the desk, then opened the diary and placed it on the writing surface where it had been penned nearly thirty-nine years earlier.

He heard her voice as he read.

Dear Diary,

It's October 13. Two days old, he is, and it seems as if a month has passed since Mercy's telephone call. I want to record the boy's name, but Father does not approve of the parents' choice, and I am unsure whether Mercy will kowtow to the pressure of continuing the "Mercer" tradition.

Jeff rubbed his eyes, then turned the page and continued:

I channeled my pent-up energy into preparations for their return home — baking, airing the nursery, then giving the rocker, the little bureau, and the crib yet another dusting. (Ellen has teased for months that I'm going to love the paint right off that furniture!)

When Father returned to the office after lunch, I called a cab and went down to Frederick & Nelson's, where I purchased a blue layette and blanket for the baby. This is more excitement than I've had in years! I cannot wait to hold this precious, long-awaited child in my arms! One can only imagine how exciting it must be for Mercy and Ellen.

Jeff squeezed his eyes shut, then brushed at his face with the back of his hand. He closed the back cover of the diary and locked it inside the desk.

Thirty

AROUND
THE CURVE
LICKETY-SPLIT
IT'S A BEAUTIFUL CAR
WASN'T IT?

— Burma-Shave

Candy-colored hot rods nested on bright green grass, making the city park look like an Easter basket filled with jelly beans and dyed eggs.

Jeff joined the line of cars entering through the park's gates. He'd tried to stay busy since returning from California a couple of weeks earlier, but it had been a challenge. Sheila's suggestion that he search out a weekend auto show (following her comment that he was obsessed lately with old cars) actually appealed to him. Cars *were* what crowded his brain lately.

The gate worker, a kid in a scalp-hugging

ball cap with the bill shaped into an upside-down U, approached the car.

Jeff rolled down his window.

"Morning." Ball Cap's green nylon windbreaker was dotted with sprinkles of rain. "You'll need to display your ID card in the windshield."

Jeff raised his brows.

"You know, your entry card?" Ball Cap said.

"Oh, not entering; just here to check out the cars."

The gatekeeper gazed at the woodie and shook his head, said, "Man, you gotta be kidding," then took Jeff's general admission money.

Jeff parked, grabbed his jacket from the backseat, and drifted over to the displays.

The most popular accessory seemed to be fuzzy dice. The rods had them, the bobby sock buggies had them, the pickups had them, even some of the cars that looked like they'd been driven straight from 1930 to the present had them. There was chrome, too, and lots of it. Now, *that* was what newer models were missing.

Jeff wandered through, admired the entries. He was surprised that most of the owners seemed to take the weather in stride, so he mentioned it to a man and a woman sitting in lawn chairs drinking coffee and looking like they'd been fixtures there since Harley Earl invented the annual model change. "You seem pretty laid-back for someone in competition. Some of these guys are driving themselves nuts trying to keep the sprinkles off their rides."

"That's the new ones," the woman said. "They always take it a might serious."

"And you don't?"

"Not these smaller shows." This from the man. "Now, Snohomish — that's one where you'll see me get serious."

Jeff raised a brow and nodded before moving on. He had the feeling a lot of things were going to get serious in Snohomish.

In a world paranoid about privacy and identity theft, Jeff couldn't believe what he was seeing. The entry forms displayed in the windows were complete with the names and home addresses of the owners. *Might as well just hand your keys to a thief and be done with it,* he thought.

There weren't many vanity plates. He'd seen quite a few on the woodies in Santa Barbara: WAVCHSR, SAPLING, KNOT ROD, even BOARD, which covered the wooden car *and* the longboard strapped on top. The plate on his woodie's twin read

4T8 WOOD. Jeff was trying to remember others when a guy pushing sixty with a bulldozer walked up to him. "Saw that sweet woodie you drove up in," he said with an appreciative nod. "You'd better get her parked right, though, before the judges come around."

"Oh, I'm not entered. Just here to take in the show."

"You're missing a bet by not competing with that one."

Jeff shrugged. "Just observing, doing my homework. I thought there'd be more vanity plates."

The guy pointed at two cars parked side by side. "You mean like those? Most folks would rather go with historical — costs less."

The cars he'd indicated — one a classic Jaguar with RAGS JAG on its plate, the other a baby-blue Thunderbird with BLU BIRD — reminded Jeff of Donna. So many things did. He'd come to expect it and, in order to avoid emotion, he'd created mind jogs. Now, for instance, he compared this car analytically to Donna's, tried to determine design differences. The only one he pinpointed was that this one didn't have the portholes.

"Historical might cost less," Jeff finally

said, "but, when you're into the old car circuit, what's another few bucks thrown into the money pit?"

"I noticed your plate when you drove in. Where's your vanity?"

Jeff watched a turquoise and white Apache pickup cruise by. "It got slapped down by my grandfather thirty years ago."

Jeff walked away, left the man scratching his head.

When he returned home, his own place looked like a car show.

His Jimmy and the PT Cruiser, along with Gordy's rental and Fleming's sedan, were head to nose at the curb. Backed into the driveway was a flatbed truck. Chained to its bed was Greer's Cadillac.

Jeff parked the woodie across the street and walked up to Gordy and Fleming.

"Hey," Gordy said, "just in time."

Greer and two men stood at the open door of the carriage house, obviously planning an approach. Jeff looked the car over. She was just like Greer described her: suicide doors, chrome-trimmed running boards, free-standing headlights like torpedoes, egg-crate grille. The gunmetal-gray paint was in decent shape, with only a few areas of surface rust, some dents here and there.

The chrome was pitted but looked to be complete, right down to the winged goddess hood ornament. As far as Jeff could see, the only exterior part missing was the right taillight assembly.

They stood back and watched as the two delivery men guided the Caddy off the flatbed, with Greer directing the move into the carriage house.

"I swear," Fleming said, "that nose will reach the next county twenty minutes before the driver does."

Gordy said, "I never would've took Greer for a gearhead."

"Listen to him for two minutes," Jeff said, "and you'll believe he can make a Jeep out of your Swiss Army knife."

"What kind of restoration is he going to do?" Fleming said. "Original, I hope."

"I think so," Jeff said.

Fleming moved toward the back of the flatbed. "I saw a maroon-colored Cadillac like that one a few months ago."

"Everybody had a maroon," Gordy said, "whether they called it Monarch, or Military, or Moselle."

Fleming said, "Not very creative with the names."

Jeff said, "I wonder if it all came out of the same vat?"

Gordy said, "I wonder who Moselle was?"

Fleming shook his head. "Who used Moselle?"

"Mercury."

"Well, there you go," Fleming said. "Nobody cares about Mercury anymore."

"Unless it's a forty-nine lead-sled." This from Gordy.

Jeff said, "And there's that country song, 'Crazy 'Bout a Mercury.' Big hit for Alan Jackson."

"Okay," Fleming said, "so two or three people care. I'll bet even they don't paint their cars Moselle Maroon."

"Moselle Maroon." Gordy held it on his tongue, like chocolate. "Sounds like a blues singer, doesn't it?"

Jeff gave him a shove. "You guys here for the auto show, or is something up?"

Fleming sighed. "We got stuff."

They passed through the kitchen, each grabbing a cup of coffee on his way through to the place that had become their conference room: Jeff's library.

After they were seated, Fleming reported the latest. "I was at the PD this morning when one of the uniforms mentioned a kid he found last night in pretty bad shape. Hospital said he'd almost asphyxiated himself.

"Sometimes, we get lucky," Fleming continued. "Turns out, the kid was one of Michael Stella's friends that I'd questioned earlier. So I paid another visit to the others. One of them finally admitted that Michael was into whippets — aka huff, rush, hippie crack. Nitrous oxide."

"Well, well." Gordy exhaled. "Michael liked his balloon hits, huh? Wonder what else he was into?"

Jeff said, "I'm out of the loop, I guess. Isn't that what dentists use?"

Gordy said, "Better trust your dentist."

"Dental professionals mix it with oxygen," Fleming said, "and are supposed to keep a close eye on things. Their problem is theft, and the thieves are only taking the nitrous tanks. They're leaving the oxygen behind.

"One Saturday night a few months ago, two tanks of the stuff — valued in the thousands — were taken from a small-town Washington dentist office. Next morning, a beat cop in Seattle found dozens of used balloons around a couple of trash cans in a downtown alley. No telling how much that thief made for one night's work."

"Nitrous bottled for the dental industry isn't easy to get hold of," Gordy said, "but the restaurant stuff is, especially with the Internet. As long as a company issues proper warnings about misuse, it's not illegal."

"Have you checked your suspects' records?" Jeff said. "Phone, charge card, computers?"

Fleming shot him a look. "Do you think we're stupid? Of course we've checked. Your computer is probably the only one we *haven't* checked."

"If the truth were known, you've probably checked it, too."

Fleming chuckled but didn't deny the accusation.

"Nitrous has a long history," Gordy said. "It was used in medicine shows back in the eighteen hundreds."

Jeff said, "I'll bet teenagers who abuse it nowadays think it's something new, just for them."

Fleming pulled a notebook from his pocket. "They think everything is."

"Isn't that the damned truth?" Gordy said.

Sheila entered, handed Jeff a slip of paper with a phone message written on it. "Did I hear somebody say nitrous? I've got some."

"You do? Why?" Fleming said.

"I'm a chef. I buy whippets for whipped-cream desserts."

Sheila left.

Jeff played his FBI acronym game on the back of the paper. He started several, drew lines through them till he landed on one.

Gordy nudged him. "You still doing that?"

"What is it?" Fleming said.

"It's something he's done for years, claims it helps him order his thoughts."

"What's it say?"

"FBI: Frantic But Intuitive."

Fleming nodded. "Thought-provoking."

Greer entered with a coffee carafe and set about filling mugs.

Jeff said, "Fleming, you may be on to something with the nitrous angle. The killer would've needed a lot, right? What about the nitrous used for cars? You know, for giving them that extra boost?"

Gordy took a drink. "Trouble is, all the suspects — vics, too, for that matter — know, or knew, this car stuff. Kind of puts things back at square one."

"Sir?" Greer poured a warm-up into Jeff's mug. "Most nitrous oxide made for cars also has hydrogen sulfide. We didn't smell a rotten-egg odor when we arrived at the shop that morning."

Fleming and Gordy looked like they'd been tapped with a stun gun. Gordy surfaced, raised a brow at Jeff. "Greer's right. We smelled lots of fumes, but no rotten eggs."

Fleming said, "The auto-grade stuff is probably out of the picture. I'll work on the whippet theory.

"Talbot." Fleming took the floor again. "Are you entered in the big auto show at Snohomish?"

"No." Jeff had toyed with the idea but hadn't made a decision yet.

It was made *for* him. "I'd like you to. If this case is still hanging fire then, it'll help to have you there watching for Tony Stella."

"Greer," Jeff said, stopping the butler, who was on his way out of the room, "can I put you in charge of this? Registration forms, rules, whatever."

"I'd be happy to, sir. If you don't mind, I'd like to attend with you, assist in getting your entry ready."

"Good idea. That'll free me up to look for Tony."

Fleming drank down half his coffee. "Michael said something else, according to one of the friends. Wouldn't give me any details, just told me Michael said he knew that his big brother would be in charge of the shop when their old man died, so he needed some insurance."

"Insurance?" Gordy said. "Maybe our hunch about Louie covering for one of his kids was right."

Fleming said, "Sounds like a little sibling jealousy, too. Might've escalated into something else."

"I don't buy it," Jeff said.

Fleming tapped the old family Bible on the coffee table. "Let me introduce you to Cain and Abel."

Thirty-one

IF DAISIES ARE
YOUR FAVORITE FLOWER
KEEP PUSHING UP
THOSE MILES PER HOUR

— Burma-Shave

Jeff watched the clock, anxious for the midday news to air. Only a week till the Snohomish show, and Fleming hadn't found anything new. Or, if he had, he wasn't sharing.

Finally, the string of commercials wrapped up. Jeff punched Mute, brought back the sound.

The over-the-shoulder graphic behind the anchorman was the same one the station had used a few weeks earlier, only now they'd added the word *Murders* in a sinister-looking font under *Four on the Floor*, and had replaced the gearshift's cue ball with a skull.

"What officials first believed were the bizarre but accidental deaths of four men has now been ruled a multiple homicide. The Four on the Floor Murders took place August second at a small auto repair shop in a remote area south of Seattle."

Jeff clenched his jaw. Louie's "small" shop — as the anchor put it — cleared, easily, six figures a year. Louie wasn't one to flash his wealth around.

The anchor reported the names and ages of the victims, adding, "A fifth employee, the owner's eldest son, Anthony Stella, twenty-eight, has not been seen since that fateful morning. The police are searching for him at this time, and it's unknown whether they believe he's in danger, or whether he's being sought as a suspect. Investigators are not saying yet what evidence they've uncovered, but ask that if you have any information in the case, please contact the King County Sheriff's Office."

He turned off the TV. So, Fleming was keeping the nitrous info close to the vest. Jeff wondered if that meant he was following some major lead.

He went toward the kitchen, heard Sheila and Greer descending the back staircase, talking. Sheila sounded irritated about something.

Jeff looked up. Each carried a white plastic bin marked United States Postal Service in navy blue. The bins were full of packages.

He grabbed Sheila's, then followed Greer's lead and set it on the refectory table.

Sheila said, "I have no sympathy for the U.S. Postal Service. You know how they're always complaining about all the money they're losing due to E-mail? Double news flash: Number one, a lot of those people never wrote to each other via snail mail in the first place and, number two, the post office is making a *killing* off eBay shipments. A killing! Hasn't it dawned on them that without the Internet, they wouldn't have eBay-generated money at all?"

Jeff had never thought about that, but she was absolutely right. He told her so, then added, "I wonder if anyone's written to them and pointed that out?"

"I don't know, but I don't have time to. I'm too busy helping them make money."

After lunch, Sheila said, "Do you feel like going through some of the stuff I've unpacked in the basement?"

Jeff reviewed a mental list, found nothing that couldn't wait. "Sure, why not?"

"Great! My virtual shelves are almost bare."

The large room of the basement where Sheila and Greer had been unpacking the past reminded Jeff of a church bazaar. Rows of long tables, butted end to end, were crowded with china, glassware, toys, figurines, textiles, books, ledgers, women's accessories, men's accessories, dressing table accessories. Two wheeled racks held clothing — both men's and women's — covering a hundred years of fashions. Dozens of cartons were piled in the corners, and several old steamer trunks marched along the far wall.

"For crying out loud, Sheila. Where'd you find all this *stuff?*"

"It does look like a lot when it's all packed into one room."

He wasn't sure where to start. Every time he reached for something, though, he couldn't decide whether or not to give it the boot. He had to be careful. His mixed feelings over the discovered family secret might be clouding his judgment. A part of him was tempted to tell Sheila to sell it all, and start over. Fortunately, he recognized his present vulnerabilities and avoided giving her carte blanche.

In all that, though, he knew one thing:

He wasn't going to grip the past as tightly as he had before. Collecting was one thing; obsessing bordered on madness.

Sheila handed him an old jewelry box, ivory with a filigreed border stamped in gold. "*Please* tell me we can sell this stuff. It really creeps me out."

Jeff opened the box, and a ballerina began twirling to tinkly music. Inside were several pieces of Victorian hair jewelry. "I don't think I told you who collects this stuff."

Sheila unpacked a large vase and put it with a like group on one of the tables. "Who's that?"

Jeff toyed with a bracelet he'd chosen from the box. "Donna."

Sheila stopped what she was doing. "Do you want to give it to her?"

Jeff moved a shoulder. "Maybe. I don't know."

"You said she's coming up for the Snohomish auto show, didn't you? Why don't we invite her over for dinner?"

"But, what if I'm wrong about her? What if she *is* involved somehow in the murders or the car theft ring?"

Sheila clasped his shoulders. "Sweetheart, you need to stop second guessing yourself. You told me that you'd practically stake your life on her innocence. Have you changed your mind?"

"No."

"Well, neither have I, and I haven't even met the woman. She shares your blood, your parents trusted her, and Louie and Marie Stella were friends with her since before you were born. I don't buy that she's capable of murder."

Jeff wished Marie would talk to him, but she kept making excuses when he called to inquire about coming for a visit. "But, would it be, I don't know, weird to have her here?"

"Not if you concentrate on the sunshine instead of the dark closets."

That was a good way to look at it, and he suspected that Sheila told herself the same thing every day. "Are you sure you're comfortable with having her in the house?"

"Yes, I am. And, think about this: Gordy will be here, too. You said yourself they might hit it off."

"You're not that into company, hon."

"This situation is a little different. Jeff, neither of us has parents left, and I'm not suggesting that you substitute your mother with this woman. But, wouldn't it be easier to be friends than to continue this . . . avoidance thing?"

"You're probably right, and she does seem like a great person."

"She sounds a lot like you."

He smiled, hugged his wife.

"Your aunt knew her, too, right? Why not just give this hair jewelry to Donna?"

"You're right. Why not?"

When he dialed Donna's cell phone, he got voice mail. This relieved him. He wasn't sure whether he was ready to speak with her directly. He left a message inviting her to dinner on Sunday evening after the show.

She returned the call while he was gone to an estate sale. Again, relief.

Sheila talked to her, reporting afterward to Jeff that they'd had a fascinating conversation, had talked about so many interesting things, and that they couldn't wait to meet each other. "And I'm not as creeped out by that hair jewelry. We had a bit of a debate, but all I had to offer were my feelings, my personal reaction. She knows the entire history, the techniques, what it meant to people back then."

"So you want to keep what you found?"

"No. I may know more about it, but it still creeps me out."

Despite the hair incident, Sheila was ecstatic about Donna's forthcoming visit. She perused recipes, fretted over the menu, planned flower arrangements, ordered things off the Internet. She even sent Greer to Bon Marché to purchase outfits from which she could choose for the festive evening.

Just watching all the activity distracted Jeff, helped make the time pass before the big show.

Thirty-two

WHEN YOU DRIVE
IF CAUTION CEASES
YOU ARE APT
TO REST
IN PIECES

— Burma-Shave

Fleming said, "The lab found a black, greasy contaminant on the vics' faces."

"So?" Jeff studied his library walls, contemplated a different paint color. He'd spent so much time in here he was getting tired of how it looked. "They were in a car repair shop."

"It's different from what was on their hands. The kid who almost asphyxiated himself the other day had the same contaminant. Somebody at the hospital lab was talking to somebody at the ME's lab, and before you know it, they were comparing cases and sharing findings. It's the same stuff: residue from being closed up with the nitrous."

Fleming held up something that looked like steel fittings or some sort of nozzle for a sprayer. "I took this off the drug paraphernalia board we use for training seminars."

"What is it?" Jeff said.

"It's called a cracker. No nitrous cartridge in this one, though."

Jeff had seen the cartridges Sheila used in the kitchen. They were silver, looked like miniature oxygen tanks. "Hard to believe that one of those little things could kill someone."

Fleming said, "They can if you use enough of them without getting any oxygen into your lungs."

"What about the oxygen?"

Fleming said, "Different percentage from what the body requires. Try this on: Somebody who knows the routine at the shop puts GHB in the coffeepot. Everybody there knows him, no one feels threatened. They're drinking their coffee, and soon they're sedated."

Jeff said, "But, Michael —"

"Right. I'll get to that. Okay, sedated. Now, Michael's working with a sprayer under the truck, doesn't know the rest are napping. Remember, no threat?

"Back to the kid in the hospital. His

close call made him a believer, he can't stop talking. Said that Michael liked to 'fish out,' which is to take in nitrous till it drops you cold. You flop on the floor like a fish."

"Where's the fun in that?" Gordy said.

"Fun, nothing. Talk about loss of dignity."

Fleming popped around in front of them like a motivational speaker. "Are you with me so far?"

Jeff and Gordy nodded.

"Okay. Our killer then starts Michael with the whippets, tells him something like, 'Hey, thought you were coming to the party last night. You missed out, so I brought you somethin' special.' Maybe Michael comes back with, 'I can't, man. You know Dad's in his office.' And, Killer says, 'He's on another one of his long phone calls, you know how he is. C'mon, I've got your back, just like always. It'll only take a few seconds, and you'll have a honey of a Friday.' "

Fleming's voice switched from singsong to the punch. He pounded fist to palm. "*Bam.* One down, three to go. And those three are already in snoozeville."

Jeff said, "Okay, but how'd he contain it?"

"My guess? Plastic bag around the head. Crack a whippet, throw it in. When the kid's out, put another cartridge in. One down. Move to the others and do the same thing. Two, three, four. A few more rounds like that, and by the time the killer makes his cleanup round to gather the evidence, they're all asphyxiated."

Fleming took a deep breath, let it out. "Four crackers — one for each — and no telling how many cartridges. It explains the residue that the lab originally thought had something to do with the shop."

Gordy said, "Any chance the killer slipped up? He had to be scrambling, juggling everything in four different rooms, trading out cartridges, messing with the crackers."

Jeff said, "Sounds complicated; first the GHB, then the nitrous stuff. Why all the layers?"

"Who knows? My guess is he either likes games, or he thought that having the exhaust off and the nozzles going full force would cover his tracks."

"Wouldn't it?" Jeff said.

"You've got to hand it to the ME on this one: Tox tests didn't show any of the typical inhalants you'd find around an auto shop. They didn't inhale those, because . . . ?" He pointed to Jeff.

"Because they were already dead when the fumes were released."

"Exactly. Add to that, this, which most people don't know: When you draw blood for volatiles — procedures used if inhalant abuse is suspected — the blood has to be put in teflon-lined tubes, and the tubes have to be completely filled so the volatile agents aren't lost. Has a lot to do with how much oxygen is in the blood. A tube half-filled with blood is compromised, because the other half contains oxygen."

Fleming rubbed his fingers over his mouth, obviously considering something else. To Jeff, he said, "Have you talked to Marie Stella?"

Jeff exhaled. "I've tried, believe me. She keeps telling me she doesn't feel like company."

"From our standpoint, it's not a social call. Drop in on her, catch her by surprise."

"Fleming," Jeff said evenly. "I'm not on your payroll."

Fleming raised his hands. "You're right, you're right."

Jeff sighed, checked his watch. "Greer already got the woodie ready for the big day tomorrow. I suppose I could take the Jimmy, go to Marie's. Maybe I'll catch her right after dinner."

"Good, thanks." Fleming stood. "Let me know if you learn anything."

The look on Marie Stella's face when she opened her front door and found Jeff on the porch made him feel like a kid who'd thrown a rock through a window.

He'd considered all this on the drive down. Now, he said, "I'm sorry for dropping in like this, Marie, but you've had me worried. I just wanted to make sure you're okay."

"I'm holding up." She led the way back to the kitchen. "Coffee black, right?"

"If it's made." He sat at the table, rested his hands on the red checkered oilcloth. "Don't go to any trouble."

"No trouble." She poured two mugs, then joined him at the table. "So many police, so many questions. I keep a pot going all the time."

Jeff knew what she meant. "At least they're trying to get to the bottom of things."

"I suppose. I'll be glad when it's done, and we can put it to rest."

Jeff tried to think where to start. "I hope Guy's been checking on you. He told me he had been."

"He has."

"Did Tony and Guy resume their friendship after Guy's release from prison?"

"Sure. You know how kids are. It burned Louie up, though. He was always chasing Guy off, away from the shop, away from the house. Said he was scared to death Guy would pull Tony into some sort of trouble."

"Do you mean before prison, or after?"

"Both, I suppose. Why all the cop questions?"

"They have to be asked. They might be easier coming from me."

She sighed, nodded.

Jeff remembered something Fleming had mentioned. "Doesn't Tony have his own apartment?"

"He does, takes good care of it. I'm proud of him."

"Did Michael ever consider going out on his own?"

"No, he never did. He seemed content, and he was younger, you know. We didn't push."

She'd used present tense when she talked about Tony, past tense with Michael, and hadn't even noticed.

"Guy's been out of prison for a little more than a year. Has he been coming over here much?"

"Sure." She smiled wistfully. "He goes on and on about my cooking. I think the boy would starve if he weren't eating here."

"Did Louie get upset over Guy's friendship with Michael? Like he did over Guy and Tony?"

"He never mentioned Michael, no. We never had any trouble with that one, though. Tony, now, he got into his share of trouble with Guy before. You know that."

"Marie, you've heard from Tony, haven't you?"

She didn't respond.

"He can't hide forever. We can help him, Marie."

Still no response.

"Marie." Jeff exhaled. It wasn't easy, badgering a woman who was going through hell. "I hope Tony isn't in any danger, but I can tell you right now: If he's mixed up in this somehow —"

"How dare you accuse him of such a thing!"

"Marie, that's not what I mean." Whether or not Tony had snapped and killed four people, Jeff needed a different tack with the boy's mother. "If he knows something and he's either hiding it to protect himself, or to protect you, if he's taking matters into his own hands, if he's out for revenge — I understand the motivation to do that, but he's not equipped. He might end up getting himself killed, too. Or, inadvertently putting you in danger."

"He would never do that."

"Intentionally, no. Please, Marie. Give me *something.* I'll talk to him first, without letting the cops know."

She gazed into her cup.

Jeff understood Marie's adamancy about taking a secret to the grave. It was how he'd felt about his agent-informant relationship with Louie. Fortunately, though, keeping that secret had never endangered anyone.

"Marie, I know what it's like to lose loved ones. You know that no one's left of my family."

Marie looked up, held his gaze till her eyes seemed to glaze over. He assumed that she was wondering if she, too, had no one left. Sure, she had in-laws and second cousins, nieces and nephews, no telling how many in the large family. But her husband and one son were dead, and, with the whereabouts of her other son unknown . . . did she believe he was dead, too? Would she *know,* inside her heart, if that were true? He'd heard people say it's a reliable feeling: that certainty, that premonition, that a loved one's life is no more.

Jeff was about to ask her, when she said, "Your parents were friends of ours."

"I learned that recently."

"I talked with Donna today." Marie set her cup on the table, scooted it around till it fit in a worn groove of the cloth. "Your mother wanted a baby — wanted you — more than any woman I'd ever known. I'd miscarried three — that's why I had my boys later in life — but your mother, she couldn't even get that far."

Jeff was anxious to learn if Marie's story would fit the grooves Donna had made in his life with her version. "Still, I can't imagine how my parents got from toe-the-line Talbots to California beach bums."

"You practically answered your own question. Not everyone cottons to toe-the-line tactics. Between your grandfather's pressure for a grandson, to his preaching about everything else, they were going crazy. Remember, it was the sixties. They'd already gone against the old-school convention of your grandfather and moved into a little apartment down by the waterfront. Your mother loved the water.

"Anyway," she continued, "the surfing

craze was going strong, The Beach Boys made everything about cars and surfing sound fun, and those wooden station wagons were the ticket."

"But my grandfather wouldn't have let them take his pride and —"

"You better believe he wouldn't! He didn't, either. They snuck out one night after he went to sleep. Had everything ready, promised your aunt they'd be in touch, and off they went to California — with a stop here on their way."

She picked up her cup, then set it down without drinking. "Ellen was beside herself, she was so excited, giggling, glowing. She was free. Free! For the first time in years. Neither one of them was thinking about repercussions." She chuckled, shook her head. "I remember how silly your dad looked. They'd dressed the part, to fit in, you know, once they got to the beach. Your mom had long, straight hair, but your dad had the military cut your grandfather required in the office. I teased him, but he said, 'It'll grow fast.'"

Jeff reached back, felt his own hair, thought about how he'd changed his own looks to fit in, how much his California venture mirrored that of his folks.

"Did you know Donna Tiajuana before

my parents met her on the beach?"

She shook her head. "After they got back home, they told us about all the people they'd met, particularly the girl who was such an influence, sweet, yet so independent, so . . ."

"Bohemian?"

"That sounds about right. When they'd told her their background, about the conventionalism that was being forced on them, she came up with a plan, convinced them that it would fill everyone's needs."

Everyone's needs, Jeff thought. Whether they were real needs, or believed to be real, was something he wouldn't try to discern. His grandfather needed an heir. His father needed independence and some way to get the family patriarch off their backs. His mother needed a child. The subsequent actions took care of all that: independence, a child, an heir, someone to carry on the Talbot name. The *Talbot* name.

"So, what she said was true. I *am* a Talbot."

Marie smiled. "The three of them met at the Casa del Desierto for your birth. And, of course, for Mercy and Ellen to bring you home."

"Did it bother my mother — Ellen — that she hadn't given birth to me?"

"Not in the least. You were hers, pure and simple. She and your aunt got everything ready beforehand."

"How, without my grandfather finding out?"

"That was the easy part. He spent at least twelve hours a day at the plant. When your parents returned, old man Talbot had Louie give that woodie a thorough going over, even paint it black. It was as if he believed he could expunge the wildness from it. He was an eccentric old coot."

"He was that, all right. I asked him once why he'd changed the original color of the car. I was half-grown, had been playing with something in the carriage house. I don't even remember now what it was. But it had got away from me and chipped the paint job." Jeff shuddered slightly, remembering the thrashing he'd gotten. "I think Grandfather was more angry about my question than about the damage I'd done."

"I doubt he answered you."

"Oh, he answered me. He said, 'Because I could.' "

"Control. That was your grandfather. Louie and I talked about your decision to have it put back to blue. We hadn't thought of that old car's California adventure in years."

"Okay, that was when my parents left the first time. How'd they get away again to pick me up?" Even as he said it, he knew how strange it sounded.

"The first trip was sort of a wake-up call for your grandfather. He realized that he couldn't completely control his grown son. When it was time, your parents announced that they were going on a vacation to see the redwoods. Nice touch, wasn't it? The redwoods? Your grandfather couldn't argue too much, since his son had earned vacation time at the plant, and was showing an interest in something that kept the family business going: trees."

"So how did you meet Donna?"

"She came up here. Your grandfather arranged for her to fly in. It was her first time on a plane, and it absolutely terrified her. So, she bought a car that Louie had just finished restoring."

Jeff smiled. "And she's been buying cars ever since."

"Ever since."

He wondered how much Marie knew, hoped she could back up Donna's story about not really wanting anything. If that part were true, it would tell him a lot about her character. "Why would my grandfather bring her up here?"

"After he found out what had been done, he insisted on 'containing the situation.' He all but forced Donna to take a sizable sum and sign some papers so that she couldn't change her mind. None of it was legally binding, of course, but your grandfather felt as if it gave him the upper hand. He had no idea what Donna was really like as a person, and he didn't care to. In his eyes, she had served a necessary purpose, and he had wrapped up the loose pieces in a wad of money.

"Poor thing wanted none of it," Marie continued. "Finally, it was your aunt who convinced her to take the money. Told her to use it wisely, so that she'd never have to depend on anyone.'"

Marie took Jeff's mug to the coffeepot and refilled it. When she spoke again, her words were stern. "Don't get any of those silly ideas about the woman who 'gave you up,' either. It wasn't like that. It was one of the most selfless acts I've ever seen."

"I understand." He really *was* beginning to understand. "Still, Grandfather must've gone crazy when they showed up with a baby."

"At first, you bet. But when Mercy assured him that you were a true Talbot, he accepted you."

Jeff remembered what Donna had said about the effect that had had on Ellen. His chest tightened as he thought about his mother's feelings being hurt like that. Until his bizarre past had been revealed, he hadn't realized the extent of his grandfather's attitude, how he'd looked upon women as second-class citizens, conduits to keep the family name going, servants to keep the household running.

Now, memories of Ellen surfaced. Even though she'd only been there the first eight years of his life, she was his mother. She was the one who sat up with him nights when he was sick, who helped him hunt with flashlights for closet monsters in the middle of the night when he'd have nightmares. She was the one who took him to the library and the beach, who taught him his letters and numbers. Nothing would alter it: Ellen Talbot was his mother.

He felt better prepared to face Donna now. She was a friend.

Thinking about all this — about the things Ellen had done for him, the things Donna and his aunt had done for him, about mothers and sons — made him understand something: No amount of pleading was going to make Marie give up her only remaining child.

"Marie, do you think Tony's somehow involved in what happened?"

"No. That's the one thing I *am* sure of."

"Remember, though. He's going to have to talk to Detective Fleming. We don't know but that he has crucial information. The cops need evidence against the k—" he almost said *killer,* realized who he was talking to — "against whoever did this. And, remember that I'll help Tony if he's in danger."

"I'll remember."

"Do you think he'll surface for the Snohomish show?"

"It'll break his heart if he can't, but he'd just started working on his entry for this year. I see no way, now."

Jeff nodded, leading Marie to believe he understood. Actually, though, there was *one* way.

Thirty-three

WHY IS IT
WHEN YOU
TRY TO PASS
THE GUY IN FRONT
GOES TWICE AS FAST?

— Burma-Shave

"Jeff," Sheila said as he walked in the door, "you'll never guess who was just here!"

He didn't have time for guessing games. "Who?"

"Miss Tiajuana. She apologized for stopping by unannounced, but —"

"Donna was *here?*"

"Jeff, you were right. She's delightful."

"But she's not supposed to be here till tomorrow night."

"Oh, she's still coming tomorrow. She brought you a present, though. When you see it, you'll understand." Sheila led him to the laundry room, where a longboard was balanced across the washer and dryer.

"She said it belonged to your dad, and she thought you might want it for tomorrow. Besides, it looked rather silly strapped on top of that *gorgeous* luxury car she was driving."

Jeff stroked the surfboard's waxed finish, its fin. "Which car?"

"The Graham Hollywood. She let Greer sit in the driver's seat. He said there's a big colored disk in the center of a cliff-like dash, and in chrome across the disk it says *Hollywood.* She bought the car after she'd made her first really good Hollywood money."

Jeff nodded, but he was more interested in the board. "This is really something."

"Sheila?" Gordy's voice boomed from the kitchen.

"We're back here."

Gordy stood outside the door. "I'm afraid that pie will have to wait till I get back."

"Don't worry, I'll save you plenty." To Jeff, she said, "Oh, I made a Key lime pie. Want some?"

"Later, okay? Gordy, I just came from Marie's."

"Got something?"

"I think so."

"Me, too. I just got a phone call, might

be the break I need in the theft ring case. Task force in Memphis recovered one of the stolen cars, and a source said I'd find the same VIN on a junker in the Stella graveyard. You?"

"I think I know where Tony Stella is." Jeff filled Gordy in on his conversation with Marie, and his resulting suspicion that Tony had been secretly working in the shop, restoring his entry for the Snohomish show.

Gordy said, "I'll call Fleming, see if he can meet us down there."

"Suggest to him we park in the grave-yard, so Tony doesn't see our cars if he drives up while we're there."

"Good idea."

It was dark and quiet when Gordy drove down one of the grassy paths between rows of rusted-out junkers.

He stopped the car, killed the engine. "Fleming could be in here, and we'd have no way of knowing it. You got those flash-lights ready?"

"Got 'em." Jeff had grabbed two from the house, along with a fresh pack of batteries. He handed one to Gordy.

When they got out of the car, a voice called in a half-whisper, "Guys, over here."

"That wasn't Fleming," Gordy said in a low tone.

"It's Cookson," the voice said.

"I'm here, too."

"*That* was Fleming."

They walked deeper into the graveyard, in the general direction the voices had come from, keeping the lights' beams low. When the four men were together, Gordy gave them the news.

Fleming said, "What do you say we go up and check out the building first, then Cookson and I will give you guys a hand with the VINs?"

"Works for me." Gordy led the way. He'd walked about thirty feet when he stopped in his tracks.

Fortunately, Jeff's eyes had adjusted to the dark. He avoided bumping into the wall that was Gordy.

Fleming said, "Easthope, what are you doing?"

"Do you smell that?"

The other three in unison: "What?"

Gordy sniffed loudly. "Mexican food."

"Gordy," Jeff said, "you should've eaten Sheila's pie. You're just hungry."

"It's coming from right over there." Gordy stepped a few feet to the right, sniffed again, walked until he was up on an old panel wagon. He shone a beam of light through the window.

"I'll be damned. Fellas, you've gotta see this."

They converged on the wagon, and shone beams of light through the windows. Inside was, effectively, an apartment. A pallet, made up of sheets and a quilted comforter, was on the long stretch of floor behind the driver's seat. On the other side was a blue and white cooler with a crumpled sack from a local taco joint on top, and an orange plastic milk crate containing individually wrapped packages of snack crackers, half-eaten bags of chips, and a box of cereal. Near the passenger seat was a large vinyl suitcase, its lid propped open to reveal men's T-shirts, underclothes, and jeans in neat stacks.

"Looks like another correct hunch, Talbot," Fleming said. "Tony's been hiding out right under our damned noses, sleeping out here at night, and working on his car during the day."

"Yeah," Cookson said, "but what kind of car?"

Fleming said, "Let's go find out."

They started toward the building when they heard the rumble of an engine, then saw the headlights of a vehicle as it shot off the pavement and headed toward the graveyard.

"Get down," Fleming said.

They crouched.

Gordy said, "Wouldn't you know it, he's pulling in where I'm parked."

The driver of the car obviously saw the rental. He slammed to a stop, threw her in reverse for a turnaround, then barreled back onto the highway.

Everybody moved.

Jeff and Gordy trotted toward their car, shining their flashlight beams in front of them to avoid tripping over fenders no longer attached to bodies and tires hidden by overgrown grass.

Fleming and Cookson ran toward their own car, Cookson yelling, "I'll put out an APB!"

"On what, damn it?" Fleming's voice. "What kind of car was it?"

"I don't know, but I can tell the boys in town that he's moving fast."

"Okay, okay." They were in the car now. "Easthope," Fleming yelled out the window, "you two stay here, in case he doubles back. We'll be back in a few."

Gordy and Jeff pulled up, walked the rest of the way. "We might as well drive around to the building and wait," Gordy said.

"It's not like we have to sit back here."

After they'd parked behind the shop, Jeff said, "He won't go to Marie's."

"No."

"He's good. Quick."

"Yeah."

"Maybe they'll find him."

"Sure." There was no emotion in Gordy's voice.

Their partners in crime-stopping returned after a few minutes.

Nobody said anything, which said everything.

Once they were inside, Fleming cursed, paced, then grabbed a wrench and slung it against the far wall. "Four against one, and he got away."

"Yeah," said Jeff. "Second time that's happened at this place."

The detective looked at him and raised a brow, effectively switching off his anger. "I don't get it, but he obviously built a car. A red car."

Cookson elaborated. "City cop saw a blur. Said he thought it was a tricked-up Chevelle, sixty-six, maybe."

"Tricked-up?" Jeff said.

"Lot of custom work. And it sounds like he's got the power under the hood, too, ready for a getaway."

Gordy said, "Or a hit-and-run at to-morrow's show, if you get my drift."

Jeff considered all he'd learned over the past weeks, all the people he'd met who were obsessed with their old cars, obsessed with cruise nights and auto shows. Heck, he'd gotten caught up in it to some extent, had been drawn to the meets. The car players were like any other collector who got caught up in that have-to-do-it, have-to-have-it mentality.

"They'll all be there," he concluded.

"What?"

"Tomorrow. Snohomish. All of your sus-pects will be there."

Fleming said, "What makes you so sure?"

"They're obsessed, like any collector. Trust me. That obsession is how I make my living. If they think you don't have any evidence — and, so far, that's what they think — then they'll risk it."

Fleming lowered his head in thought. "You know, you may be right. That show's big. Crowd of about ten thousand people, hundreds of entries. I don't know if they'd risk entering, unless they did so under someone else's name, but, yeah. They won't be able to stay away."

After that, Fleming walked along the

worktables against the wall, browsing, inspecting tools and car parts.

Cookson said, "I don't know what you expect to find. The team went through all that junk."

"You've got an evidence kit in the trunk, right?"

"Sure, you find something?"

"Ever notice how many things in an auto shop look like other things? Look at this. You're telling me they checked every *scrap* in this building?"

Cookson sighed, lumbered toward the exit. "I'll get the kit."

The detective didn't respond. He went to the break room, flipped the switch, and went inside.

"Looks good to me," Gordy said, following the detective's trail. "I could take a load off."

Jeff drifted to a worktable stacked with binders, glanced inside a few. They held owner's manuals, diagrams, price sheets, and the like.

Cookson returned with a steel case, pulled a perplexed expression, like someone left behind at the train station.

"Break room," Jeff said.

"Right." Cookson turned, headed that way.

Jeff turned back to the binder he was opening. On the first page was a photo of the red Chevelle.

He scooped it up and loped to the break room.

"Look at this." Jeff spread the book on the round table next to the open evidence kit. "That red car was Tony, all right. I found his build book."

They formed a crescent beside Jeff, who flipped pages as he spoke. "I learned about these from this couple in Santa Barbara with a car like mine. It's a build book, documents the restoration."

Gordy leaned in, pointed to a photo. "Look at that. Police caution tape in the window. He's been in here all along, building this car."

Cookson said, "There was a junker under a tarp the day of the murders. We made a note of it, but nobody gave it any thought after that."

"There's probably a start date." Jeff flipped to the inside front cover. "Yep, looks like he put her in here first of that week."

Gordy went to flip a page when Jeff stopped him. He glanced in the kit, grabbed a magnifying glass, and scrutinized the box with the yellow car on its label. "See that old cigar box?"

While the others took turns with the glass, Jeff said, "I shelved this weeks ago, because I couldn't come up with anything solid. Hollister mentioned it that first night when I saw him at the Stella house, said that *it* was what Tony found in my door panel with the stuff in it."

Fleming said, "You mean the stuff in the envelope? The one I gave you that morning?"

"Yeah. Hollister said Tony had shown it to him. I remember wondering whether Tony kept the cigar box for himself because it's his car — the thirty-six Olds. But I couldn't see him stealing it. On the other hand, he's done his share of pranks, so?"

"Could be nothing," Cookson said, "or, it could be a lame attempt at some clue."

Gordy grunted. "Lame is right."

Jeff said, "Yeah, well, picture Tony coming in here, finding what he found. He freaks out, he's looking around in a panic, scared for his life, and his eyes light on that box. He thinks, *I showed this to Guy, and it's from Talbot's car, and maybe . . .*"

Gordy said, "I think he's proved that he wasn't in his right mind. If he *is* innocent, then I say it's a textbook case of shell shock. After what he saw, he climbed into the only safe place he knew: cars."

"So you think the cigar box means nothing?"

"Or, it means he's pointing a finger at Guy. But if he was in shock, that gesture could've meant anything."

"At least, with this —" Fleming thumped the build book with a knuckle — "we'll know what to look for tomorrow. We'll ask him then what the hell it meant."

Fleming left the room. Cookson picked up the steel case and followed.

When they were out of earshot, Gordy said, "I should've thought beyond Louie. He wasn't the only person working here."

"You and I both knew we could trust Louie with our lives."

"We thought so, anyway. It's cliché, but it's true: Blood is thicker than water."

"You ready for tomorrow?" Jeff said.

"Oh, I'm ready. You know all the cars, right? The Tiajuana woman — sorry, pal, but I have to keep an open mind."

Jeff had told Gordy all of it, but he hadn't wanted Fleming to know yet. He nodded, and Gordy continued.

"She's entered the dark blue Graham Hollywood, Tony'll show up in this Chevelle, and, as near as I can find out, Hollister only has that pink hot-rodded thirty-one Model A."

"Hey!" Fleming yelled. "You two want to come back here?"

They stood, followed Fleming's voice to the supply room.

Gordy said, "When are we going to check those VINs?"

"We'll get to that."

"Where are you?" Jeff stooped, trying to see through the rows of shelves stacked with cartons of all sizes.

"Down here."

Jeff spotted him on his hands and knees between shelves about halfway into the room. He pointed him out to Gordy.

Fleming stood and stepped from behind the row of shelves. With a gloved hand, he held up a chunk of metal that matched one he'd shown Jeff and Gordy in the Talbot library.

"Polly want a cracker?" Fleming said.

"You found that in here?" Jeff said. "How?"

Fleming took something from his pocket, held it next to the one in the baggie. "I started thinking about the killer and his round robin. Say he or she was finishing up back here, got distracted by something. He trips, nitrous cartridges and crackers go flying. Remember, he's got multiples. He tries to find all of them, but he knows he's on a tight clock. Finally, he has to figure that if *he* can't find the last cracker among tens of thousands of bolts, spark plugs, engine parts — you name it — nobody else will."

Cookson said, "He was almost right. We got to talking about the search, figured most of this had been covered — the few empty shelves, the space under the shelves, the gaps between the hundreds of boxes — but nobody looked that closely *in* the boxes."

Fleming wrapped it up. "A cracker's heavier than a spent cartridge. We narrowed the search to everything below three feet."

Gordy said, "Who'd you use, Mickey Rooney?"

Thirty-four

IF THESE
SIGNS BLUR
AND BOUNCE AROUND
YOU'D BETTER PARK
AND WALK TO TOWN

— Burma-Shave

Downtown Snohomish was an antique-lover's dream. And, on the last Sunday in September, those dreams manifested themselves as dream machines.

The town, known for its turn-of-the-century charm and antiques shops that virtually filled every block, came alive each year on this designated day with oldies music, street food, hundreds of old cars, and people. Ten thousand people, to be exact.

Unless it rained.

Today, it was raining.

"Greer, don't drive yourself crazy over the sprinkles after we get parked. Everyone's in the same boat."

"Yes, sir."

Jeff checked his side-view mirror as they slowed, caught up to the mile-long row of art on wheels that filled Lincoln Avenue.

Behind them, a black GTO wheeled in and out of line, its driver obviously anxious to get in place on his designated street. The guy had looped "Little GTO" on a sound track, and Jeff wondered whether he was now stuck with the lyrics looped in his own head for the rest of the day.

Greer twisted around. "Look at that goat, sir. Stacked headlights, modified hood scoop; GTO's new look for sixty-five."

"I hope he doesn't hit the surfboard." Jeff's woodie didn't have brackets on top for it, so he'd draped an old beach towel over the tailgate and secured the longboard through the open window. He'd considered leaving it behind because of the weather, then, embarrassed, remembered that it *was* made for water.

The butler faced forward, checked the map. "Turn here, sir, then you'll need to stop at the registration booth and give them this. It's your confirmation post-card."

"Okay." Jeff hid a smile as he took the

card. Greer's folders of maps, directions, instructions, rules, and who knew what else, probably weren't necessary. All they had to do was tailgate, stop for instructions like everyone else was doing, and go where they were told to go. But the butler was beside himself with excitement and, Jeff had to admit, it was contagious.

If by some chance the woodie went home with a trophy, he'd give it to Greer. After all, he was the one who'd done all the work for the show.

A young woman in a ball cap and vest over jeans and a T-shirt from the previous year's show approached the window. She took the postcard and told Jeff to drive to Union, where someone from the parking crew would show him where to park.

The volunteers were organized, kept things moving, and had a spot for Jeff in no time.

After the woodie was in place, Greer sighed elaborately. "Okay. The car can*not* be moved, or we're disqualified."

"Yes, sir," Jeff said, which clearly flustered the butler.

Jeff shrugged. "Equal ground. You're not dressed like a butler, you're not to act like a butler. We're a team today, got it?"

"Yes, s— I mean, got it. And thanks for the Hawaiian shirt."

"When *can* the car be moved?"

"Let's see." Greer checked his notes. "Judging ballots must be returned to the information booth by one p.m., vehicles cannot be moved until the awards ceremony is completed at three-fifteen."

"It could be a long day."

Greer opened one of the folders and removed an index card. As he marked a tiny red X on it, he said, "We're parked here. The entry packet needs to be picked up at the information booth, number seven in the legend." Greer handed the card to Jeff.

"Thanks. This'll come in handy, especially if I'm summoned by Gordy or Fleming. Speaking of which." He picked up a small walkie-talkie and hit the button. "It's Talbot. Anyone on the scene yet?"

"Watching the cars roll in." Fleming's voice.

Gordy said, "Hot-rod alley. You got a trophy yet?"

"Not the one we're looking for."

Everything had been worked out the night before. After quick success with the VIN search, Fleming had called the ME and set up a midnight meet at the lab to check for prints on the cracker. Before he and Cookson left, he also called the Snohomish police and mapped out a plan. Both Cookson and Fleming would have police radios, but Fleming had also put into play the three walkie-talkies so he could keep Gordy and Jeff informed.

Jeff took a deep breath, exhaled. All angles seemed to be covered.

They crawled out of the car. While Greer propped open the hood, Jeff went to the back and refilled his travel mug with coffee. He walked past the Lion's Club Weenie Wagon, where a group of men and women busily prepared food for the expected throngs. The aromas made him hungry, and he realized that he hadn't eaten yet. He checked his watch, amazed that it wasn't yet eight a.m.

He strolled to the information booth and, while he waited in line, watched a stage crew across the street trying to protect speakers and a platform full of electronic equipment from the drizzle.

He found a couple of vendors open for business, bought doughnuts from one, two ball caps from another. After snugging a cap on his head, he took his purchases back to the car to share with Greer.

By midmorning, the streets pounded with music, chatter, and tides of people coursing through as if carried by some undercurrent, like a slow-moving river. Some exhibited spirits as damp as their hair, but most were true Northwesterners, taking it in stride as they admired the rows of antique and vintage cars.

Nearby drivers grumbled about the rain, blaming it for the relatively small attendance. But Jeff couldn't imagine adding many more people to the crowds.

Jeff recognized lyrics from several songs, and lots of passersby sang along to the music that filled the streets: "I Get Around," "Little Deuce Coupe," "Maybelline," "Dead Man's Curve," "Mustang Sally." When he heard "Fun, Fun, Fun" he thought of Donna's T-bird.

"Where do you think Donna's group is?" Jeff asked.

Greer said, "My guess would be either exotic or orphan."

Jeff wasn't sure whether the words fit the car, but they seemed to fit the woman. "What's orphan?"

"Anything no longer produced: Packard, Studebaker, her Graham Hollywood."

"Why don't you take a break, go around and look at some of the other entries?"

"Are you sure?" Greer's excitement was evident.

"Yeah, go ahead. If you see Donna, tell her I'll be by in a little while."

The longer the morning dragged on, the more nervous Jeff got. He'd been on the alert, constantly scanning the scene for Tony, Guy, even Donna. Any or all of them were likely on constant move. The two men wouldn't realize that Jeff knew a fundamental truth: Obsession is a predictable bedmate. They were here *somewhere.*

Greer returned, bringing lunch and a report that he'd spoken with Donna Tiajuana. "She's looking forward to seeing you, and is very excited about dinner tonight."

Jeff had almost forgotten about the evening's plans, he was so caught up in the present.

They sat on the tailgate and ate hot dogs, then Greer told Jeff where Donna's car was parked.

"I think I'll go over there, touch base."

He didn't make it.

The walkie-talkie squawked. "They're on the run." Gordy's voice.

A gun's report sounded, then another, bracketed by screams. Jeff estimated its location, started toward it as he hit the speaker button. He was at least a block away, maybe two.

"Gordy?" He moved in fits and starts, slowed by knots of spectators.

"Tony and Hollister, both armed."

"Which one's shot?"

"Neither. They were deadlocked, then Fleming tried to make an arrest. Hollister ran inside that big antique mall on the corner."

"I know the one, know the layout, too." *An opening.* He broke into a full run, slipped on the rain-slick pavement, went down. The radio skittered to the gutter. He popped up and grabbed it, then took off again. He was almost there.

"Jeff, stay out of there. You aren't heeled."

"Back me, then."

"I'm chasing Tony."

"Talbot!" It was Fleming.

"Yeah?" Jeff shot up the stairs and through the entrance. Inside, he was double-blasted with the sounds of glass shattering. It reverberated in the stairwell and the walkie-talkie, covering Fleming's words. More followed, this time without the transistor, just sickening waves of glass crashing, as if a display case had been pushed and the domino effect put into play. Random screams resonated from the rafters three floors above, then nothing.

The noise stopped, leaving him with an echo in his ears and the sensation that the rest of the world had stopped. He crept toward the wide old staircase, listened, debated his next move.

More crashing, this time someone running down a flight of stairs, then another, and they were almost on him before he remembered Gordy's warning about no gun. He ducked into a side room with a decent view of the large foyer.

Hollister landed practically in front of him, as if he'd dropped from the ceiling. Jeff's heart pounded: telltale heart. Hollister *had* to hear the thing.

Hollister turned his back on Jeff's vantage point, swung open a door that led to the adjoining restaurant, and disappeared.

Jeff gulped air, started after him.

The transistor sounded, Fleming said, "Where is he?"

Jeff said, "Back on the street." When he didn't get a response, he figured Fleming was on the police band, orchestrating moves.

Most of the spectators had taken cover. Jeff spotted Hollister rounding a corner, took off after him.

Halfway into the next block was the pink Ford. Hollister ran toward it.

He opened the door when he got there, but hesitated. He looked up at Jeff, took off again on foot.

Jeff ran after him, wondered where the others were, Fleming, the cops.

"Jeff!" A new voice.

Donna Tiajuana climbed out of her car as Hollister ran past it. Clearly, she hadn't seen him. She smiled at Jeff, waved, jogged toward him.

"Get down!" Jeff yelled, running toward her, watching Hollister pivot, watching him raise the gun.

The warning was too late, the words severed by a gun's report.

Donna's face registered shock, surprise, as her body was propelled forward and knocked to the pavement. Before she hit the ground, a second report sounded. Its tone was different. Jeff turned toward its source. Gordy was lowering his weapon, moving across the street.

Hollister was down.

Two city officers closed the distance, joined Gordy with Hollister.

Jeff carefully rolled Donna to her back. She was losing a lot of blood, but she was conscious, taking in rapid, shallow breaths.

"Sorry," Donna said, raspy voice through gritted teeth.

"Don't talk." Jeff cradled her head.

She shook her head, spoke again, each word an effort. "You told me. Cover my back. Didn't listen."

"More likely, you wouldn't believe there was this much evil in the world."

"Car." She raised a fist.

He took the ring of keys from her grip. "Don't worry. Garbo's in safe hands."

People poured into the street. An ambulance's siren changed from a steady shrill to rhythmic whoops as its driver worked to clear a path.

"Break it up!" Gordy's booming voice did more good than the ambulance's noise-makers. People parted like the Red Sea. Two paramedics, one on either end of a gurney, rushed to Donna's side.

Gordy told them, "Gunshot in the back," then stooped over, hands on thighs. He was breathing hard.

Jeff said, "You okay? Sounds like *you* need an ambulance."

Gordy stood, waved him off. "Eight hundred frigging cars, and we have a foot chase."

Jeff stood aside for the medics, crossed his arms over his chest, held on. "What about Tony and Hollister?"

Gordy exhaled. "I think I just winged

Hollister; saw him shoot her. Fleming and another pair of medics have him. City cops are holding Tony till Fleming has a chance to talk to him."

One of the medics broke free, jogged toward the back of his panel wagon.

"What was that about a deadlock?"

"Saw it with my own eyes. Tony drew a gun on Hollister, who returned the favor. It was knee-jerk, though. Hollister looked stunned, hurt. Tony paused, like he couldn't follow through. Hollister lowered his gun and took off."

The medic came back through with more equipment. Both men stepped aside.

Donna winced as the two medics lifted her onto the pad, then again when they lifted it with the force needed to lock it into position.

Jeff stared at the pavement where'd she'd lain, surprised that she was still conscious, considering the amount of blood she'd lost.

"Jeff?" Her voice was weak.

"Right here." He took her hand in both of his, walked along as the medics wheeled her toward the back of their wagon.

". . . proud . . . how you turned out . . . had good parents. . . ."

"Yeah." Jeff kissed her cheek. "All three of you."

After they'd loaded her, one of the medics said, "Are you a relative? She's going to need a transfusion, they'll need to do a cross-check at the hospital."

"Yeah," Jeff said, handing Donna's car keys to Gordy, "you can check me."

"Climb in, then."

Thirty-five

ROAD
WAS SLIPPERY
CURVE WAS SHARP
WHITE ROBE, HALO
WINGS AND HARP

— Burma-Shave

Jeff inched the woodie along the narrow dirt lane as the procession slowly made its way toward a tented area in the back corner of the cemetery. The cars in the procession reminded him of the Snohomish auto show. People from all along the West Coast had made their way to Seattle for the funeral, driving their classics out of respect for the departed.

As per her request, Donna Tiajuana's resting place was to be in the Northwest, her last ride to be in a vintage hearse.

Jeff felt loss. Not the loss one would feel for a mother who had raised him, but loss, all the same. She was connected to him by blood, and that connection had been severed.

He'd learned that she was the last of her line. And, since he had no blood relatives left, she truly was the last of him.

They'd been up all night after the car show — Jeff at the hospital, Fleming in interrogation rooms, Gordy bouncing back and forth between the two.

Tony was the link to everything. He'd known his brother, Michael, was part of the car theft ring, that their father had found out and had, subsequently, set up Guy as a stall. He'd also known that, after all these years, Michael was still vying for Guy's friendship. He'd looked up to Guy, had practically followed in his footsteps, and was always trying to gain his approval, his friendship, his acceptance. This was an important factor in Guy's plan that morning at the shop.

Tony had seen Hollister there, something Hollister was not aware of.

Tony knew that Guy wouldn't miss Snohomish, so he made plans to take his revenge there. But he wasn't a killer. He couldn't follow through.

Capitalizing on Michael's tag-along syndrome, Hollister learned of Michael's nitrous habit and used it to gain his trust with the whippets.

Hollister was in the supply room when he heard one of the garage doors opening, then the car start up. He panicked, headed to the window to see who it was, and tripped — just like Fleming figured.

Partial prints on the cracker matched Hollister's and, in the end, he confessed. He'd killed all four men as a cover for killing Louie, not only for setting him up, but also because Tony was the only real friend he'd ever had, and Louie had been trying to take that away from him since first grade.

Hollister acted on the mistaken idea that Louie had set him up as a way to sever his relationship with Tony. He didn't know Louie was trying to cover Michael's crimes.

Finally, and ironically, Hollister didn't realize he was killing every chance for the friendship he was so desperate to preserve.

Rather than prove his innocence, he did something far worse than the crime for which he'd been set up. Louie had prevented friendship with Tony, but he didn't know that Michael and Guy had been friends, too. Michael was the one who told Guy that he heard his father blame him.

The L.A. freeway incident in which Donna Tiajuana was run off the road turned out to be random. LAPD made an arrest after tracing the man who had rented the car.

So, Hollister's claim that shooting Donna was accidental might prove true. Jeff didn't know; he'd lost all perspective. Let the jury decide.

Jeff rolled down his window, glad to be alone, and welcomed the breeze as if it could blow the cobwebs from his mind.

He'd gotten a haircut before the funeral. He had considered waiting, sort of as a nod to Donna's wild side, but realized that her wild side was a result of what she'd taught him: the freedom to choose, to be yourself, whatever that might be.

This was him, the man who looked more like an FBI agent than a beach boy, the man who functioned better if he followed a routine, the man who wore socks.

Most of the time, anyway.

Sheila had insisted he keep some of the strands of hair. At the time, he didn't know why, but before he left for the funeral, she'd given him a locket containing it, and had asked that he put it in with Donna, along with a chosen piece of the Victorian hair jewelry.

After the service, he stood graveside for awhile, spoke briefly with people who had known her much longer than he, and with friends who had come to support him: Blanche, Gordy, even Detective Fleming. They drifted through, one by one, until everyone had gone.

"Mr. Talbot?"

Jeff wheeled, a little startled. "Tony? I didn't expect to see you here." Jeff extended a hand, and the young man shook it.

"I needed to be. She was the last person who saw Dad and Mike. Except for Guy." He was quiet a moment, and Jeff left it that way.

Tony continued. "It's easy to get lost in the memories, isn't it? I've been spending a lot of time at the cemetery where they're buried. You know, taking Mom out there. Funny, what you remember that you haven't thought about in years."

"True." *Very true.* "Were you at the church during their funeral?"

Tony smiled. "There's a removable panel under the stage that leads to the pipes for the organ."

"That's where you were?" Jeff nodded his appreciation. "You must have a good relationship with the church employees."

"I guess so."

"How'd you keep from going deaf when the organ played?"

"Brought along the earphones I use at the shop."

"Good thinking." Jeff remembered the panel wagon. "If the navy finds out you like small spaces, they'll put you to work on a submarine."

"I'll make sure they don't. I'd rather stick to cars."

They walked toward their own cars, the only ones left on the lane that bordered the cemetery grounds. When they reached the woodie, Tony brushed a fallen leaf from the hood, then took a handkerchief from his hip pocket and buffed the spot he'd touched. An image flashed in Jeff's mind of Guy Hollister doing that with his Ford flamingo.

"I haven't had a chance to thank you, Tony. Your restoration work on her is top-notch. You're a true artist."

"My pleasure. She's a real beauty."

"You know, if you hadn't been so thorough, I might never have known about my past."

Tony stuck his hands in his pockets. "Do you wonder if that might have been a good thing?"

"In ways, sure. I suppose I always will. But it's all a part of living, unless you're living in a vacuum."

"Yeah."

"Will you keep the shop going?"

He moved a shoulder. "I don't know how to do anything else. Besides, it's what Dad would've wanted."

Tony looked away, toward the paved road that ran in front of the cemetery. "You know, it's weird, but all the media attention put the shop on the map. People have been showing up from all over the country with their old cars, wanting me to restore them. It freaked me out at first, but Mom said . . ." He paused, imitated his mother's voice and hand movements: " 'It's a blessing, bambino. You need to stay busy — busy to the point of exhaustion. It's the only way to get through these first few months.' "

"Your mother is a strong and wise woman."

"Yeah, she's a tough one. Michael's death has been harder on her than Dad's. She says that a woman subconsciously prepares herself to be a widow. Never to outlive her children, though."

"Well." Jeff clasped Tony's shoulder. "Take care of yourself."

"You, too." Tony nodded. "Oh, I almost forgot." He sprinted to the Chevelle and reached inside the window. He returned with the cigar box. "This was in your door panel. The pictures and stuff were in it." He handed it to Jeff.

Jeff studied the labels. The car looked a lot like Greer's Cadillac, and exactly like Tony's car that he and Gordy had seen at the cabin.

"I was pretty messed up after what I . . . well, afterward. I saw that cigar box and remembered that Guy had seen it, had said something about it looking like my car, a few days earlier. I don't know, I just hoped it would come up, and you'd know it meant something. Pretty stupid, when you think about it."

"No, it's not. Any attempt to leave a clue in a case like that is worth it. I'm sorry I didn't piece it together."

"Weird, though, what crosses your mind."

Jeff looked at the box again. Without research, he had no idea of its value. Twenty dollars? Fifty? Two hundred?

He handed it back to Tony. "You keep it. It belongs with your thirty-six Olds."

"You sure?"

"Sure."

"Thanks, man." Tony admired the box. "You did the right thing in all this, Mr. Talbot."

Jeff wasn't sure what he meant, but he said, "You, too, Tony. You, too."

★ ★ ★

After the funeral, Jeff drove by the house, where he changed out of his suit and into cargo shorts, deck shoes, and an Aloha shirt.

From there, he drove down to Alki Beach, and sat in the car for what seemed like hours, lost in thought, staring at the horizon. His mother brought him here when he was a child.

A couple of rollerbladers shot past on the path in front of him, broke his stare. He grabbed his keys and headed through the sand, toward the waterfront, toward the ocean that had brought his parents in contact with the orphan girl turned beach bum turned self-made woman, the ocean that had then taken their lives. Donna had said she used to like the water, till she'd learned of Ellen and Mercy's deaths. After that, she'd stuck to dry land. She'd wanted to feel the sensation under her of wheels on asphalt, of hot desert nights, of the effects of the ocean — without giving it a chance to swallow her up.

He'd always had the same sensation, of the ocean swallowing him up if he gave it the chance. Since then, though, he'd been thrown into the deep. Nothing would have that effect on him again.

This wouldn't scare him anymore.

He kicked off his shoes and waded into the water.

Recommendations from Jeff Talbot

Dear Reader,

Many things besides cars were mentioned in the preceding story and, on the following pages, Sheila and I will provide you with resources on a variety of subjects.

But the fact remains: Automobiles changed the face of America, and that change affected — and still affects — all of us. It doesn't matter whether you're leasing the latest SUV, driving a reliable ten-year old, waiting at a Walk/Don't Walk in New York, or scooting downtown for a weekend cruise night in a sweet little vintage number, your life is almost constantly touched by transportation.

In its heyday, that changing face was evident, tactile: more diners, drive-in theaters, a different kind of music, those Burma-Shave signs, motor courts — the list goes on and on.

Our interstate highway system changed

all that. The faster cars could go, the faster people moved, a stress-related phenomenon that created a desire for everything faster. No longer were the days of curb-side service for a burger and malt; the cineplexes and multiplexes booted out the drive-ins. It's all coming full circle. Antique, vintage, classic — no matter which sobriquet you apply to old vehicles, people are into them more than ever before. More books are available about the subject, and the Internet has made it easier than ever before to locate a club or organization that you and your wheels will fit into.

Cruise nights and auto shows are bigger than ever, too, and the reach back to a nostalgic time has spurred huge interest in collecting all those things tied to it — from hood ornaments to gas pumps, from state tablecloths to state maps, from license plates to Burma-Shave signs to Route 66 memorabilia to soda fountain supplies. It's all being scooped up like ice cream on a summer day.

You'll find crossover information between my quasi-bibliography and Sheila's webliography. Whichever source you choose, we hope you have fun learning more.

A final note: Keep in mind that the

prices in a price guide might be a year old when it's published (many books have a year's lead time).

Till next time, watch those curves!
Jeff Talbot
(Proud member
of the National Woodie Club)

Several types of ephemera are in the preceding story (postcards, stationery, cigar labels), and a stellar source for those and many more forms is *Encyclopedia of Ephemera: A Guide to the Fragmentary Documents of Everyday Life for the Collector, Curator and Historian*, by Maurice Rickards (edited by Michael Twyman; Routledge, 2000). Rickards, one of the leading experts in the study of ephemera, spent more than twenty years compiling the sourcebock. For more information, check the Web site Sheila lists for the Ephemera Society of America.

You're in good company if you enjoy deltiology (the study of postcards); postcards are very popular collectibles. A couple of good collector sources for postcard enthusiasts are: (1) *The Postcard Price Guide, 4th Ed., A Comprehensive Reference*, by J. L. Mashburn (Colonial

Press, 2001; updated with new values and listings in all chapters); and (2) *Encyclopedia of Antique Postcards*, Susan Nicholson (Wallace-Homestead Book Company, 1994; includes preservation, restoration, and framing guides, as well as a glossary and an *extensive* bibliography).

A postcard note: There are many Fred Harvey designs, in addition to the map of Santa Fe Railroad routes found in my car's door panel. Recently, Sheila purchased a similar — and interesting one — in an online auction. It was written in French in 1921, and mailed from Gallup, New Mexico, to a woman in Paris, France. Exciting, isn't it, that this small piece of pasteboard crossed the Atlantic more than eighty years ago, and somehow found its way back! Also, it's historically exciting to think about a French woman traveling our Southwest rails not too many years after that region was frontier.

Collector's Encyclopedia of Hairwork Jewelry, Identification & Values, by C. Jeanenne Bell, G.G. (Collector Books, 1998). This book has over five hundred photos, vintage illustrations, and images. Hairwork is featured in one of four categories: memorial, commemorative, sentimental, and purely decorative. There's also a list of criteria to aid in evaluating, identifying, and pricing pieces of hairwork jewelry.

The Victorian Home: The Grandeur and Comforts of the Victorian Era, in Households Past and Present, by Ellen M. Plante (Running Press Book Publishers, 1995). This coffee table book takes you through the Victorian home one room at a time. You'll find many color photos, the history of each room, as well as tips for creating those looks today. The author has also provided sidebars throughout the book, which quote from such Victorian sources as *Godey's Lady's Book*, Charles Eastlake's *Hints on Household Taste*, and *The American Woman's Home*, by Catharine E. Beecher & Harriet Beecher Stowe. A glossary of Victorian terms, a chronology of Victorian Furniture Styles and Trends in Interior Design, and an extensive Source Directory complete this valuable look at Victoriana. Author Plante's column, "Collecting Victoriana," is a regular feature in *Victorian Homes* magazine. She's also the author of *Kitchen Collectibles: An Illustrated Price Guide*, and *History of the American Kitchen.*

If you're interested in learning more about automotive history, start with these fascinating books about the auto industry and the Motor City: *On a Clear Day You Can See General Motors*, by J. Patrick Wright, (Wright Enterprises, 1979); *The Fords: An American Epic*, by Peter Collier and David Horowitz (A Touchstone Book published by Simon and Schuster, 1987); and *Detroit Goes to War: The American Automobile Industry in World War II*, by V. Dennis Wrynn (Motorbooks International Publishers & Wholesalers, 1993).

Car Memorabilia Price Guide, by Ron Kowalke and Ken Buttolph (Krause Publications, Inc., 1996), offers info on automobilia, petroliana, license plates, hood ornaments, and more. Also, a large segment on toys, and some interesting photos of pedal cars.

Pickups: Classic American Trucks, by Harry Moses with photographs by William Bennett Seitz (Random House, 1996). Eye candy for the truck lover.

American Muscle Cars, by Jim Campisano (Michael Friedman Publishing Group, Inc., 1999). Back when high-octane fuel cost about two bits a gallon and America had risen as the world power, there was the muscle car. And, there was another war on, this one to see which automaker could cram the most horses under the hood. Here you'll find a great combo of history, photographs, details, and specs.

There aren't too many books out there about funeral vehicles. Here are two to check out: *Classic American Funeral Vehicles: 1900 Through 1980 Photo Archive*, by Walt McCall and Tom McPherson, (Iconografix, 2000); and *American Funeral Vehicles 1883–2003: An Illustrated History*, by Walter M. P. McCall (Iconografix, 2003).

For more on those catchy road signs that became one of the most successful advertising campaigns in history, find one of these: *Burma-Shave: The Rhymes, the Signs, the Times*, by Bill Vossler (North Star Press of St. Cloud, Inc., 1998); or *The Verse by the Side of the Road: The Story of the Burma-Shave Signs and Jingles*, by Frank Rowsome Jr. (Plume Reissue edition, 1990).

You can usually locate bits of information about those Southern sugar chests in general antiques books on American furniture. But for a great article on them, check the September 2003 issue of *The Magazine Antiques*. (Use your favorite search engine to see if the article is still on-line.)

Two works to aid you in fairings and world's fair history are: *World's Fair Col-*

lectibles: Chicago, 1933 and New York, 1939, by Howard M. Rossen (Schiffer Publishing, Ltd., 1998; thanks to Susan Gibberman for the recommendation!); and *Fair America: World's Fairs in the United States*, by Robert W. Rydell, John E. Findling, and Kimberly D. Pelle (Smithsonian Institution Press, 2000).

You'll want to have either a diner nearby, or the fixings for your favorite pie, when you peruse *Diner Desserts*, by Tish Boyle (Chronicle Books, 2000). The recipes, combined with San Francisco-based Clark Irey's stylish black and white photography, are a treat for the senses. You'll get hungry just thumbing through it. Excuse me while I break for an Eve With a Lid Oh, and a cup of Joe. . . .

Okay, I'm back, and there's nothing like having your dessert first. If you'd rather start with the main course, though, try one of these:

Blue Plate Special: The American Diner Cookbook, by Elizabeth McKeon and Linda Everett (Cumberland House Publishing, 1996); introduction by *Roadside Magazine*'s Randy Garbin. Included is a glossary of diner slang, a copy of the menu from Mel's Diner (circa 1957), and profiles of diners and the people who run them. A fabulous collection that offers over 450 secret recipes.

A Second Helping of Murder, by Jo Grossman and Robert Weibezahl (Poisoned Pen Press, 2003). If you missed my recipe for Talbot's Three Can Chili in *The Marriage Casket*, you can find the quick concoction in this collection of recipes from mystery writers. A portion of the profits from this cookbook goes to From the Wholesaler to the Hungry, a national organization that helps cities across the country develop systematic programs to distribute nutritious, fresh produce to low income adults and children.

Lidia's Italian-American Kitchen, by Lidia Matticchio Bastianich (Knopf, 2001), is one of Sheila's favorite Italian cookbooks. She particularly likes the layout, with categories such as "Quick-Fix Dinner," "The Bumper Crop," and "A Midsummer Meal." The author is a restaurant owner and hosts a PBS cooking series.

Since many readers have written to say they're now interested in antiques after reading about my adventures for the mystery elements, a fun place to start learning is with *Antiquing for Dummies*, by Ron Zoglin and Deborah Shouse (IDG Books Worldwide, 1999). Another one of the wildly popular ". . . For Dummies" series, *Antiquing* provides loads of information, such as The Care, Feeding, and Deleting of Antiques (Part V). These five icons used throughout the text are invaluable: Tip, Warning!, Repro Watch, Remember, and Check it Out.

As long as I'm mentioning this series of books, Sheila recommends *Starting an eBay Business For Dummies*, by Marsha Collier (Hungry Minds, Inc., 2002). Here, Collier (who also wrote *eBay for Dummies*) offers loads of helpful information, and four of those helpful icons (Tip, Remember, Warning!, and Auction Anecdote).

Traveling Route 66, by Nick Freeth (University of Oklahoma Press, 2001). Don't let its size fool you. This chunky postcard-sized book provides a fantastic state-by-state peek at The Mother Road. The aesthetics are great: retro colors, a few well-placed roadfood recipes, cars, and motorcycles. It's a perfect blend of history, nostalgia, and graphics.

Cars of the Fascinating '40s: A Decade of Challenges and Changes, by the auto editors of *Consumer Guide* (Publications International, Ltd., 2002). This book gives a timeline overview, and segments are presented by year (with the exception of 1943–45, when automakers turned their assembly lines to the war effort). Hundreds of color photos, several woodies, lots of info. Curious about what my car looks like? Check out the photo on page 246. Donna's Graham Hollywood? Page 93.

The American Diner (MBI Publishing, 1999) is one of several books on American culture by Michael Karl Witzel. This book gives extensive history and many great photographs of diners across the United States. Great bibliography, too. Witzel's other books from MBI include: *The American Drive-In: History and Folklore of the Drive-In Restaurant in American Car Culture* (1994); *Route 66 Remembered* (1996), and *Cruisin': Car Culture in America* (1997).

Although German photographer Gerd Kittel barely got his feet off our Atlantic shoreline (the back cover claims he scoured the American city and countryside) for his collection of photographs in *Diners: People and Places* (Thames and Hudson Ltd., London, revised edition, 1998), the resulting photos are worth a look. They're the grit, the melancholy, the real diner — no spruced up, stash-the-detritus, homogenized-for-a-photo-shoot view. If you want to see realism, this one's worth checking out.

Celluloid Collector's Reference and Value Guide, by Keith Lauer and Julie Robinson (Collector Books, 1999), offers a fascinating history about this nineteenth-century invention. Originally meant as a substitute for elephant ivory, celluloid's clear make-up made it the perfect base for dyes. It was used for many things that are desired collectibles today, including the boxes Sheila mentioned selling (for handkerchiefs, collars, neckties, and gloves), men's collars and cuffs, corset boning, vanity items, hair accessories, and toys. Hundreds of color photographs included, as well as a bibliography.

Two resources available for locating flea markets are the *Official Directory to U.S. Flea Markets*, by Kitty Werner (House of Collectibles, 8th edition, 2002) and the *U.S. Flea Market Directory* (Griffin Trade Paperback, 3rd edition, 2000), by Albert LaFarge. Lots of information for the flea market fan.

A good, general guide about silver is *Miller's Collecting Silver: The Facts at Your Fingertips*, by Jill Bace (Special Consultants: Alexis Butcher and Juliet Nusser; Antique Collectors Club Ltd., 1999). Includes a segment providing many sources for further reading.

Encyclopedia of American Silver Manufacturers, by Dorothy T. Rainwater, Judy Redfield (Schiffer Publishing, Ltd., 4th edition, 2002). More than 2400 marks illustrated, and brief histories and cross-references of more than 1600 manufacturers.

If cigar art is your interest, one of these three titles from Schiffer Publishing might prove beneficial: *Cigar Box Labels: Portraits of Life, Mirrors of History*, by Jerry Petrone (1998); *Great Cigar Stuff for Collectors*, by Jerry Terranova and Douglas Congdon-Martin (1997); and *Gals and Guys: Women and Men in Cigar Box Label Art*, by Jero L. Gardner (1999).

The Harvey House Cookbook: Memories of Dining Along the Santa Fe Railroad, by George H. Foster, Peter C. Weiglin (Longstreet Press, 2001). Over 200 vintage recipes, many period photos, and the fascinating story of Fred Harvey.

For extensive history, consult *The Harvey Girls: Women Who Opened the West*, by Lesley Poling-Kempes (Marlowe & Co; Reprint edition, 1994).

These two books published by Motorbooks International are definitely worth a look. Author: Mike Mueller. *Motor City Muscle: The High-Powered History of the*

American Muscle Car (1997) and *The American Pickup Truck* (1999).

American Muscle Cars, by William G. Holder, Philip Kunz (McGraw-Hill Professional, 1993). Information broken down by division: Olds, Chevy, Pontiac, etc., and an extensive index.

If, like Greer, you're inclined to tackle your own car restoration, don't miss Jim Richardson's *Classic Car Restorer's Handbook* (HP Books, 1994). Good photos and diagrams, lists of supplies needed to tackle any of a number of jobs (from overhauling the engine to detailing the interior) including reconditioning the steering wheel and restoring the radio. A concise guide, with great tips throughout. Many of Richardson's restorations have taken first-place honors at prestigious concours shows.

In addition to Barbara Conroy's books on restaurant china (see Sheila's webliography), Blanche also lists these as invaluable: *Dining on Rails: Fourth Edition*, by Richard Luckin (RK Publishing, 1998); and *The Official Guide to Dining Car China*, by Douglas W. McIntyre, (Golden Spike Enterprises, 1990; updates available).

Sheila Talbot's Webliography

www.aaca.org

The Antique Automobile Club of America, founded in 1935, is the world's largest automotive historical society with over 60,000 members and 400 regional clubs worldwide. The AACA is dedicated to perpetuating the memories of early automobiles by encouraging their history, collection and use.

www.barstowrailmuseum.org

Housed in the Casa del Desierto, the Western America Rail Museum (WARM) shares the building with Amtrak, Greyhound, the Mother Road Route 66 Museum, and several art groups.

www.cardisplay.info

The Web site for the Snohomish Classic Car and Hot Rod Display. Get your entry information here!

www.cigarlabelgazette.com

An impressive on-line newsletter about those artistic, collectible labels. Several informative articles on the site.

www.cityofsnohomish.com

Good-looking site, with several links to other Snohomish Web sites. Extensive shopping guide — check out the antiques!

www.deborahmorgan.com

New! Photos of the 1937 Cadillac that's being restored, more recipes in Sheila's Recipe Box, and news of what's next for Jeff.

www.dinermuseum.org

Go to the segment on diner culture for an interesting story about the Englewood Diner used in the movie version of Max Allan Collins' novel *Road to Perdition*. Also from the culture page, check out the diner slang. Other things at the site: the history of the diner, diner locator, lots of information.

www.dinercity.com

On-line guide to classic diners and the American roadside. Includes a diner directory, many photos (including Route 66), classic gas stations and motels, recommended reading, diner reviews, just loads of stuff at this site.

www.driveintheater.com
Whether you're feeling nostalgic for a taste of the past, or you've never experienced the drive-in theater craze, go to this fun site and learn whether there's one near you.

www.eisnermuseum.org
From the menu, choose "exhibits," then "on-line exhibits" for a great, animated look at Burma-Shave.

www.ephemerasociety.org
The Ephemera Society of America, Inc. has an appealing site offering lots of articles and information. Scrapbooking has experienced a resurgence in recent years; thanks to its current popularity, I've been able to get many supplies for making greeting cards. There are dozens, if not hundreds, of online sources. Here in Seattle, we have a great little chain of stores called Impress. I shop at their Web site: *www.impressrubberstamps.com*

www.fleamarketguide.com
A good resource for finding flea markets is this Web site.

www.gramasattic.net

A wonderful resource center, this site belongs to Pamela Glasell (author of *Collector's Guide to Vintage Tablecloths*, Schiffer, 2002). Glasell formed the Vintage Tablecloth Lover's Club, and her site has many links to other TLC members who sell vintage tablecloths. Informative newsletter articles on-line, too.

www.hanlonassociates.com

The Web site for Classic & Antique Car Drawings by Greg Hanlon. Loads of paintings and drawings (many of woodies), great car links, and an extensive list of books (with a segment devoted to books on woodies).

www.harveyhouses.net

A good place to start for brief history, links to other web sites about Harvey Houses, and a list of publications.

www.hubcapcafe.com

"An Online Classic Car Show and Events Calendar." Check "Resources" for an extensive alphabetical list of auto museums in the United States.

www.miniusa.com

If you like those MINI Coopers, but aren't in the market for a real one, check out the remote control version, which goes up to nine miles per hour! Cool site.

www.motorbooks.com

The Classic Motorbooks catalog offers the world's largest selection of automotive books. In addition to how-to books, there are books on racing history, trucks, motorcycles, pretty much anything with tires, from your Hot Wheels and Matchbox cars to eighteen-wheelers. Also includes books on diners, gas stations, the American motel, and other road stuff.

www.national66.org

Here's a fantastic Web site from the National Historic Route 66 Federation. Extensive links, current events, history, even a segment with photos of original Route 66 postcards, and a fabulous photo gallery of sites along the route.

www.nationalwoodieclub.com

This official Web site of the National Woodie Club is impressively designed, and has much great information. There are links to the regional club sites, and to several other sites about the wooden-car world. Also, details about Woodies on the Willamette, Woodies on the Beach, and many other woodie-related events.

www.oldwoodies.com

A great site with lots of info, and a recommended reading list (several books on woodies, of course).

www.parishotelboutique.com

A good place to find (and research) hotel silver. Typically, pieces are marked with the name and/or logo of the hotel, as well as the silver marks from the popular companies that made the heavily plated pieces for hotel use: Gorham, Reed and Barton, R. Wallace, and International Silver. I like that there are several photos of the pieces for sale at this Web site, and there are even postcard images of some of the hotels! Adds a nice bit of history.

www.railroadcollectors.org

The site of the Railroadiana Collectors Association Incorporated (RCAI) offers extensive information about all aspects of railroadiana; I mention it here for its china details, including a date code for Syracuse China (Syracuse made the exclusive peacock china for The Milwaukee Road that Jeff and Blanche discussed).

Almost a thousand members belong to this association. Web site also offers lots of information on fakes and reproductions.

www.recipegoldmine.com

It's true! A gold mine of recipes. Extensive index.

restaurant-china.home.comcast.net/home. htm

Author Barbara Conroy, whose books Jeff mentioned, has a wonderful Web site chock full of information. You'll benefit from her extensive research in the restaurant china field (she even offers guidelines on describing and photographing items for Internet auction). Also data on reproductions, fakes, and commemorative commercial china. All in all, a wealth of information.

www.restaurantwarecollectors.com

Official Web site of the Restaurant Ware Collectors Network. Forums, fantastic pattern ID reference pages, and many links listed according to category (thanks to Lynn Stein for introducing me around).

www.roadfood.com

This award-winning site offers restaurant reviews, forums, suggested reading, and much more. Among the board members are Jane and Michael Stern, the co-authors of over two dozen books about food and popular culture, including the guidebooks *Roadfood* and *Eat Your Way Across the USA.*

www.victorianhairartists.com

As you've learned, I'm not personally a fan of hair jewelry, but many, many people are. To learn more, visit this site. It offers many links, too.

www.wavecrestwoodies.com

This official Web site for Wavecrest, the world's largest gathering of wooden-bodied automobiles, provides the scoop, along with contact information for more details.

About the Author

Before moving to Michigan, **Deborah Morgan** was managing editor of a biweekly newspaper located on the fifteen miles of Kansas Route 66. As with most editors of small-town papers, Morgan wore the reporter's and photographer's hats, too. She's currently restoring the 1937 Cadillac you'll find in this story. Morgan and her husband, author Loren D. Estleman, go antiquing every chance they get. For more information, visit her Web site at www.deborahmorgan.com.

We hope you have enjoyed this Large Print book. Other Thorndike, Wheeler or Chivers Press Large Print books are available at your library or directly from the publishers.

For more information about current and upcoming titles, please call or write, without obligation, to:

Publisher
Thorndike Press
295 Kennedy Memorial Drive
Waterville, ME   04901
Tel. (800) 223-1244

Or visit our Web site at:
www.gale.com/thorndike
www.gale.com/wheeler

OR

Chivers Large Print
published by BBC Audiobooks Ltd
St James House, The Square
Lower Bristol Road
Bath BA2 3BH
England
Tel. +44(0) 800 136919
email: bbcaudiobooks@bbc.co.uk
www.bbcaudiobooks.co.uk

All our Large Print titles are designed for easy reading, and all our books are made to last.